Glaston

C.C. Lynch

ISBN: 1517126843
ISBN-13: 978-1517126841

To the people who taught me that the extraordinary does not exist solely in fiction.

ACKNOWLEDGMENTS

This book began as a dream and evolved into a full manuscript in a matter of months. Thank you to my mother, Lorelei, who dealt with my constant nagging and updating while I wrote the book. She put in countless hours adding suggestions and comments to the writing, for which I will forever be grateful. Thank you to my loving husband for his patience and support throughout the entire process.

CJD -

We both kept our promise.

1

He was perfect. Everything about him was flawless from his straight hairline separating chestnut tendrils and a broad smooth forehead down to his gently pointed chin at the corner of an exceptionally chiseled jaw line.

"Are you okay?" Brown strands fell into serious but kind eyes that bore into me.

Though I willed my body to move, I was frozen and captivated in his features. I searched for words, anything to say to him, but I lay there motionless staring into the eyes of this familiar stranger.

I woke up startled and sweating, the equal mix of fear and trust I had felt in the dream was still palpable. His face was seared into my memory, a result from seeing him in my dreams each week for a decade. Despite my trepidation, I wanted to fight consciousness and hold onto the intense and irrational adulation for him that would dwindle as my cognizance increased.

I walked begrudgingly down the sea foam rugged stairs to find my mother enthralled by her tablet. I wanted to confide in her the deepest part of the dream that I kept to myself, to tell her how strong and real my emotions were whenever I saw the man. Whenever I divulged any information about my dreams it was met with her pretending to be interested by providing appropriately emotional "oh?" and "wow!" statements when she felt necessary. She could not be bothered to give me her full attention; she just wanted to return to whatever she was doing before I began speaking.

Sighing, I closed my feelings into an internal box and plucked some ripe strawberries from the refrigerator. Each morning was the same, I would eat some assortment of berries and my mother would ask if that was all I was going to eat only to hear me grunt a "yes" before running out the door to go to school. On rare occasions she would yell out "I love you" but it was typically an aggravated and expectant shout as if I had greatly offended her by not saying it first.

In an effort to counter any passive aggressive statements of affection I shouted "bye mommy, I love you," before darting outside.

"Hey girl," my best friend Steph wrapped her arm around mine when she found me in the school parking lot. "Can you believe we are back in school already?" She tilted her head on my shoulder, her perfumed curls bounced off my arm. Steph's static perfume was comforting; it seemed that all of our best memories were wrapped in that scent.

"I feel like summer was barely two weeks," I grumbled. "I just want to be back on the beach."

Truthfully, I loved school and the idea of summer break being over was more pleasing than anything. I hated days that were free and unstructured and summer break was two months of the fruition of my fear. Steph, on the other hand, could spend her entire life lying on the beach. She could easily be one of those trophy wives that starred in a reality television show with her perfect hair, makeup, and rich husband.

She scoffed at the lie that I had murmured in my effort to be more normal. "What, so you can lie there for half an hour then leave to go and get some ice cream?"

"Whatever," I laughed and shook my head. "I love the sound of the ocean but that sticky feeling makes me want to jump in the shower A.S.A.P." I shook my body as if trying to rid myself of the imaginary salt.

"Maybe you could try relaxing for once in your life," she smirked, skipping ahead towards the door with perfectly curled ringlets bouncing off her shoulders.

I envied how she could curl her hair with no effort and paint on a perfect face. Without makeup we could be sisters. Our face shape and expressions were the same; it was our eyes and personality that were different. My eyes were blue with green swirls as if my irises were made of marble and hers were a solid deep brown.

Those brown eyes seemed to command trust

from everyone, any person that met her practically fell to her heels, including me. I adored both her and the fact that everyone around her loved her. While Steph seemed to be able to lasso every human with her charm, I kept people at a distance only making room for Steph and our friend Nicholas. Growing up with telepathy makes it hard to trust anyone. It was not that I disagreed with what people thought, or even tried to read them for that matter, I was just afraid that if I let someone in they would know I was different.

I followed Steph up the stairs as we greeted peers we hadn't seen in months. In the middle of catching up with Steph's newest infatuation an announcement came on the intercom directing everyone to go to their homeroom.

"Wait," I began to panic, "we have a homeroom?" After three grueling years we were finally seniors. We had been assigned our share of gossip, homework, and teenage columniation, but never a homeroom.

With a seductive grin she nodded a goodbye to the guy then turned to give me her full attention. "Something new they're trying I guess," her tone was beguilingly blasé. "Didn't you get the letter in the mail telling you where to go?"

"No," my chest started to rise and fall quickly, "my mother never said anything." Of my few fears in the world, being late was high on the list.

"Calm down Abrielle, I'm pretty sure

Nicholas is in your homeroom with you. Your last names are like a letter away from being the same."

My muscles relaxed as relief washed over them. Nicholas was walking into the school at that moment. I leaned over the balcony railing willing him to locate me and almost on cue his eyes found mine. A smile spread across his face before he hopped up the stairs, two steps at a time.

"Please tell me you know where our homeroom is," I pleaded, grabbing his hands.

Calloused palms squeezed mine gently in reassurance as he nodded. I mouthed a silent "thank you." Nicholas snorted, adjusting his backpack, "the ice queen didn't give you your mail?"

"Oh she is not that bad," I looked towards the people flooding into the school to avoid eye contact. I could never lie while looking a person in the eye. I would make a terrible lawyer, doctor, or anything sort of professional that could make an impressive amount of money.

"Right," he snickered grabbing my backpack, "this way my dear."

"Um, why isn't anyone carrying my stuff?" Steph planted her feet and crossed her arms.

"You never bring a backpack," I pointed to her empty shoulders.

"Yeah, but my purse weighs a ton," feigning difficulty she shrugged it off and handed it to me.

I lifted it as if I was doing bicep curls. "Did you bring hand weights to school?" Her purse was heavy like she had shoved all of her school books into the designer handbag.

"A curling iron," she rolled her eyes as if I should have x-ray vision. "First day of school, duh." She scrunched her nose then sauntered after Nicholas.

"Silly me," I shook my head, laughing.

My homeroom was deafening with excitement. Everyone shared their summer stories with one another in competitive volumes. Nicholas had his shoes up on the chair in front of him saving my seat. I had only taken a minute to put my notebooks into my locker and Nicholas already had an admirer trying to take my seat. Long blonde beach waves hung in front of his face as Lisa flirted and chewed her gum loudly. My handsome best friend had his very own fan club and she was a customary admirer. Though Lisa was beautiful, she was a bit too dim for Nicholas's taste.

I watched his hand intently. If he wanted me to save him from the situation he would tap his finger on the desk three times. We had been friends since we were nine and somewhere in those eight years we came up with the three tap code.

I sat down facing the front of the class waiting for the final bell to ring. "Hey Abrielle," Nicholas tapped my desk from around my shoulder, "how was your summer?"

The three taps. Mischief curled my lips and I turned slowly and traced his fingers delicately with mine, "you tell me, I was with you the whole time." I leaned in towards him and plopped my head on my hand blocking Lisa from his view. I batted my eyes and sighed deeply. "How was your summer?" I winked suggestively. Lisa exhaled annoyed and walked off to find her next victim. We fought to suppress the laughter threatening to abrupt from the outcome of our scheme and continued on with catching up with one another.

Nicholas, Steph, and I were so close that no one knew if either Steph or I were dating Nicholas, which made these scenarios immensely entertaining. We had faked relationships and break ups on numerous occasions. I loved Nicholas and treasured our friendship, but I always blurred the lines between friends and more. Faking relationships with him had burned me in the past. He never blurred the lines though, Steph and I were his friends and that would never change in his mind.

A man in his fifties adorning a tweed jacket holding a tin travel mug in one hand and a briefcase in the other made his way into the room. "I'm Mr. Murphy. Good morning, pleasantries, summer fun, yada yada. Unless you have a class with me I won't see most of you again until the last day of school when we meet in this room next. I'll do a roll call and go over safety procedures then please head to your first class." The new teacher did as he promised and Nicholas braided my hair while he spoke.

The homeroom erupted once Mr. Murphy

finished speaking but I waited for Nicholas to finish the braid he had started before leaving to find my class. I rounded the corner and bumped hard into Samantha Basil, a girl with the same gift that I had. There were few people I ever met with telepathy but whenever I was around them I could hear a strange buzzing sound similar to the noise a light bulb makes when it is about to blow out. Samantha and I could tell we had the same ability the first time we laid eyes on one another freshman year of high school. Our friendship only extended to friendly acquaintances but we had a silent respect for one another.

When she first moved to the town her gifts were on display like a street performer. The first day of school she had brought in tarot cards and started doing readings for people. Though she hid her telepathy in her tarot card façade, most everyone got a kick out of her talents and our peers would ask her to perform on a daily basis. If Samantha and I were in a class together she would look over to me for a nod of approval to make sure she was saying the truth. I could never tell why she looked to me since it seemed that her skills were far superior to mine.

Unlike Samantha I never told anyone that I had telepathy. I figured that the moment I mentioned to anyone that I could read another person's thoughts or feel what they were feeling a plethora of medications would soon follow. Being an empath was difficult enough without throwing telepathy in the mix. In fact, I had tried to squash my gifts because I was too empathetic. Being around other people would alter my emotions so much so that oftentimes I could physically feel the pain of others. My mother would scoff at me because I was too sensitive of a child and when I told her why I was crying she threw me into every therapist's office she could. I made it through eight psychiatrists before I learned to put a wall up and keep everyone else's thoughts and feelings out of my head.

When I got to my first class of the day I took out a notebook and saw a piece of paper fall out of my bag. It was a note written by Samantha that read "switch out of calc." My chest tightened and I looked at my schedule. Third period was A.P. Calculus. I knew that if Samantha was urging me to drop a class it was serious. Mrs. Walters went over the Latin syllabus and once she finished I asked to go to the guidance councilor.

"You want a study period instead of math?" my guidance councilor asked tilting her head to the side. Kerry Flannigan was a flaky redhead with good intentions oozing from every pore.

"Yes. I should have enough credits to warrant me a study period."

"Ha!" Kerry slapped her hands together triumphantly. "Do you have a job?"

"Uh, yes. I work the filing at city hall and I do a few hours at the pharmacy." I spoke cautiously not understanding where she was going with her sudden epiphany.

She turned to her computer and underlined a section of my transcript with her finger. "You have enough credits to graduate right now. We have a work program that would allow you to leave school early to go to your job." She winked suggestively, as if I would possibly go somewhere else after school. "State law mandated that you have an English and math class for both semesters, but tutoring freshmen for their standardized testing counts as a math requirement. We would have to get you a study for third period because we technically have to feed every pupil lunch but you'll be out by eleven." She laughed and tilted her head to the side again.

"Oh no, Miss Flannigan, I just want to switch out of calculus. I'll gladly tutor students though, that sounds like fun."

"Oh we just have a very different definition of fun, don't we Brianna?" She chortled and began typing.

"Abrielle," I corrected her, "my name is Abrielle." She flipped her hand in the air as a response, not caring that she had gotten my name wrong.

"So I will sign you up for tutoring and a study period." She clicked and bounced around in her seat as if there was a song playing in her head. Inhaling deeply, I reminded myself that she was just a happy person and had good intentions. Kerry printed out my new schedule and handed it to me, satisfied with her work. I looked over the paper to find that she hadn't changed my calculus class.

It took three more print-outs for her to finally arrange my schedule to something that was acceptable. Before leaving I turned to her and quietly asked if it was possible for my college packets and responses to be mailed to the school instead of my house. I did not want any college replies to get lost like many of my parcels that passed through my mother's hands had.

She straightened her face and gave me a solemn expression. "You need to put a permanent address on all of your applications but each of your schools will have an early admissions meeting and I will receive the answer that day." I nodded a silent thank you to which she responded with an exuberant, "Have a great day Brianna!" I smiled and waved as I shut her door.

The rest of the day was underwhelming. By the time I got to my second to last class it seemed that the summer excitement had already come to a halt. I had a study period for the last two classes which translated to 120 minutes of social interaction. I crossed my fingers as I walked into the room hoping that Steph or Nicholas would be in there with me.

A retractable wall had been folded to allow the high number of students to fit in the class. I took a seat in the back of the room and watched as my peers shuffled in just as the bell rang followed by yet another new teacher.

"Hello everyone," an older lady with a perfectly straight salt and pepper bobbed haircut spoke as if she was commanding a dog to sit down, "this is study period. If the noise level becomes too high we will separate the rooms and all pupils will study with their head on their desk for the rest of the year."

"That makes no sense," I muttered irritated by the woman's superior attitude. How could someone study with their head down on a desk? We were high school seniors, not toddlers.

"A problem?" she arched an eyebrow my way.

I twisted my tongue over in my mouth calculating my response. "There shouldn't be," I smiled and shook my head.

"Good," she tapped her fingers together.

The seats were filled with acquaintances, not a best friend in sight. Declining any social interaction I began creating study sheets for my Latin class. In the middle of my notes an abrupt voice came from my side. "Why were you not in class, Abrielle?"

I jumped at the slightly familiar voice and looked up to see Mr. Murphy. "I'm sorry, what do you mean?" I mentally kicked myself for the way I spoke. People always looked at me funny because the two most common words out of my mouth were always spoken in succession: I'm sorry. I was trying to delete those two words from my vocabulary, but not with any success.

"Advanced placement calculus, you were on my roster. Was there a reason that you skipped my class?"

"Oh, no, I changed my schedule." I sunk

down under his gaze and handed him my new schedule. I felt someone staring at me from my right and turned quickly to see Samantha's eyes glued to me. I wanted to put my wall down and listen to what she was trying to tell me but I decided against it and planned to ask her once Mr. Murphy walked away.

"So many study periods will not look good on a college application." His lips twisted in disappointment.

"I have a 4.2 grade point average and hundreds of volunteer hours. I am certain that if the college I want to go to overlooks my community activities because of a couple study periods then it probably is not the place I want associated with my higher degree."

"That's a very egotistical point of view, Ms. Abbott." He sneered at me with condemnation.

A light air brushed by as I felt someone stand beside me, "altruistic is Abrielle's middle name, I don't know how 'egotistical' could ever be associated with her." Steph flipped a perfectly curled lock over her shoulder and crossed her arms over her chest. She glared at Mr. Murphy until he finally decided to walk away at which moment I jumped up and hugged Steph tightly.

"I am so glad you are in study with me!" I gave her another quick squeeze before pulling away.

"Me too," she smiled calmly, "but first I need to take care of something." A look of determination came across her face momentarily before an angelic pout replaced it. "Mrs. Anderson," she raised her hand.

Unenthused cold eyes scanned the room slowly until they fell on Steph. "Yes, what is your inquiry Ms. Fields?"

"I can see at least five other students in this class that are in physics. That just so happens to be my friend Abrielle's specialty. I feel that if the other students agree, it would be enormously beneficial if we were able to reserve a spot in the library to dedicate to her tutoring us."

The teacher's stony face never faltered and I thought for sure that she was going to decline her request. *History is about to be made*, I thought to myself, *someone is actually going to say no to Steph Fields*. Instead Mrs. Anderson replied, "For today you can just put the desks together. I'll talk to the principal about allowing you a table in the library."

With that, social hour commenced.

2

The next day Mrs. Anderson told us that the principal had approved a library study session under the stipulation that a volunteer teacher was to look over said session. Steph's lips twisted into a smile knowing that she had effectively granted a group of our friends a free spot in the library to gossip for a majority of the week.

Mrs. Anderson adjusted her pale yellow business suit and then pointed her nose towards the door just in time for another teacher to enter the room. "Please remember to thank Mr. Murphy for volunteering to overlook your library sessions."

I could feel eyes bearing into me from my side again and I realized I had forgotten to ask Samantha what was wrong the day before. Drawing in a breath, I began to take the wall down so I could figure out what she needed to tell me. Closing my eyes, I imagined the psychic wall I built flowing down gently like a curtain then I focused my attention on Samantha and I heard her say one word: *dangerous*. I shuddered at what she could have possibly seen to be so adamant about this warning.

What is the matter? I asked her and all I received in return was that word "dangerous" yet again. I was getting frustrated trying to figure out how Mr. Murphy was threatening. As my frustration began to build I heard the man in question mutter something about Stephanie being my best friend.

"Her name is Steph, not Stephanie. On her birth certificate is says Steph." I was irritated but remained polite as possible. The class went silent. Looking around I realized that he had never said it out loud. The edges of his lips twitched into a strange and accomplished smile. Thanks to my telepathy I had made myself look insane in front of the entire class aside from Samantha.

Steph muttered a "huh?" before I said, "Oh, I thought I heard someone say Stephanie and you know how I love to correct people." She looked at me quizzically then shrugged.

I looked back to Samantha who was staring at her desk in a hard concentration. Mr. Murphy was watching me with a satisfied grin that sent a chill down my spine. With my wall still down I tried to connect to him somehow and see if he was like me, but there was no buzzing sound like I typically heard from other telepaths.

I shook my head from the paranoia then rubbed my temples to rid myself of my irritation. He probably enjoyed the fact that I had embarrassed myself like that. Mr. Murphy was a new teacher and so far he did not seem to enjoy his work nor did he seem particularly fond of students. Until I found out what bothered Samantha about him, I decided I would keep my wall down.

When the teachers were occupied I wrote her a note. *What did you see?* I studied her closely as she responded to my question. She was wearing her typical outfit consisting of black jeans, black boots, a crimson bohemian shirt, and a bronze amulet dangling from her long slender neck. Long blonde hair was as usual, worn down and stuck to her back like it was glued in place. My eyes twitched as I studied the dark circles that hugged the bottom of her turquoise eyes. She was normally happy, not exuberant, but happy. Whatever she had seen bothered her enough to cause her face to wear the worry.

A few minutes later scribbled underneath my question read four words that made my stomach drop and limbs shake: *I saw you die.* The room felt like a vacuum, I could hardly breathe. Death was Samantha's specialty. It was something she abhorred, but her abilities were uncanny.

Once I realized I was staring I swallowed the dry lump that had formed in my throat and searched for an explanation for my awkward gawking. "Samantha," I stretched back nonchalantly to hide my discomfort, "I ripped my favorite shirt last week. Is there any way I can bring it over to your house to get it repaired? I'll pay you."

"Yeah," she was emotionless. "My grandmother will be home. If I can't fix it, then she can."

"Hello," I spoke politely to Samantha's grandmother. The humming vibration of telepathy was palpable and I was overwhelmed by the strength of her powers. I felt like I was in the presence of a queen. "I'm here to see Samantha."

Her wrinkled face formed a gentle and wise smile as she ushered me into the house. I smiled back with adoration. Though age brings devastation, I find unequivocal beauty in it and I found myself envious of the wisdom that gleamed through those amiable eyes.

Her flat palm slid gracefully from her diaphragm then towards the stairs directing me to Samantha's room. "The first room on the left," she nodded graciously then walked back to the kitchen where an amazing and unique aroma was emanating.

Delicately, I slid my hand along the thick wooden railing as I ascended slowly up the stairs. I could feel eyes upon my back, however Samantha's grandmother was nowhere in sight. When I entered Samantha's room I was completely taken aback by the contents. Though I had expected to see a library with a bed and an altar, her lavender walls were covered in posters of handsome models and artists. Aside from one small section it was just like any other teenager's room filled with posters and knickknacks.

In the corner of her room by a window was a single shelf dedicated to a snow globe. Inside the globe was a barren tree with two ravens perched on a limb. Light danced in the globe in such a way that the birds almost appeared to be moving.

"How long has your wall been up?" I turned to see Samantha walk in, her nose deep in a novel.

Embarrassed, I fidgeted with the hem of my shirt. "I've kept it up for a while. It was getting too difficult feeling everything everyone else was feeling."

"Why not just put a wall up against the empathy?" She seemed annoyed.

I shrugged, "I don't know how. It seems like it is all or nothing with me. I wish I had some way of practicing."

Samantha arched an eyebrow. "You really just need to accept your gift and it will become a lot easier for you."

She was right. Sighing at her truth I decided to get to the point of my visit. "Samantha, what exactly did you see?"

The book was placed gently on her nightstand and she took a seat on the edge of her bed. Her lips pursed as if she was contemplating something and then she finally took out a small pocket notebook. "Have you noticed there are a bunch of new teachers this year?"

"Yeah," I shrugged thinking about how often new teachers came to our high school. It was nothing out of the ordinary. "Mr. Murphy, Mrs. Anderson, and Mr. Brown, right?"

"There are three more as well, all with equally as unimaginative names." She put the pocket notebook flat on the bed and pushed it aside. My eyes were drawn to her stick strait blonde hair that never seemed to shift no matter how much movement she made. "I was suspicious when I saw the new lot of teachers here and more so when I got a vision of Mr. Murphy trying to kill you. You ran through a door, it was strange," she searched her mind for the right words, "like it was just a door on a ledge or something. Anyway you were trapped and couldn't escape him. He threw you from the ledge."

"Why?" I was flabbergasted that anyone would ever want to harm me.

"I don't know, but you should start keeping that wall down so you can read people. It might be the only thing to save your life."

I nodded and stared at the snow globe again. Without lifting my eyes from the object I asked if she had noticed his reaction when I mentioned Steph's name. Though it had been more of an observation than a question she agreed he had acted strangely and hypothesized that he must know about my telepathic abilities and perhaps it was part of the reason he pushed me in her vision. After her statement she quickly told me I needed to leave and ushered me out of the house. Her grandmother nodded her head in a polite goodbye and Samantha rushed me though the foyer.

I shouted a "nice to meet you," seconds before Samantha slammed the door behind me.

Her curt goodbye only solidified the sense of

dread that filled my chest as I walked to my car. My mind raced trying to picture the door Samantha described as I fumbled about for my keys. I had never seen a door that led to a ledge, not even the one on the school roof matched the description.

Before getting into the car I started to assess if there was anyone following me. My senses were heightened and the crackle of a leaf blowing along the sidewalk made me jump and in the process my car keys fell from my hand.

Quickly I picked the keys up and scanned my surroundings once more.

"And the paranoia begins," I muttered as I plopped into the front seat of my small sedan.

3

"Hi mom," I shouted as I walked through the door.

As I listened for a response a glut of emotions began to trickle in. Quickly I put my wall back up and made a mental note to try and let the wall down when I left the house and put it back up when I returned. My mother's emotions ran high, too high for an empath like me to deal with.

"How was school? Why are you late?" Her questions came in an abrupt tandem. She wrung her hands in a towel as she came into the foyer to watch me kick my shoes off.

"Remember, I have clubs Monday through Friday. I have math club, honor society, robotics, year book, and future philanthropists, respectively." I counted the clubs on my fingers. Looking up while I counted helped me to hide my lie.

I did have clubs every day, but they would not start for another two weeks. She would not have cared if I had gone to Samantha's but explaining what

I was doing there would have been a bigger lie than just saying I had gone to one of my afterschool activities.

She ignored what I said and went back in the kitchen only to yell from the other room. "So, how was your day?"

"It was productive." I followed on her heels. "I tutored Mrs. Gambale's kid today and turned in essays to six different scholarships."

"Susan's *child?*" She hated when people called humans "kids."

"Yes, Susan's daughter." I spoke eloquently and with a fake accent.

"You left your dirty napkin on the table today. You're seventeen and I am not your maid. Clean the table and do your homework. Dinner will be ready at 7:15." Wrinkles rose between her brows from her scowl.

"Okay, mother," I smiled sweetly.

"The term 'mother' is for women who beat their children, I do not beat you." With that she left the kitchen and went to the living room to watch television.

"I love you," I sang as I walked up the stairs to my room.

When I got up to my bedroom Nicholas was sitting on my bed with a finger to his mouth signaling for me to be quiet. I rolled me eyes and tip-toed across my room. I could not figure out how he was able to open my bedroom window but I sighed in relief because it felt so nice having a friend that I could hug after finding out a telepath had seen my imminent death.

"I don't know how you got in, but I am so happy you are here," I smiled hugging him before gracefully falling on my back and looking up to the plastic glowing stars on my ceiling.

He followed my gaze then glanced back at me in adoration. "I'm here for an entirely selfish purpose."

"What's that?" I pushed myself up onto my elbows.

"I need someone to go to a concert with me tonight." Silence fell as he looked around the room before adding, "Steph bailed."

"Talk about second choice," I scoffed and rolled my eyes. I did not blame him for not asking me before since I was typically too involved with homework to do anything once the school year began. My schedule was so light now that I actually had the freedom to hang out with him. Shrugging, I smiled, "yeah, I'd love to."

"Cool, meet me at the corner at seven and I'll take you. I know your mom would never let you go out on a school night so tell her you're going to Steph's, or the library, or some genius convention." He waived his hands in the air as if he was doing magic while coming up with silly excuses.

"I'm not a genius," I chuckled, playfully sending an elbow to his shoulder. "The Steph excuse will work fine."

"See you soon Abbs," he said before rustling my hair and jumping out the window.

"Abbs?" I laughed after him, "Abrielle, never Abbs." I rolled my eyes at his strangeness and watched to see him land gracefully outside my window.

Our trio was exclusively anti-nicknames and the fact he just gave me one did not sit right with me. I shrugged and pushed the feeling aside. Perhaps the pet name and climbing in the window was a strange teenage boy phase.

When I told my mother I would be going over Steph's she put up a fuss because she had already began cooking dinner. Eventually she ended her own argument by saying "fine, I guess I will have lunch for tomorrow. Go have fun at Steph's and call me if you're going to stay there for the night."

When I got to Steph's her mother embraced me in a warm hug before ushering me to her daughter's room. Steph was on her bed painting her toenails a glossy cherry red. "Hey love," she smiled tossing her hair over her right shoulder. "To what do I owe this pleasure?"

"I came to trade." I grinned, pulling out a paper bag filled with fresh fudge.

Her eyes grew big with anticipation and she inched closer to me. "You have my attention."

"I need to borrow an outfit for tonight. Something that says I'm at a rock concert and I'm hot but not easy."

"Oh. My. Gosh! You know that giving you a makeover is a dream come true. You don't ever need to give me fudge for that." Delicately she took the bag from my hands, "but I am grateful nonetheless." She jumped up and began rummaging through her closet pulling out random clothing articles and tossing them on the bed. Once she accumulated enough for four choice outfits she pulled out a pair of sandals and a pair of heels.

I grabbed a pair of jeans, a tank top, a leather jacket, and the heels and began changing. Once I was dressed she nodded her head in approval and grabbed her makeup bag.

"You have been here for like twenty minutes and haven't told me who you're going on a date with yet. Do I need to stab you in the eye with mascara to find out?" Her eyes gleamed with anticipation and excitement.

"It's not a date, it's just Nicholas." I rolled my eyes.

She froze for a brief second, almost too quick for me to take notice before she continued. "Where is my ticket?" I could hear a hint of jealousy in her voice.

"He asked you," my brows furrowed, "he said you blew him off."

Just as I said the words I felt how ridiculous they sounded. Steph had never learned how to say no to anything. I began to realize how strange the entire situation was. Nicholas had snuck into my bedroom to ask me to go to a concert instead of calling or knocking on the door and he hadn't invited Steph. He had given me a nickname *and* told me to meet him at the corner of my street rather than his house or Steph's like usual.

I slammed my palm into my forehead as soon as I remembered that my wall had been up. There were two possibilities to what had happened. Either Nicholas was going through some really strange phase or someone had come into my room looking like him. I had never known anyone to be able to look like another person but I was sure that a strong enough telepath could alter what another person was experiencing. My heart started racing at the possibility that this could have something to do with what Samantha warned me about. Steph was staring at me, most likely trying to figure out why I slammed my head.

Lie. "I just realized, that I had answered the phone while I was studying and I never even looked at who had called. I just assumed it was Nicholas because no one else ever calls me."

Steph began jumping up and down with excitement. "You have a date!" She yelled and danced around her room. "Oh my gosh! I want to know who it was! I bet it was Steve. No wait, it could have been Matt, he sounds just like Nicholas." She was dancing around her room, eyeliner still in her hand.

"Jeez Steph, it's not like I've never been on a date before. You make it seem like I was the ugly duckling that just transformed into a mediocre swan."

"No," she laughed grabbing my hands, "it's the anonymity of it all. A mysterious phone call, a date to a concert," she stopped midsentence and wrinkled her nose. "Wait, he said I already told him no?"

"Oh," I searched quickly for another explanation, "I asked if you were going to be there and he said no, I guess I just assumed."

"Anyway," she waved it off, "the unknown admirer, taking my best friend on a date." She looked me over in her outfit, "what are you wearing for underwear?"

"Black cheekies," I blushed.

"Hot mama," she slapped my rear before continuing to finish my makeup.

4

I stood at the corner of my street promptly at seven waiting for whatever may be in store. Standing there in high heels and a full face of makeup made me feel too noticeable, like I could actually be in the spotlight for once in my life. I enjoyed being hidden and having Steph get all the attention. I sucked down my discomfort for my appearance and focused on the unknown that lay ahead that evening.

Though I should have been terrified at the possibility that I was being tricked into some sort of dangerous situation, I was actually a bit intrigued. Nicholas's black sedan pulled up to the corner and I mentally let the wall fall then got into the car.

"Whoa," Nicholas guffawed, "is there something other than sneakers on your feet?"

"Yeah," I giggled nervously, "I let Steph do the makeover she's been dying to give me all these years."

His knuckles went white for a moment as he gripped the steering wheel harder when I mentioned

Steph's name. Closing my eyes and sighing inwardly I tried to pick up on the emotions around me. I felt excitement, nervousness, and giddiness. Being able to decipher which emotions belonged to who would have been easier if I hadn't been feeling those exact ones, or if I hadn't spent most of my life trying to keep people's thoughts and feelings out of my head.

"You car smells good," I sniffed honing in on what exactly I was sensing. "It's like mint and tea tree oil." Nicholas's car usually smelled like a bag of dirty gym clothes with a few sprays of cologne to mask the foul scent. Another detail that was different about the man I was in the car with.

"Okay?" His voice was barely audible and he adjusted his hands on the wheel.

The rest of the ride was filled with small talk about our first days back at school. My hands were tucked under my thighs, a nervous habit I had developed years ago. As the ride became more comfortable I played with my gift and I repeatedly began to push into his mind then retreat slowly. Nicholas was one of the easiest people to read and after nearly twenty minutes of effort I had no luck penetrating his mind.

Pain gripped my stomach as the tingling sensation of fear raced from my toes to my face. The man I was in the car with was clearly not Nicholas and I had no idea why someone would want to impersonate my best friend. I jumped when he suddenly asked me what was wrong. His eyes searched my face and I looked away quickly.

"I forgot cash," I stammered slowly looking at him. *Relax,* I told myself. "Man, I forgot how easily my expressions give me away." I shook my head at myself. It was far more difficult acting normal around an imposter than I could have ever imagined.

"Don't worry about it," he tapped his hand on my leg quickly, "tonight is on me."

I said nothing more about the situation and spent all my energy trying to calm down. The man did not feel threatening, but it was definitely not Nicholas. My mind was either being tampered with to make me see my friend or this person could change their appearance. The first one sounded extremely invasive while the second was just utterly impossible.

We parked a few blocks away from the concert and stopped at a pretzel cart on the way. My senses were heightened as we ate our snack at the octagon fountain in the town square. I tried to keep calm and act as natural as I would if Nicholas was in front of me but my lying was outright terrible. Silence fell between us just long enough for me to notice a boy playing guitar on the other side of the fountain.

"You've been staring at that kid for ten minutes now." Fake Nicholas raised an inquisitive brow while he crumpled up his napkin.

"Watch him," I whispered.

"Yeah, he's good," he shrugged disinterestedly, "so what?"

"You're looking at him, but you're not seeing

him." I shook my head in disbelief. "Watch when someone talks to him."

Almost on cue someone put money in a cup by the boy and began speaking to him. The boy strummed his guitar while the person spoke. "He's not playing a song to that person, he's translating." I was utterly amazed by what I was witnessing.

"I don't…" fake Nicholas began to speak before I took his hand and brought him around the octagon to take a closer look.

I knelt down to eye level with the young oriental boy. I smiled and spoke softly, "Hello. You play extremely well."

The boy's fingers broke from the song he had been strumming to pluck a few random notes as the words left my mouth. He grinned and nodded before continuing on with the song he had been performing.

"He doesn't speak English." I looked at fake Nicholas and giggled disbelievingly. "He's translating everything he hears to the notes that he understands. It's absolutely beautiful." I was in awe. "Could you imagine? What an incredible mind!"

Fake Nicholas was smiling at me. He seemed proud, as if he was approving of what I had just said. "Come on," he squeezed my hand, "we're going to miss the headlining band." I took another look at the boy who gave me a thankful nod then followed Nicholas.

The moment we stepped into the arena I was

hit with a flood of thoughts and emotions. Putting up the wall was a tempting idea but I was afraid to be so remiss in the presence of the fake Nicholas. I danced and sang along with the band for an hour until the crowd was drunk. Drunken emotions were the worst to deal with because they ran higher than sober ones. My chest started heaving and the edges of my vision began to grow dark. I had waited too long and fake Nicholas knew something was wrong.

"Are…" he began to speak but I cut him off.

"It's just really hot in here, can we step outside?" He nodded and took my hand leading me to a side door.

Once we were away from the crowd I rested my hands on my knees and looked up at the person pretending to be Nicholas. "Sorry about that, I don't know what came over me. I must be coming down with something."

"No problem," he shrugged, "the band was playing all new crap anyway. Only the old stuff is good."

I nodded in agreement. Sucking in a large breath I stood and gathered my strength to walk back to the car.

"Thank you for tonight," I smiled when we were halfway home, "I'm sorry about not feeling well."

"No problem, I had fun." He looked over and smiled the same big goofy one that Nicholas so often flashed.

For a second I forgot that it wasn't Nicholas I was in the car with but when I remembered a wave of anger washed over me. "So who do I tell Steph I went with?"

"What?" he seemed completely baffled and the leather of the steering wheel squeaked as he squeezed it tightly.

"I obviously borrowed clothes from her and told her I was going tonight. When I said you had told me she bailed on you she said that you never asked her. You put me in a pretty awkward position so I had to lie and say that I got a phone call and I just assumed it was Nicholas." I was careful to say Nicholas instead of "you," a verbal push into his subconscious so he knew I was onto him.

"Oh," he licked his lips nervously.

Calm down. Though I did not feel threatened by this man, I still had no idea who he was and I was in a car with him. My life was in his hands and pissing off a stranger after I had just gotten a warning from a telepath about my death was at the top of the list of stupid things I could do. I inhaled and calmed myself. "Look, I know she can be a bit exhausting to take to these things. She's always finding a way to get alcohol, is pushing the limits, and we end up just being babysitters. This is the first and last time we lie to her. I'll tell her I went with some guy I tutor and we will never mention tonight again. Deal?"

Relief washed over his face and he nodded in

agreement.

"I'll see you tomorrow?" I asked before getting out of the car.

"See you later Abbs," he winked.

"Abrielle," I corrected him before shutting the door. "See you later, whoever you are," I grumbled as he drove off.

The visit was bothering me so much so that I fought myself for an entire hour before calling Nicholas.

"Yeah?" he answered in his typical way that annoyed me greatly. Was it so hard to just say hello?

"What are you doing right now?" my eyes were closed and I tried to read him through the phone.

"Just studying for this exam tomorrow," he huffed. "Actually, what can you tell me about quantum mechanics?"

"Oh you have Warner for the wonderful you-should-have-studied-all-summer exam?"

"Yes ma'am," he huffed.

"Don't worry about it," I laughed sitting up, "I've got the exam right here and he never changes it. I'll email it to you right now and you can just tell him I tutored you if he gets suspicious."

"Thanks, Abrielle!" A sigh of relief followed.

"No problem, Nicholas. I'll see you tomorrow."

"Goodnight, Abrielle."

I smiled and hung up. I would always be Abrielle to my Nicholas, but I would be "Abbs" to fake Nicholas.

5

Walking towards study hall I felt arms wrap around my waist. "You are the best Abrielle," Nicholas said over my shoulder. "Thank you so much for that test."

I smiled and slowly read him. It was the real Nicholas, easy to read and said my full name. "If you ever have questions about Warner's class, always ask. I have all my old tests, essays, and notes."

"You're my girl," he squeezed me tightly and kissed my right temple quickly. "I'll see you Friday at Steph's."

With that he jogged off to catch up with some blonde girl I had never met before. His friendship loyalty lay with Steph and me, but he had girls chasing him from every angle. With a strong jaw, dimples when he smiled, dirty blonde hair, and green eyes, Nicholas belonged in a magazine posing for underwear advertisements. Whenever I watched him with other girls I could not help but think how the woman he married would be unbelievably lucky. She would have an incredibly handsome husband that was sweet, smart, affectionate, and entertaining. He had a nearly perfect personality wrapped in a handsome body.

"That was very intimate," Steph glowered at me as I sat down next to her.

"What?" Nicholas was like that with both of us and it was not meant in a romantic way. "Oh, oh my goodness, I forgot to tell you about last night. Yeah, it was not Nicholas, it was this guy Rodney that I tutor in math."

"Rodney?" Steph snorted, "Who knew we had anyone named Rodney in this school?" She rolled her eyes and pulled out her pocket mirror.

"Don't be so shallow," I scolded. "I had a really good time. He was sweet and is super handsome."

"Well does *Rodney* know that you and Nicholas are so touchy-touchy?" Steph gave an exasperated sigh.

Why was she getting so weird about Nicholas? He was our friend that was overly affectionate since the day we met him. "Who cares? He's not my boyfriend and you and Nicholas are just as… oh my gosh!" I shrieked quietly, "you like Nicholas! That's why you seemed so upset last night and why you are getting so catty right now!"

I could see she was just about to defend herself when a student knocked on the door. "Is Abrielle in here?" She was a petite and sheepish sophomore wearing a neon yellow volunteer tag.

"Yes?" I hesitated.

"Oh, um, Miss Flannigan needs to see you." She held her elbow and swayed nervously.

The class erupted in quiet mockery of drawn out "ohs" and "trouble."

When I got to Miss Flannigan's office she ushered me right in. "Come in, come in!" She was bouncing in her seat excitedly. "I have wonderful news!"

"Oh?" I had no idea what she could be so excited about.

"We had a representative from Glaston Academy here and they did an on-the-spot admissions interview. They want to take you in next week! They know you have enough credits to graduate here and they are willing to do a pre-college year where you finish off this year's necessities but enroll you in college classes too. They even said they will provide a full boat based upon your scholarship essay!" Miss Flannigan was bouncing in her seat so much that her computer was wobbling on her desk. "I already notified your teachers and your mother!"

"Wait, what?" I practically yelled in her face. "I've never heard of Glaston Academy, I did not apply there, and I never accepted their offer." The news felt more like punishment than good news, like I was being sent away. I began to pace about her office, furious and confused.

"Oh don't worry dear, since you are not legally autonomous your mother signed the consent form." She tapped her finger on a file placed on her desk. "You are the first student here accepted to a college! Hooray!" She clapped her hands together in excitement. "We already made you a star and it is hanging on the wall outside the principal's office. You'll have to quit your jobs and volunteering because the school is an hour or two... was it four? Either way, no work, just study, study, study. How exciting is this?"

"No, I need to think about this." I ran shaky hands through my hair. "I would be leaving my school, my friends, my life. What about graduation? I deserve to graduate from here."

"Honey, your mother already signed all the necessary paperwork. You're starting college next week. Go say goodbye to your friends because you are living on campus like a big girl soon." Her voice was serious and strict but her vivacious smile was still in its usual place.

"This isn't legal, Miss Flannigan. There is no way. It's just some sort of sick joke." I was planning on going to Yale or Salve Regina; some beautiful college where I was only a small drive from a beach. Sweat beads were beginning to form along my hairline as the panicky feeling intensified. "And why is it so damn hot in this office?"

I fanned my face with my hands and I could feel the sting of the tears that threatened to erupt. I ran out of the office and down to my class before I would let her see me weep. I got into the class and I could feel the eyes of the other students on me.

"I need Steph to take me to the nurse. I'm not feeling well." I turned on my heel and waited for Steph to come to my side.

"What is wrong?" Concern strained her voice.

"I got accepted into college." A laugh erupted as I realized how preposterous that sounded. "My mom signed the paperwork already. I go next week."

"Abrielle," she looked at me pointedly, "you realize how illegal and ridiculous that sounds?"

"That's what I said to flaky Flannigan, but I'm not autonomous yet, I turn eighteen in six months. Honestly, if my mom signed the paperwork my only chance is seeing if I can argue with her." The chance of my mother changing her mind about anything was slim to none. My spirit was breaking and tears began to slide down my cheeks. "I have never even heard of Glaston Academy." I shook my head and laughed at the absurd circumstances through sniffles.

"That sounds like an English boarding school," Steph muttered wiping away a few stray tears. She straightened herself out and her voice became firm like a mother. "I will see you every other weekend and you will do your best. You will become a brain surgeon someday and use that academy as a stepping stone to do so. When you are done there you will work for fifteen to twenty years until you make enough money for us to both retire on a beach on some tropical island in the South Pacific." Her eyes began to well up. "Go say your goodbyes to the friends you have here. Nicholas and I will throw you a going away party this weekend. You are going to have fun at this new place and when Nicholas and I go to visit you we'll get drunk at some sorority where we can make bad decisions."

She kissed my cheek quickly as an older sister would do to her baby one then twisted her arm in mine and walked me down to the entrance of the high school. There she sat with me until I calmed down enough to make myself believe that the entire afternoon had been part of some strange bad dream.

I sat on a radiator with my legs crossed underneath my body undisturbed. The longer I sat with my chin propped up on my hand the more disbelief was replaced with excitement. Not finishing my senior year of high school in the town I grew up in was surreal.

A few minutes after our last period began I felt someone staring at me. Soft footsteps came up and sat beside me. I finally looked over to see Nicholas.

"Steph told me what happened," his voice was gentle and he put a hand on my shoulder.

"I feel like I'm the butt of some sick joke," I shrugged my shoulders.

"Anyone would be excited to be in your place, Abbs." His voice was reassuring and supportive.

I sat up slowly and went over to a set of doors that led to a fire escape stairwell. "Come here, let's talk where no one else can hear us." I mimicked the crooked grin that was on his face.

He walked through the doors after me and I looked up at him innocently. Nicholas's face was so handsome and sincere. Quickly I pushed him against the wall using a tactic I had learned in a self defense class. "Who the hell are you?" I gritted.

"What's your problem?" he pushed against my grasp. "I'm your best friend, I've been your best friend since elementary school." His tone sounded rehearsed and bored rather than threatened.

"*My* Nicholas only calls me Abrielle and would never bring me to a concert without Steph. Now I'm a pretty easygoing person but I've had a particularly upsetting day and I'm kind of pissed off. If you would kindly tell me who you are and what you're doing taking on the image of my best friend it would really make my life a lot easier."

He laughed and pushed me away like I was a feather that had fallen upon his arm. "You'll find out soon enough."

He began to walk away but before he reached the door I yelled for him to stop and much to my surprise he froze.

"Look at me," I growled as tears began to form, "please." He turned slowly to face me. "I… I can't read you," I stuttered. "But I trust you. I'm hoping it is not just because you look like Nicholas, but because you're trustworthy. So is there anything you can answer for me. Like, do you have something to do with this Glaston Academy place?"

He looked over to his right and shrugged, "I can't say anything. You weren't really supposed to be able to tell I wasn't Nicholas." He ran his hand through his hair then looked back to me. "I guess I can say that I'll see you in school next week. You just might not recognize me."

"Are you a guy?" I chortled at my own question.

Amusement met his eyes. "Yeah I am."

"Okay, then why can't I read you?"

"I have to get back to class, Abbs," he raised his hands with a mischievous look before leaving the stairwell.

Somehow the conversation had put me at ease. I was glad that I would have someone at the school that I actually knew, sort of.

6

I walked into my house and stormed my way into the living room where my mother was wrapped in a blanket watching a Lifetime movie.

"I am cross with you," I put my hands on my hips. "You did not even discuss the Glaston Academy decision with me. You just signed my life away. I may not legally be an adult but I at least deserve some input in my own life."

I felt strong and powerful for those few moments while I spoke right up until she slowly pulled the blanket off of herself. "Abrielle," her face was tight and her voice was exacting, "until you pay all the bills in this house you have no right to make financial decisions. That school offered you a full scholarship including tuition, books, a meal plan, and housing. No one else would have given you that."

"I do volunteering, I single handedly started a local shelter for abandoned animals, and I have saved an entire year's worth of tuition to an Ivy League college. Any school would have been fortunate to have me as a student."

My mother rolled her eyes and I thought for sure I was going to get a lecture about my inheritance. I had not actually saved any money but I did get a healthy sum from my grandparents when they passed away.

"I never got a written form from any Ivy League school saying that I will not have to pay a dime." She pulled her blanket back onto her signaling that she was finished with our conversation.

"Acceptance letters won't come in for at least another four months!" I yelled throwing my hands up in frustration. "If someone hands you a platter that has 'too good to be true' written all over it, you should probably ask a few questions."

"Go do your homework Abrielle." She put the volume of her movie up a few notches louder.

"I don't have any homework because I'm not going to be at school next week, mother." I threw my backpack on the floor dramatically. "Steph is throwing me a going away party, so I'll be away this weekend. Two days less that you have to spend with the biggest mistake of your life before you send it away to some fake school." I turned around and stomped up the stairs to my room. I made it three steps before guilt surged through my torso.

My mother had me when she was only seventeen and she worked hard to make sure we both had a good life. She may have been strict, but she never physically hurt me. Every bit of strict parenting I received from her was only to make sure that I never made the mistakes she had made.

I plopped onto my bed thinking of how horrible I had been just when I got a text from Steph.

Lance Sinclair's parents are away this weekend.
Pick you up at 7 Friday for your party.

Love you!

Lance was the football team's quarterback who had prestigious lawyers as parents. He had an older brother that bought him kegs whenever his parents went away, which was at least once a month. The parties always ended with people passed out and others vomiting on the lawn. I typically snubbed my nose at the concept, but since I was about to begin college life a year early I figured Lance's house would be good practice.

I'll be wearing your heels and tank top.

I smiled to myself as I threw the phone down on the bed knowing she would be proud.

As soon as I got home that Friday I jumped into the shower then began doing my makeup and hair as Steph had done when I went to the concert. I curled the ends of my long dark hair, the curls bringing out the natural red and blonde highlights that hid in my brunette tresses. My eyes glowed blue between the curls that framed my face. The heels and jeans helped to accentuate the right parts of my body making me wonder why I did not wear them more often.

Steph picked me up at half past seven and gave me a once over before throwing me an approving nod. I slid my bottom into her jeep casually, making sure not to disrupt the work I had done on my hair.

An incredible wrap-around porch hugged Lance's three story snow colored house. Drunken guests mingled underneath the hanging plants paying no mind to a couple that were making out on one of the rocking chairs. It was strange seeing drunken teenagers stumbling about the house before the sun had fully set.

Steph tried to get me to walk in front of her into the house but we finally settled the wrestle with us walking in together. I was greeted by thirty familiar faces all saying a variety of things including "hey Abrielle," "congratulations," and "surprise." Lance quickly came up to me and pulled me into the kitchen where a large plastic tub with rope handles was filled with some sort of an alcoholic beverage.

"My brother and I made this for you. Well his girlfriend and I. It's called," he paused dramatically, "Abrielle's Awesome Punch." A wide and proud smile showed off his perfect teeth. "Everyone else has to pay two dollars to have a cup, but you can drink all you want for free all night. Because it's," he paused again, "Abrielle's Awesome Punch." I spoke the name of the drink with him feigning excitement and quickly grabbed a cup to appease the host.

"This is awesome," I smiled hugging Lance tightly. Lance and I barely ever spoke, but our interactions had always been pleasant, but I just figured that he had no idea who I was. I thought I had done a relatively good job of staying under the radar, but I suppose being attached at Steph's hip was bound to get me noticed.

As I was enjoying several cups of "Abrielle's Awesome Punch" I looked around and realized how much I would miss the people in the house; but in strange ways, almost as a security blanket. I could always count on Lance having parties just when things were about to become boring, Stacy and Ben breaking up only to get back together a week later, and all those habitual things that became everyday high school gossip. I was scared to move into a place where I would have to find new friends, gossip fountains, and hangout spots.

A strange mix of angst and happiness were bubbling together and the room was slowly beginning to appear fuzzy. I excused myself to the bathroom, by unappealingly yelling to Steph, "I've got to pee." Ten steps and a right turn later I found myself in the bathroom mirror and forced myself to smile.

"Even a fake smile will make you happier," I told my reflection and began making ridiculous smiling faces in the mirror. Just as I began laughing at myself someone knocked on the door. "Just a second," I muttered as I tried to grab the door handle, but missed. "Second time's the charm," I said opening the door abruptly with drunken ineptitude.

Nicholas was casually leaning against the door frame with his hands tucked into his jean pockets.

"Nicholas!" I wrapped my arms around his neck and pulled him in for a wobbly hug. "I was so nervous I wouldn't see you tonight. You know I found out I have a lot more friends than I thought, but you're my favorite guy friend ever, in the whole world. Let's be best friends forever."

He gave me a quick squeeze before he let go. "Obviously I wouldn't miss your going away party. Looks like you started drinking without me. Guess I'm going to have to catch up."

"Oh you will. Let's have a toast, a best friends forever toast with my own punch. Lance made it. It's called Abrielle's Awesome Punch." I slurred my own name so it sounded like "Arbrielleb."

"That sounds awesome," he smiled tugging my hair affectionately. "I'll meet you downstairs in two minutes Abbs."

He began to close the bathroom door but I jammed the heel of my palm into it. "What did you just say?" A wave of angry sobriety momentarily replaced my drunkenness. I stepped closer to him and poked my finger into his chest. "How dare you come to a party full of *my* friends pretending to be *my* Nicholas? What are you doing here? What is your obsession with disguising yourself as him anyway?"

"Whoa, Abrielle," he put his hands up, "you're acting crazy." He looked genuinely concerned and I wondered if I had heard him wrong. I looked around but fortunately there was no one else within earshot.

"Sorry," I muttered, "I guess I drank way more of the punch than I realized."

"It's okay, just switch off water and alcohol from now own and eat some snacks." He kissed my forehead quickly. "We'll make that toast in a minute, Abbs." He winked and swiftly slammed the door shut.

My jaw dropped and I punched the door. "You're a really rude man," I slurred at the door. "I'm going to tell Lance to make all the rude people leave." I stuck my tongue out then went down the steps to find Steph.

Steph was in the kitchen leaning against the counter laughing with Lance, Nicholas, and a few of the guys from the hockey team. Seeing Nicholas made my heart jump and heat rose to my face. It was unfair that I was having a hard time figuring out if I was looking at my friend or the stranger. The imposter was so good at acting like the real one that the only true way I could tell the difference between the men was by using my telepathy.

I was so comfortable around everyone at Lance's house that I hadn't thought to read anyone. Waves of nausea hit when I wondered if anyone else at the party was a fraud. Was it just the one person or was my mind being manipulated more than I already thought it was?

Unanswered questions were instantly wreaking havoc on my sanity so I tapped into the minds of the students at the party. As far as I could tell there were no emulators near me, though I did not know where the man that was just in the restroom had gone off to. For the rest of the night I stood with my shoulder against the real Nicholas in hopes that keeping constant contact with him would keep me from bumping into the fake one at any point.

The rest of the night was an Abrielle's Awesome Punch induced drunken festival complete with one noise complaint and three people vomiting before midnight. Lance's brother was offering free rides to anyone that lived within a five mile radius and was too drunk to drive home. Steph and I were the third pair to take his offer. Despite how intoxicated Steph was she managed to get into the backseat gracefully. I opened the front door feeling awkward but grateful that he had offered the ride.

"Who was your friend that was hanging out in the living room tonight?" Steph had directed the question at Lance's brother. He replied with a confused "huh?" and with a dainty sigh she replied, "There was a guy hanging out in the living room most of the night. I have never seen him before so I figured it was one of your friends making sure the party didn't get too crazy."

Her ability to hide her slurring amazed me. She had much more to drink than I did but could hide it when she wanted to. I stared at her reflection in the mirror to see that she was swaying ever so slightly. "He was watching you all night, Abrielle."

My mind began to race as I tried to remember

all the faces I had seen at Lance's house. I did not remember seeing anyone that I did not recognize in the living room, especially not one that was staring at me. Just then I realized that what I was seeing, or wasn't rather, had most likely been altered. "That was Rodney," I replied softly.

"You've been holding out," she clucked her tongue in a disapproving manner.

"He's annoying, Steph, you would hate him."

I felt both Steph and Lance's brother look at me. I waited for Steph to say something but a welcomed silence greeted me instead.

I stayed at Steph's house for the weekend watching slapstick comedies, eating junk food, and playing out future scenarios. Sunday night Steph, Nicholas, and I got together for a nostalgic sleepover at my house. By ten o'clock Nicholas was snoring softly while Steph and I lay on the bed staring up at the ceiling.

"You know my favorite thing about you?" I did not look over at Steph, just waited for her to respond.

"What's that?" her voice was quiet, as if she was about to fall asleep.

"I understand the whole idea of people following a crowd as a deep and primal survival instinct. Throughout history social pariahs do not do well on their own, they get killed or just have to live without the desired amount of human interaction.

You know who you are and you would survive no matter how far from the crowd you went." I looked at Steph, "I think it's awesome that you are so confident with the person you are."

Steph chuckled lightly, "I guess I make it look easier than it really is."

"How exactly do you think the crowd decides the direction it goes? Is it just a collective consciousness that strives for progression or is there a particular voice that we are programmed to listen for and follow?"

She stifled a yawn and rolled onto her side to face me. "Is there any way we can save the existential discussions for another time?" I giggled and nodded only to see her face fall somber. "You know what my favorite thing about you is?"

"My long glorious locks," I tousled my hair about faking excessive vanity.

Ignoring my feigned narcissism, "it's your faith in humanity. No matter how many bad things happen in this world you still believe there's good in everyone. You're like the little kid that stares outside waiting to watch Santa's reindeer fly over. The rest of the world is bitter and materialistic but you still see the magic in it all."

I was not sure what to say so I nudged her lightly, "I guess we're both pretty awesome."

7

My mother's voice was shrill at quarter to five in the morning. "Nicholas, would you please help Abrielle get her bags into the trunk?"

Nicholas grunted before responding with a polite, "Yes ma'am."

My lids fell shut and when I opened them next all the luggage was gone from my room. Steph was spread out across the bed next to me and Nicholas was sitting at my desk staring at taped pictures that lined a whiteboard hung above my computer.

Walking to his side I admitted, "I can barely remember a time before we were friends." The three of us had been friends for so long that it seemed like my memories began with them.

"Don't get all sentimental on me. You're going off to college before the rest of us are even graduating and we're stuck in high school rubbish classes. I'm not going to feel bad for you." He smiled but dark circles under his eyes made them look sad.

"You're just cranky because without me you will have to actually tell girls that you're not interested in them." I put down my wall to check that it was the real Nicholas and was happy to see that he was easy to read as ever.

"Being my fake girlfriend was the highlight of your day." He smirked and puffed his chest.

"Don't give yourself so much credit. It was, but only because I loved to see the looks on the girls faces when they thought that I actually might be with you." I chuckled to myself before a despondent silence fell upon us. "Take care of Steph," I squeezed his arm. "You may be fine without me, but she might actually miss me. Make sure that she is safe and happy and don't let anyone break her heart."

"I'll be fine," Steph muttered with her eyes still closed. I smiled and hugged her tightly. "Brush your teeth, sicko," she grunted before grabbing me in a tight hug. Not to be left out, Nicholas jumped on top of us to join in on the hug.

The departure was an emotional one. Steph and I both cried and my mother's eyes were watery. I read Nicholas again quickly just to make sure that it was him. I had to suppress a laugh when the thought I barged in on was him saying to himself, "the ice queen is melting."

My mother and I rode in silence with the exception of a drive-thru coffee stop halfway to Glaston Academy. I forced myself to eat in fear of the devastating embarrassment that would come along with low blood sugar on my first day at college.

Once we got off the interstate we took a right turn onto the road the school was on. I fidgeted with anxiety and studied my acceptance letter. Twelve miles from the interstate the street turned into a gravel road hugged tightly by trees.

"Did we miss it? I haven't even seen one building since we got off the highway." My stomach and throat were clenching in apprehension as my mom continued driving. She did not respond, only fueling my anxiety. "Mom, we are going down the scariest road in the continental United States. We were obviously picked by cannibals for some cruel joke. Let's turn around."

"Don't be so dramatic," she shook her head irritated, "we will keep driving for a few more minutes and if we don't see anything then we can call the school." After a long pause she looked at me in confusion, "why the continental United States?"

"I've never been to Hawaii or Alaska," I shrugged.

"Neither have you been on every road." She pinched her lips in annoyance.

"Touché, mother, touché."

We drove for another ten minutes until the road ended at two large iron gates with the letters "GA" curled into the ironwork. Beyond the closed entrance was a long path that led to a building that seemed more like a mansion than a college.

Hesitantly, I got out of the car and walked to the iron letters and pushed on them lightly only to find that they did not budge. There was no keypad or speaker in sight to prompt our entry onto the grounds. After a moment of searching for some way to get in I ran back to the safety of the car.

"I don't see anyone outside." Hardly a second passed after I spoke those words and the gates opened. The car rolled through and I took a deep breath, squeezed my eyes shut, and exhaled, "One... two... three. Three... two... one. " My words were barely audible but my mother asked what I had said. "I gave myself three seconds to be scared and let fear take over. It didn't help so I gave myself three seconds to become brave."

She slowed the car to a stop and stared at me quizzically. It was tempting to shrink under her scrutinizing gaze. I chewed on my bottom lip then whimpered, "Mommy, will you come get me on the weekends if this place is horrible?"

"Of course, honey." She squeezed my hand reassuringly. It was so seldom that she was supportive that when it happened it was pleasantly surprising.

"Here goes." I sucked in a breath and memorized the grey stone building in my mind before jumping out of the car.

I loved the way the stone dust crunched and moved beneath my feet. The sound calmed my anxious mind and I fell into step next to my mother who did not seem to be bothered at all by the strangeness of the situation. We both stopped in front of two large oak doors. I went to grab the handle but as I did the door opened slowly.

"Good morning!" A tall girl not much older than I with a tiny frame stood in front of my mother and me. She wore a light blue plaid dress that reminded me of a table cloth and matching high heel shoes. Where did she get a dress with matching shoes? "My name is Rebecca," she put her hand out to shake mine, "and you must be Abrielle. What a unique name!"

Rebecca was personable, but there was something about the way she spoke that made me uneasy. Gently and cautiously I tried to read her. Suddenly she stopped speaking and narrowed her eyes at me as if she could tell what I was trying to do. I jumped at her reaction. As far as I knew, no one could tell when I tried to read their minds but it definitely seemed like she knew.

Random facts about Glaston Academy were spoken almost in a sing song manner while Rebecca brought my mother and me to the Dean's office. Since it was a college I had expected to see hung over students, people making out, sorority pledges, and the token gritty student that was still in pajamas but everyone was engrossed in their studies rather than social interaction.

"Here is the dean's office." A flat palm traced the way from our view to the open door. "Go right in, he is ready for you." She smiled and gave a brief curtsy before walking away.

We walked into the office and I froze. What I was witnessing held my body captive; I could not compel any of my limbs to move. I blinked rapidly to try and determine if I was seeing the person sitting in the Dean's chair correctly.

"Pleasantries, Mrs. and Miss Abbott, please come in." Mr. Murphy ushered us into his office. "I am Professor Horicon, the dean of students here at Glaston Academy. Now, seeing how Miss Abbott is not yet eighteen I just need you to sign some paperwork and then we will get her to orientation right away."

I was going crazy; it was the only explanation. That was why there was a fake Nicholas, why I was suddenly accepted into a college before I was supposed to finish high school, and why the dean at the college was my homeroom teacher. Glaston Academy was just a mental institution that my mother was dropping me off at. There was no other explanation.

My mother signed the papers and everything seemed to move quickly but in slow motion all at one. Once she was finished I took deep shallow breaths expecting a strait jacket to be put on me. "Bye sweetie. Good luck," my mother hugged me quickly and tightly.

"Mrs. Abbot one of our students, William, will be waiting in the foyer to assist you with Abrielle's belongings." The man had his hand resting lightly on his diaphragm as he stood waiting for my mother to leave the room.

Tears threatening to escape stung my eyes and I searched for something in the office to take my attention away from the horrible feelings welling within my chest. Mr. Murphy, or Professor Horicon, shut the door behind my mother and went back to his seat.

"Take a seat, Abrielle, I'm sure you have a few questions."

"First and foremost being, who are you? Are you Mr. Murphy or Professor Horicon?"

Amusement tugged his lips upwards. "Glaston Academy is a college for young adults that are gifted. Part of my job is to perform clandestine scouting for gifted individuals at other schools that are deemed worthy of Glaston Academy. Due to the sensitivity of the gifts that our students possess it is critical that I hide my identity while I scout. Mr. Murphy is my alias but Professor Horicon is my true identity."

"Gifted? I have good grades but I'm second in my class at a public school. I'm not anywhere close to gifted. Mensa not Mega," I clarified. Had my high school teachers not been so eager to give extra credit my GPA would have been under a 4.0.

"We do indeed look for intelligent students. You will find that Glaston Academy has an extremely rigorous curriculum and if you cannot find a way to keep your grade point average above a 3.0 then you will lose your scholarship." He stood and looked outside. "The gifts I am speaking of are much more arcane in nature. I am talking about telepathy, telekinesis, one's ability to manipulate energy, and so on." He turned to me for a dramatic effect. "We even have a student here who has perfected invisibility."

"Professor Horicon," I spoke cautiously, "did you say this is Glaston Academy or Glaston Asylum?"

"Very clever, Abrielle." He scowled and cleared his throat. "We had a few scouts at your previous school. We sensed telepathy, empathy, healing, and possibly replication." He gave me a moment to allow his words to sink in. "Here at Glaston Academy we will help you further develop your skills, among other things."

"Among other things?"

He ignored my question and continued on as if his introduction to the school was previously recorded and was simply playing through his mouth. "I'd like to show you some figures. You were given a full scholarship your meal plan, books, tuition, even a small clothing allowance." He put a sheet of paper in front of me that showed the sum of charges that added up to a figure that my mother made in a total of twenty years. "Now, if you fail one class you are put onto academic probation. Fail two classes and you are on an academic warning. In the fashion of our all-American past time, three strikes and you lose your scholarship."

"I lose the scholarship, but I am not expelled?"

"Heavens no," his lips curled into a smile that

would be painted on an evil clown doll, "the material we teach here is much too sensitive to be only partially taught. We cannot have gifted individuals running amuck with just part of their talent polished. It could create chaos." He paused and pursed his lips together, "we... Glaston Academy cares about each one of its students."

"Three class failures in one year or in the entire four years we will be here? Do I have a major? I never signed up for one."

"Wonderful questions, Abrielle. The failures are for your entire education here. The academy is not necessarily four years because each person has a different gift and it takes some longer to perfect that gift than others. We give you a major based upon your strengths. It is not the typical way that universities do this, but we find it works well for our students." He stood up and straightened out his tweed jacket. "So that we are clear, if you fail three classes while you are here your mother is responsible for your tuition. Plenty of extra credit opportunities will be given so I should hope this will not be an issue for you."

"The worst grade that I have ever received was a C+ in junior high because I kept burning things in my cooking class. I cannot imagine that I would fail anything."

He held the door open for me so we could begin the tour. "Classes at Glaston Academy are taught at an exceptional level. You are all intelligent so we teach the classes for our brightest pupils.

Receiving a C is a mark that you are average. Failing simply means that you had the lowest score on the test in that class. You will understand soon enough."

Since the entire Glaston Academy ordeal was entirely too good to be true and there was so much emphasis on the three failures policy I figured that this was the one visible blemish on their beautiful façade.

The inside of the academy was breathtakingly intricate in an old mansion sort of sense. Stunning dark hardwood floors lay beneath elaborately patterned high ceilings. The interior style of the school reminded me of one of those old mansions in Rhode Island. My anxiety was actually diminishing as I observed the architecture.

Professor Horicon showed me where the bulk of the classes would be held, the offices of the professors, and the kitchen where we were free to make our own meals or have them made by the chef Susan something or other when she was working. We exited a door through the kitchen out to the yard. A fountain and two statues separated a long yard of perfectly mowed grass and a line of trees. To the west of the building were stables and to the east was a smaller stone building and a couple tennis courts.

He informed me that there was also a running track and swimming pool on campus but he believed my roommate would show me that in time. The smaller building was used for dormitories. The first floor of the residence hall had a small kitchen, sitting area, and another room for recreation. The second floor housed the females while the third was designated for the guys. There were about one hundred and fifty students and each shared a room with either one or two other students.

I stepped onto a slightly slanted tile floor into the recreation room of the building. A few pool tables, televisions, and foosball tables seemed brand new and untouched. The next room was a massive carpeted sitting room where a dozen people were lounged on different sofas studying. Inside the sitting room was a stately staircase leading up to the second and third floor.

We stopped in front of Room 217; my new home for the next year. He knocked on the door and introduced me to my roommate, Elizabeth. After the brief introduction Professor Horicon turned on his heel and vanished.

My new roommate had straight blonde hair that curved against her chin, an angular face, and deep green eyes that were almost brown. "Liz," she stuck her porcelain hand towards me. I took it in mine and nodded, "Abrielle."

She ushered me inside the room. An old hardwood floor was covered by a large grey area rug that disappeared beneath two beds on opposite sides of the room. Two wooden desks underneath their own windows were against the far wall separating the beds. Identical lavender duvets lay atop the twin beds and the one furthest from the door had my luggage piled atop it.

Liz shut the door behind her and squared her chin towards me. "I am going to do this the fairest way I believe possible. In the closet are your books. Once I hand you the books you become a student and then we are in competition with one another. Until you set your hand on those books you are simply an acquaintance asking questions about the school. I can give you an hour for questions, after that I will hand you the books. Fair?"

She was polite, but direct. My jaw hung slack for a moment from simply being overwhelmed. "Yes, that is fair." I moved the luggage off the bed and sat down. "So, I guess it is really competitive here." It was both a statement and a question.

"Yes. The goal is to get the best grade that you can. The classes are small and range from five to twenty students. The way they teach things here is a bit unorthodox but the main concentration is our gifts. When it comes to our gifts we are mostly in competition with ourselves, but the regular classes are not easy and are taught at a graduate level. Academia is graded in terms of your classmates. Even if you get, say, a 95 on an examination but the rest of the class scored above you, you will fail."

Liz paused for a brief moment then continued, "You will get a schedule delivered to the room in about two hours so you will have a better idea of what is in store for you. Monday, Wednesday, and Friday will have two academic classes and a four hour block dedicated to your skill. Tuesday and Thursday have three academic classes and one hour for gifted learning. The weekends are for studying and practicing."

"What is your gift?"

Emotionless she answered, "Invisibility."

"No way!" My jaw dropped with excitement. "Can I see?"

My roommate had the gift of invisibility? I had thought I was a rare gem for having telepathy but learning that there were actually people with other capabilities was incredible. I did not think I would ever have anyone to talk to about my gift let alone be able to learn how to use it or perfect it in any manner. Glaston Academy was quickly changing from a possible asylum to a godsend.

"We cannot use our gifts unless it is the weekend or we are in class." She began to fidget then pace.

I tried to focus on what I would need to know about the school. It was impossible to tell what the important questions were since I was not acquainted with the school yet. Biting my lip I searched for the first question to come to mind so as to not waste the hour. "What is replication? Professor Horicon said that they sensed replication. How do they sense what we can do specifically?" I had no idea what replication was or if I was truly able to heal organisms, but I was more interested in how someone could sense my gifts.

Her eyes grew wide momentarily. I almost thought that I imagined it because it was so quick before her face was back to stone. "Replication is the ability to mimic another person's gift. It is really rare and the only person I know to have that is the headmaster. You must have misheard him. I can see that you're a telepath and an empath. That is it."

"How can you 'see' that?" Sure I could feel when I was around Samantha that she was a telepath like me, but I definitely could not pick much up from anyone here so far.

She informed me that we were only allowed to use our gifts during particular hours and I desperately wanted to read her. The body language she was displaying said that she was moments away from hitting me but my innate senses were telling me that I could trust her and she was a friend. "You will learn it in the next two weeks, I'm sure." She then sighed and rolled her head to the side as if I was exhausting her.

"So, how exactly do you get extra points?"

She sat down on the bed across from me. Apparently I had asked a question she deemed worthy. "Extra credit is awarded by doing things that the professors highly approve of. Some professors are harder to impress than others and some things that you might do for the academy will get you extra points towards whatever class you wish. For instance, you had scouts go to your school or work or what have you. A couple of those scouts were students. They will most likely get between twenty and fifty points."

"There was a guy there that was pretending to be my friend, he was identical to him. Who, how, and why?"

"Oh," she flicked her hand in the air, "it was either Vlaine or Draxe. They are the only people here who can shift. They can take on the image of whoever they want. Vlaine is a bit more talented in the shifting department but Draxe is a better scout. For all I know it could have been them both trying to see if you were Glaston worthy."

"I don't have my schedule yet, but are there any study tips or tricks for the classes you think I might have?"

Her eyes were focused on me and she smiled for a fraction of a second. I had asked another question she approved of. "I heard they nabbed you from high school. Assuming you had above a 3.2 you will test out of your high school classes and go right to college ones. You will probably have a healthy mix of economics, physics, robotics, anatomy, and calculus. If we can finish up this painful discussion I promise to give you five minutes dedicated to this question once you get your schedule."

I nodded my head in agreement and she quickly rushed to get my books and pushed them towards me.

"Wait," I said before touching them, "just one last quick question." She groaned in response. "What is the worst thing that can happen to me while I am here?"

Liz hugged the books to her chest and her flawless porcelain complexion drained to a grey one. "You could get a visit from the headmaster. He is someone you never want to meet and if someone says that you have a meeting with him I would be very, very concerned."

I nodded and put my hand on the books that she was still clutching tightly to her chest. "Thank you, Liz."

She ordered me to get a decent meal because it would be the last enjoyable one I would have until I graduated from Glaston. I went to the kitchen and reintroduced myself to Susan who seemed thrilled to have someone to speak to. Her ruddy red hair was cut short like a boy, she was stout and homely, but her voice was entrancing. I wondered if the entire faculty was gifted as well because I was sure that if she had one it was the ability to captivate someone with her speech.

Susan put a plate of salad with diced grilled chicken and asparagus in front of me and pushed a napkin wrapped cookie towards me with a wink. I ate quietly and listened to her describe her children and what they did for a living. While she spoke I tried to study the students that shuffled by quickly. Each one had an arm full of books and there was no particular clothing style. The other girls wore anything from jeans and a tee shirt to dresses and heels. I made a mental note not to use a backpack and to keep to myself until I could figure out who was friendly enough to approach.

Just as I was finishing up my meal an older man in his forties walked through at a normal pace. His lack of rush was the first thing to get my attention and the second thing was his appearance. He was the definition of debonair. My eyes scanned his body from his shined shoes, up a perfectly ironed suit that met a clean shaven, strong chin. Raven black hair was combed into place and his dark eyes did not appear to look at anything in the room. He walked towards the side of the refrigerator and opened part of the wall that led to a hidden room behind the kitchen. I looked away, not sure if the concealed room was something I was allowed to know about.

I had been so fixated on the man that I did not realize that Susan had stopped speaking. She was frozen in place, her eyes watching me until the panel was completely closed. Once it was back in place Susan continued on with her story as if nothing had happened.

"Wait," I cut her off from telling me about her grandchild that was soon to be born, "should I pretend that I did not see that panel open up into another room?"

"The headmaster did not seem to hide it from you, but I would not go telling the entire school about it." Her mouth formed a thin line.

"That was the headmaster?"

"It sure was," she gave a quick nod before taking my plate away.

"The way I heard about him I expected a

terrifying old man, maybe with horns."

Susan put the plate down and leaned close to me. "The headmaster is not to be trifled with. He is the most powerful man here and trust me when I tell you that being off his radar is in your best interest. Now go on little missy and start your studying. Just because you are new here does not mean they will give you any leniency."

I nodded, thanked her, and headed back to my dorm room. Liz was writing notes furiously and reading quickly out loud. As silently as possible I began putting clothes away into the small section of the closet that was empty. Everything was separated into our own particular sections. I could not tell if Liz had done it because she was simply that precise or if stress made her meticulous. She did not seem to notice my presence until someone knocked on the door.

"Yeah," she yelled quickly never taking her eyes off her notes.

I opened up the door to see the plaid dress once again. She handed me an envelope and walked away without saying a word. I skipped over to my desk and eagerly slid my finger underneath the flap and pulled out three different stapled packets. One entailed the rules of the school, another highlighted the activities the school offered, and the last was my class schedule.

The activity packet noted I would have to pick three in the event that my choice was not available. I signed the rules, checked off archery, horseback riding, and then track. I wriggled in my seat with anticipation and pulled out my schedule. Monday, Wednesday, and Friday would be physics and ecology before four hours of skill broken up into two hours a piece with a one hour lunch break. Tuesdays and Thursdays would begin with chemistry, literature, followed by a lunch break and would end with macroeconomics before an hour of skill.

I pulled the textbooks for my classes out of the pile that Liz handed me and put the rest under my bed. I began reviewing chemistry, literature, and macroeconomics since they would be my classes the following day.

"Do I have a text book for my skill class?" Liz snorted in response and kept writing notes. I knew what would get her attention. "The headmaster is really handsome and he did not look mean at all." Liz dropped her pen and her porcelain face turned grey once again. I crouched towards her and whispered, "Why are you so afraid of him?"

She put out her hand and ignored my question. "Let me see your schedule," she demanded sounding exasperated.

"You can turn invisible but you are afraid of some dapper guy in his thirties or forties. That just sounds ridiculous. But I guess so does a school for students endowed with abilities that are seemingly impossible. Here's my schedule." I handed over the paper and sat back watching her eyes intently.

Her lip twitched as she read it. "Okay," she straightened herself out in her seat, "you have physics and ecology with me. I took macro and literature before but haven't taken chemistry yet. It looks like they are giving you the smorgasbord to find your potential. In macro you really want to focus on the reading. You could almost ignore his lectures and just read and you would be safe. The lit professor is one of those people who focuses on symbolism and themes. You will have a lot of papers to write and if you mess up your works cited then you fail the class instantly. We have a test in physics next Wednesday and a paper due at the end of the week in ecology. You won't get any favors but I'll let you see the syllabi for the classes so you can start getting ahead." A few seconds later she pulled out the syllabi and I copied them down and began studying.

8

In the middle of studying I got the urge to write Steph a letter. I let her know how busy I would be with school and that it did not seem like visiting would be an option for at least a month but I wished she could see the campus. I filled her in on a few interesting details about the school but kept everything else a secret.

Once I finished the letter I roamed the grounds looking for a drop box. Curiosity brought me to the stables. I walked by two students on the way who never even glanced up as I passed by them. The horses were the only things on the campus aside from the three people that had talked to me that seemed to have any life to them. I wanted to touch the horses, as if they were calling to me. I lifted my hand up towards one and realized I was still holding the letter. I heard movement at the other end of the stable.

"Hey," I spoke softly as I walked towards the movement. I turned the corner to see a student brushing a horse.

The guy had dirty blonde hair and a pleasant

face. There was nothing particularly striking about the guy, but he seemed approachable. I walked closer to him, leaving enough distance so that if the horse kicked I would be out of its reach. He looked up quickly but concentrated on his stallion once again.

"Is there something I can help you with?" I turned around to meet the face from whom the voice came from. A tall guy with dark skin and hair that was buzzed so close that he was nearly bald looked down at me with a kind smile. "He won't stop brushing that horse for at least another hour." His voice was deep, smooth, and pleasant.

I put my hand out to shake his, "Hi, I'm…"

"Abrielle," he cut me off, "we all know who you are. At a small school like this we always know when someone leaves or comes. If someone new is coming in it is our business to know everything there is to know about them."

"That is a little creepy, but I guess I understand. I was wondering if there is a drop box anywhere." I held the letter as if I needed to prove that I had a reason for looking around.

He chuckled, "You were looking for a drop box in the stables?"

Heat rose to my face, "no, well, I was walking and I wanted to see the horses. You know, on my way to find the drop box."

"I'm Will," he finally stretched his hand out to meet mine, "help me with Cinnamon and I'll take you over to the mailbox."

I took his hand and happily complied. It was nice to have another student treat me like a human. He led me to a white horse with light brown spots and handed me a brush. "Cinnamon?" I arched an eyebrow and pointed at the mostly white horse.

He nodded his head in reply and began making long strokes with the brush. "They are beasts compared to us. Push hard so that it does not tickle her." The instructions were the only thing he said while we brushed her. It was relaxing and after half an hour the anxiety from my day had completely dissipated.

The silence between the two of us was surprisingly comfortable. When we finished he led me out of the barn towards the school. Once we were clear of the barn he broke the silence. "Until people know who you really are, they are not going to speak to you. It's a defense mechanism here that works. That was Kyle back there. He's a good guy, but I would not try to be friends with him if I were you. You're aware of the competition that everyone is in with one another, and it brings out the worst of everyone. At least when the worst is out we can see the true human that lies underneath."

"That sounds incredibly morbid."

I was a nice person, but who was I when I was at my worst? I hated seeing people sad and if someone was hurt all I wanted to do was take their pain away. The most upset I could remember being was when that person pretended to be Nicholas. It was invasive and I felt betrayed. If that happened when I was in a more stressful situation there was no telling how ugly my personality could be, but I hoped that I was trustworthy and kind enough for new students to come to if they needed.

I lowered my voice. "Is there anyone I should steer clear from?"

He smirked and pulled the door open for me. "Adele is a real firecracker and she can't seem to control it when she is mad. She gets mad a lot." His white teeth seemed to glow as he laughed at a memory he was playing in his head. "I mean everyone stays to themselves for the most part but you'll learn who she is quickly and learn to take cover when she gets mad." His smile faded and he whispered so close to my ear that it tickled unpleasantly. "Vlaine."

I nodded so that he knew I heard the name. "I'm sorry if this is really intrusive, I'm not accustomed to a place that wears their gifts on their sleeves. I spent most of my time hiding and building walls for mine. What is your gift?"

He stopped walking and all emotion left his face. "Jeez Abrielle, we just met and you're asking me to take my clothes off?"

"I... I'm sorry, I," I began to stammer before he started laughing.

"I'm just kidding. I'm a telepath like you but my specialty is in mental manipulation."

Mental manipulation sounded like something a villain from a superhero movie would have. I decided not to press about it because I had no idea what the unwritten policy was for discussing our particular talents. He led me to a copper box beside the secretary desk with a flip lid that had the word "MAIL" stenciled on it. I tucked the letter into the container then he walked me back to my dorm and we parted ways.

Back at the dorm Liz was lying on her bed reading some sort of notebook. When I walked in she shielded it with her arms so that I could not see it. I shrugged it off, if she truly did not want me to know she had it I was sure it would have gone under her pillow or blanket as soon as she heard the door open.

I got into my pajamas as quickly as possible and snuggled under my new eiderdown and reviewed the notes I had taken earlier. Once I felt comfortable enough with my understanding of the material I placed it underneath my bed and turned off the light on my side of the room.

A few minutes later Liz followed suit. "Goodnight Abrielle," her words floated in the darkness.

I smiled at the glimmer of kindness. "Goodnight, Liz."

9

Liz was rummaging about the room at five in the morning. Groaning, I pulled the covers over my head and tried to fall back asleep for another hour before my alarm clock went off. The sound of Liz starting the shower prevented me from being able to fall back asleep. Annoyed with my lack of sleep from an anxiety ridden night of tossing and turning I grunted and growled with each move I made.

Steam flowed from the bathroom as Liz emerged wrapped in a bright pink towel. "Shower is all yours."

Once I got over the initial shock of seeing Liz come out in just a towel I ran into the bathroom to get ready. Our classes were not scheduled to start until eight but she seemed to be in a rush. I wanted to get out and ready quickly enough to figure out what was happening before classes began.

Five minutes had barely passed before I hurried out of the bathroom. My hair was wrapped in a towel and I was hopping side to side trying to shimmy a sock onto my damp foot.

"Don't classes start at eight o'clock?" It was only quarter to six and she was completely ready.

"Breakfast is at six-thirty and everyone congregates in the kitchen half an hour early. It is really the only social hour that we have here." She smiled and smeared a deep red lipstick on that perfectly contrasted her natural platinum hair. A sage dress hung loose on her body making it seem like she had curves in places that there really were none.

"You look beautiful, Liz," I smiled and I grabbed a pair of jeans and a tee shirt from my side of the closet.

"Thank you." She stopped applying mascara and sighed. "Today is your first day at Glaston Academy. What you wear today is how you will be remembered by most of the people including the faculty. Wear that outfit next week but for today grab my burgundy dress, stockings, and boots. No one has seen me wear it yet so they will not know it's mine. You've got me beat something unfair in the chest department, but it just might work for you."

I did as she said and we were both ready for the day within forty minutes. We walked towards the kitchen together until a girl with bobbing curls grabbed Liz by the arm and pulled her away from me as if she was saving her from some social faux pas that Liz was committing by being seen with me.

I walked into the kitchen and said good morning to Susan who was busy preparing pans full of eggs, pancakes, and bacon. Baskets of fruit sat on each table ready for the taking. There were only a few students in the kitchen so far and I felt my shoulders relax when I saw Will walk in. I did not want to disrupt his social standing with anyone so I tried to be as nonchalant and quick as possible asking him where to sit. I knew how upset people could get if someone was in their seat and I did not want to leave a bitter taste on anyone's tongue if I could help it.

"Sit over here," he pointed his chin at a small table to the far right of the room.

"Thank you," mouthed to him as I made my way to the chair he pointed out for me.

"Will!" Liz shrieked, "Would you mind not starting fire to the kitchen first thing in the morning?"

I jumped and looked over towards Liz confused by what had just happened. Will laughed so hard that he had to steady himself by putting his hands on his knees.

"Argh," Liz grunted, "that is Adele's seat. Abrielle, sit over at the table next to that one in the chair facing my table."

"I told you not to trust anyone," Will winked.

"What is your obsession with this Adele girl? Is she your girlfriend?" I plopped into the chair that Liz designated for me and watched Will try to gather himself after his laughing fit.

"No," his lips were barely hiding his bright white teeth.

"You totally like her," I gasped. "You like it when she gets mad!" I giggled and pointed at him.

"Hey," he gave me a pointed look, "spreading rumors on your first official day is no way to avoid enemies." I put my finger to my mouth indicating that his secret was safe with me.

Students began to trickle in and though Liz had helped me to find a seat I was still uncomfortable. Everyone knew who I was and I would surely be under scrutiny by the other peers. I straightened out my back and tried to put my insecurities aside and think of how Steph would act in this situation. She would sit with her back straight, chin up, and exude confidence at anyone that came in. Any other telepath could tell that I was anything but confident, but I would hold my head up and feign it for anyone else.

I found myself staring at Will's table. There were three other guys sitting with him, two of which could easily pass as his brothers. Will and the two men were tall, dark, and muscular. The other person had thick rimmed glasses, freckles, had pink toned skin, was plump, and short. Each person at the table acted the same and I wondered if it was possible they had the same abilities and it drew them together.

A familiar feeling came over me while I was people watching. Just then I saw Will stop talking and watch someone walk across the kitchen. I followed his eyes to a man that was just about to sit down at my table.

"Hello," I smiled politely hoping that Liz hadn't directed me to his seat.

I had to suck my cheeks so that I would not grin like a fool. The man in front of me was handsome and everything about him indicated trouble. Flat drawn eyebrows played a strange duality with his roguish grin. Deep blue eyes glimmered in contrast to his dark hair and fading tan. After studying his face my eyes traveled from his boots up to stonewashed jeans then lingered a little too long on his white tee shirt that hugged his sculpted torso.

The silence was making me a bit uncomfortable and I began fiddling with my orange peel as I waited for him to reply. He pulled the chair in front of me out exaggeratingly slow and just as he was about to sit down I realized why he felt familiar.

"You," I gasped, my mouth hanging unattractively agape. I was looking at the man who had pretended to be Nicholas, I could feel it.

An innocent expression came across his face. "Me?"

"You were the fake Nicholas!"

"Whoa," he put his hands up defensively. "The new girl is crazy," he muttered with a sardonic smile.

I looked over towards Will to see that he and Liz, as well as a few other students, were watching the interaction intently. The man remained in the seat across from me, much to my dismay I wanted him to stay there. His demeanor was aggravating and I hated the fact that he pretended to be my friend, but he offered familiarity in a place I felt mostly alone.

"Well, looks like you are a guy." My eyes traveled along his body once again, "Unless, of course, you took on the appearance of someone else this time." I crossed my arms against my chest. I was not backing down and he would not make me look like a fool on my first day.

"Yes I am a guy." He nodded his head as if he was speaking to a toddler. Then he switched his position to a more threatening one. "But by all means keep staring. If you don't I might just turn into a woman."

"Ugh, you are such a jerk." I snarled my lip at him. "What is your problem? Am I in your seat or something?" I looked quickly at Liz, her blank face gave me no indication either way.

He stared at me and provided no answer. "Do you pick up traits from people when you emulate them? Nicholas always gets cranky when he hasn't had breakfast. Here, eat something," I tossed an apple at him.

He grabbed the apple and threw it back at me. I caught the fruit with my right hand then took a bite of it and winked at him. I was smiling, but it was only because I was impressed with my ability to catch the apple so quickly.

Without a word he stood up and began to walk away. "See you later," I cooed before taking another bite out of the apple.

"Later, Abbs," he turned and winked before vanishing from the room.

I stared at the spot where he was when he left the room memorizing his features. When I finally snapped my attention to the rest of the room I found that a quarter of the students in the kitchen were staring at me.

Will walked past my table on his way back from getting himself a helping of pancakes. "The one person I told you to stay away from," he gritted through his teeth.

"That was your girlfriend Adele?" I was being playful but I was a bit agitated from how he had tricked me earlier.

"You just met Vlaine." There was no smile on his face this time. "Help me brush Cinnamon tonight at six."

"Sure thing," I nodded. As Will began to walk away a couple sat down at my table. They were so immersed in their own conversation that they did not seem to even notice I was there. That must have been why Liz told me to sit there. Of all the open seats in the kitchen, this table was the only one where I was invisible to the regular occupants.

I found my way to my class an hour early and began looking over my notes. Being early allowed me enough time to begin writing the paper that was due at the end of the week and read the material we would cover in class. I liked to be prepared in case I was called on for any reason. Chemistry was not my strongest area of study, but I was sure I could manage well enough.

Two draft pages were finished before any of the other students trickled in. My concentration lay solely on my paper and I refused to meet the gaze of whoever was staring at me from the other side of the room. Having another student's eyes on me was reminiscent of how I felt when Samantha was staring at me in our study period. Ignoring the prying eyes, I looked out the window and enjoyed the view of a few decorative trees lining a garden on the side of the building. A squirrel hopping along the branches stole my attention until the professor entered the room.

The professor scribbled equations across the board and the students frantically copied them down along with whatever he was saying. Halfway through the class the squirrel caught my attention once again. It scurried about and jumped to a slender branch on an adjacent tree. The branch snapped underneath the critter's weight and he fell to the ground, squirming about erratically. I must have made some noise because as soon as I saw the squirrel fall to the ground the professor asked if he was interrupting whatever had my interest.

"I'm sorry, I was paying attention." My eyes were still on the squirrel.

"What did I say then Abrielle?"

I repeated his exact words and the formula

without breaking eye contact with the hurt animal. "I'm sorry Professor B. I know this is going to sound silly, but there's a squirrel down there with a broken leg. I saw him fall from a branch and it's…" my words began to trail as I realized how ridiculous I sounded.

"Do you think you can help it?" his words were surprisingly kind.

"Yes," I whispered uncomfortably.

"Then go ahead," he nodded before returning to his work.

"Really? Okay." I walked quickly from my seat to the door then took off in a full sprint down the stairs and outside to aid the animal.

"Shhhh," I slowly made my way to the animal.

The squirrel was hobbling about frantically thrashing about his broken leg. Letting go of all precautions I had before, I let myself use the healing ability Professor Horicon declared I had. I imagined a wave of serenity flowing from me to the rodent. Within seconds it stopped thrashing and lay on the ground panting. As I inched closer his rapid breathing slowed. Finally I put my hand a few inches above his leg and imagined every cell in the little limb mending and fixing the injury.

I opened one eye slowly, afraid to find the leg still limp and twisted, but exhaled in relief when it was rather firm. Slowly I stepped backwards and retracted my influence from its mind. Once I saw that he could run away on his own without any trouble I sprinted back up to the classroom and silently took my seat.

At the end of class the other students left quickly to get to their next destination. I gathered my items and the professor called me to his desk. Worry ridden waves of nausea rolled about in my gut as I made my way to his desk. Considering the austerity of the school, the concern of a squirrel was probably on the bottom of the priorities list at Glaston Academy.

"That trick you pulled with the squirrel, Abrielle," he began before I cut him off.

"I'm so sorry for disrupting your class like that. I saw that it was hurt and I just couldn't help myself." I looked at the floor ashamed of how infantile I had acted in my very first college chemistry class.

"It was disruptive," he pulled his glasses off, "but it was superior. I will award you fifty extra credit points to the class for healing the squirrel."

"You saw that it worked?" I asked surprised.

"Oh yes, it is one of my gifts." He grinned and made a note next to my name in his roster. "The class has a paper due Friday. Since they have had an extra week to work on it I will give you until one week from today to finish it. Good luck with the rest of your day Abrielle." I tried to suck in my cheeks to hide the enormous smile that pulled across my face. I could not believe that I had scored fifty extra credit points on my very first day.

It seemed that the rest of the students in Literature had taken their seats by the time I had arrived which made it easy for me to decide which one I would take. Three open chairs were in the back of the room and I took the one closest to the window. I was easily distracted by the nature outside, but it had proven to be a good luck charm in my last class.

"Is there a bunny or something you need to go save?" The guy who pretended to be Nicholas leaned into my ear.

My heart raced at our proximity, both out of frustration and curiosity. "Ew, I have your saliva in my ear now," I laughed rubbing where he had just whispered. "How do you even know about that?"

"Everyone knows everything here." He tapped his finger on the desk. "Sort of like how everyone knows that this is my seat."

"How am I going to protect the animal kingdom if I cannot keep an eye on it, Vlaine?" It felt empowering knowing his name. Will had given me the largest piece of consolation I could ask for, the name to the man who was fake Nicholas.

"I will drag you out of that seat if I have to, Abbs." His eyes were cold, serious. I fought the chill that crept down my back.

"You still haven't eaten breakfast have you?" I stood up and walked to the seat directly next to it. "It is the most important meal of the day." I sat down gracefully not letting him know that his intimidating demeanor had me uneasy.

He took his seat and I sat through the lecture entirely aware of the daunting yet incredibly attractive man sitting next to me.

10

I was fidgeting in my seat for most of macroeconomics just waiting to get to skill. The idea of a seminar dedicated to perfecting my innate abilities was exciting. I practically skipped to Professor Horicon's office to find out where I would need to be only to find out that they had not figured out which professor would be instructing me. It was disappointing that I would have to wait to begin my Individual Skill Enhancement Seminar, but it would give me an entire afternoon to finish my chemistry paper.

With all the other students in their classes I had the entire dormitory building to myself. The silence allowed me to polish my paper before Professor B. left for the evening. Since everyone made such a big deal about failing a class I wanted to make sure the assignment was to his liking.

Though Professor B. was impressed with my initiative, he informed me that my reference format was outdated and some of my figures seemed pointless. The man was fair and made it evident that we would have papers on the most important parts of the lecture so he knew we understood the material since we would be learning so much in such a short amount of time. I did not know what my other professors would be like, but so far he was my favorite.

I left his office studying the notes he wrote on my paper and walked into a body. "I'm so sorry," my eyes met a freshly ironed three piece suit. The headmaster met my gaze momentarily and continued walking without saying a word. "Have a good evening, headmaster." I called politely to him as he walked away. He definitely did not speak much, but I still had yet to find out why people were so afraid of him.

I went back to my dorm to make the necessary changes to my paper and then met up with Will at the stables. Aside from the horses, we were the only ones in there.

"Well I did not get Adele to set a fire like you wanted. I thought for sure there would have been an explosion when I walked directly into the headmaster, but nothing happened then either."

His jaw dropped, "what did you do to piss him off?"

"Nothing, I was leaving a room and he was there but I didn't see him. I walked right into him, but look," I raised my hands in the air, "I'm still here."

"No," he shook his head, "you don't get it. The headmaster isn't seen unless he wants to be seen. Most students here stay under the radar enough so they never interact with him. You did something to piss him off."

"These freshman scare tactics don't work on me," I squinted at Will, "I'm an empath, remember? We can tell when someone is bad, it's innate."

"Your alarm bells are broken. You flirted with the one person I told you to stay away from."

"Ugh!" I sneered my lips in a repulsed manner, "I wasn't flirting. Vlaine was a scout that pretended to be my best friend. I was bitter because of that so I made sure he knew I knew it was him."

"Don't Abrielle, don't interact with him. He's bad news."

"How?" I was beginning to get frustrated with how unclear he and Liz were about their warnings.

"Vlaine is…" he searched his mind for the right word to use, "powerful."

Will put the brush down and waved for me to sit next to him. I ran my hand along Cinnamon as I walked to Will's side and sat next to him.

"I know you don't understand that everyone has different abilities here. I remember when I was new and I thought that I was the only one in the world with a talent like I had. Meeting other people that could communicate telepathically was really incredible. Then I was walking past another Individual Skill class and I saw someone that had telekinesis. I was floored."

He bumped his fist on his thigh nervously as he searched for more words to complete his warning. "Vlaine can shift how other people see him, like you found out, but he can also manipulate how other people use their gifts. It's a really, really dark talent and he does not use it for anything good."

I searched his eyes and found nothing but the truth there. "I greatly appreciate the warning Will, but I am still not convinced. Give me a reason to be afraid of him and the headmaster."

"When I first got here I saw another student stand up to Vlaine. It was nothing serious, something stupid like taking the last pretzel that Susan had made or something. Either way the kid made it kind of obvious that he was taking a stand against Vlaine. Later that day when the kid was in ISE Vlaine was in the corner watching. The other kid's skill was astral projection, see he could project on command and walk different dimensions. Well, when the kid was in the middle of projecting into the forth plane Vlaine altered him and made him get stuck there. I could feel what the guy was feeling, it was awful. I've never felt so scared or trapped in my life. That was not the first or the last time Vlaine has done something like that and he never gets in trouble for it."

I took everything in. I still had no idea what the full story was and I refused to judge anyone from another person's account. Chewing on my lower lip, I let my wall fall quickly so I could read Will, hoping he would not notice. "Why do you think the two people you have warned me about seem to be around me all the time?"

He shrugged, "no clue." *Unless they're protecting you,* he thought to himself. I put the wall back up before he knew that I had read him.

Protecting me? Why would I need protection? It was such a bizarre thought and I knew that it wouldn't leave my mind until I knew what he had meant by it. Of course if I asked, he would know that I had read him. I pushed it temporarily out of my mind knowing that Vlaine and the headmaster were the only ones who could answer my question.

The energy in the barn was getting too depressing so I felt the need to change the subject, even though I had not heard what was so terrifying about the headmaster yet. "So why don't you just ask Adele out? I saw her today, she is gorgeous. Those perfect curls, pretty brown eyes, and a super cute pixie nose." I smiled and bumped my elbow into his.

He shook his head bashfully, "no way, I think she has a thing for Robbie. He's another pyro. Besides, no one has time to date around here."

"Seems like wasted years if you don't make some sort of effort to be fully happy. She could be sitting here with you talking instead of your faux pas friendly acquaintance."

"She doesn't like horses," his smile drifted towards Cinnamon.

"That's not the point," I laughed. I stood up to finish brushing the horse. "You never know until you try."

We fell into silence and finished grooming Cinnamon.

11

The next morning Liz and I followed the same routine getting ready and then we walked to the kitchen together. When the girl grabbed Liz's arm it was less abrupt, assuring me I must have done something right to not get the complete leper treatment.

Though a huge part of me wanted to run and hide in the dormitory until classes began, I would not show the other students I was scared. I found my way to the table and began munching on some fruit and looking over my lecture notes. Halfway into my persimmon Professor Horicon called me to his office.

My throat clenched as I walked to meet him. Each time I saw the man I could only think of Samantha's warning. I felt as if I was off to the gallows with each slow and calculated step. Purposefully, I kept the door ajar when I entered the room, only to have him close it nevertheless.

"We have come to a conclusion about your Individual Skill Enhancement Seminar." Professor Horicon unbuttoned his jacket and took a seat. "A quarter of a mile down the road you will see a small path to the left and down at the end of the road is a small building. Get there around ten. On Tuesdays and Thursdays you will have archery in that same building once your ISE seminar is complete."

"Thank you so much, Professor Horicon!" I was exuberant. The anticipation to find out what the class would be like was overwhelming.

"Oh, and Abrielle," he cleared his throat just as I was about to leave his office, "many of the students are a bit superstitious here. If I were you I would not tell anyone who your professor is for that class."

"Okay." I nodded confused, but told him to have a good day. He had never mentioned who the professor would be, but I was too excited to question him.

I was nearly two hours early for my physics class and at some point during my pre-class reading I dozed off. I awoke to the feeling of someone braiding my hair. *Nicholas.* I thought to myself and smiled. I love when he would play with my hair during class. A few moments later I sat up startled when I remembered I wasn't at my old high school.

I turned around abruptly expecting to see Vlaine, but it was Will sitting in the seat behind me. "Will! You scared the crap out of me." I had my hand to my chest. He smiled and I felt instantly calmer. "Are you in this class?"

"No," he grinned and got up from his seat

and left the room.

I ran my hand through my hair wondering if I had dreamt the feeling of someone braiding my hair, but sure enough my hand brushed against a messy braid. *Weird.* I thought to myself. Will was someone I was really comfortable around and trusted, but I still did not know him well enough to know what his personality was like.

Students walked in, gossiping excitedly about something that I must have missed at breakfast. In a few minutes I would see the rest of my peers turn from normal excited college students to overly stressed individuals merely seconds away from a meltdown. Just a few days earlier I had been a physics connoisseur at another school and here I was already completely lost and beginning to understand why everyone else was so stressed all the time. At the end of the week we would have an exam on information no one seemed to understand.

Ecology was a nice mental break from physics. Just as the class ended Liz ran up to me. "Hey, so we have that project that we have to work with someone on…"

"Yeah, we can talk about it tonight, I have to run!" I squeezed her arm and rushed out of the building. I felt bad running off from her so quickly but all I could think about was getting to my skill seminar.

I jogged down the gravel road and nearly missed the turn on the left. The trees were thick on either side of me but opened up to a small field with an old brick building in the middle of it. I opened the door to find a large basketball court with a track on the second floor that circled the court. At the back of the gymnasium were a few glass doors. I made my way to those wondering if my class was in there. One glass door had a weight room inside, another had a small snack bar with a few tables, and the last one lead to locker rooms.

It was lonely and awkward peeking through glass doors in an empty building. Just as I was beginning to become self conscious I heard the door open. Completely oblivious to my presence walked in the man that I had seen in my dreams for a decade. He was even more incredible looking in real life. My heart was in my throat and I could not pry my eyes off of him.

A perfectly straight hairline separated kempt short dark hair from a flawless face. His eyes were soft, approachable. The man tucked his music player into his basketball shorts, stuffed headphones into his ears, and began jogging around the upstairs track. Never once did he look my way, but I could not help but watch him.

"Staring is impolite," someone whispered in my ear from behind me. I turned around to see Vlaine.

"It's just," my face grew hot, "never mind. I don't need to explain myself to you and you wouldn't understand anyway."

"I wouldn't understand that he's super dreamy and you just couldn't help but swoon?" Vlaine gave me a disparaging smile and pulled out his cell phone.

Dreamy. That was one way to put it. "No, well yes, but I had seen him before and I just could not believe I saw him here. Like, here at Glaston."

"Glaston is the only place you would have seen him," Vlaine muttered.

"No it's not," I rolled my eyes getting annoyed with how besieged I felt with everything. "I said you wouldn't understand."

I didn't even understand and I was getting flustered trying to figure it out. I just saw a man that I had been dreaming about walking into a school that I hadn't known about until last week. The school year had begun quite peculiarly and only got stranger by the day.

"Well maybe you can be useful," I smiled pushing away all the negative emotions, "could you tell me where there is a classroom at this building?"

"Where do you want the classroom to be? Do you want it upstairs on the track? You could have it in the middle of the basketball court. Perhaps the snack bar or locker room appeals to you."

"What?" I fought to suppress the aggravated feeling rising in my torso. "You are so weird, Vlaine." I shook my head and looked around, mostly hoping to see my dream man again.

"I'm your teacher for ISE. Well I am until your skills are deemed worthy enough for the headmaster to give you any hours of his busy day."

Giving him an incredulous look, "*you* are going to be my teacher?"

"Don't be so surprised, I'm a teacher's assistant here."

I had completely forgotten that students could be assistants to the professors at colleges. "Okay, I'll bite," I still wasn't convinced, "is there a syllabus or something?"

"Where do you want the class to be?" he crossed his arms in front of his chest. The posture did not match his rather calm voice.

I walked to the middle of the basketball court and followed the black line until it intersected with another line close to the wall and sat down. Vlaine jogged to a closet at the far end of the gymnasium and pulled out blue padded mats and brought them to where I was sitting.

"We're going to be here for a while, go ahead and get comfortable." He flashed a brief genuine smile and took a seat on a mat in front of me.

We are going to start today by practicing your telepathy since it is your strongest skill. Hopefully working on it will bring your other ones out. His voice reverberated in my head.

Amazing. I smiled at the clarity of his voice. *I*

knew that I had telepathy and was most definitely an empath, but how do you know I have other gifts?

Your voice is weak. Try to talk louder and while you are doing that try to read my thoughts.

Okay. I pushed into his mind like I had when he was taking on Nicholas's appearance but found nothing.

He waited patiently for ten minutes until I threw my hands up in the air. *I cannot read you. I never could. You obviously have some sort of block that I can't get past.*

"Sometimes when people have a really strong defense wall to their mind you have to come into physical contact with them. For instance you could try a nonchalant brush past them, anything that gives you a skin to skin connection. Here, take my hand and give it a try."

I put my right hand in his and tried to read him. I physically felt like I was walking into a wall repeatedly. Each time I would adjust my seating, take a deep breath, and squeeze my grip. Another ten minutes had passed and I still got nothing. Growling, I scooted closer to him and grabbed his other hand.

Breathe.

I opened my eyes and saw his purple fingertips from my grasping his hand so hard. Just then I burst out laughing thinking of how ridiculous we may have looked to an outsider, sitting on a basketball court holding hands. I with my eyes squeezed shut clenching his hands while he sat there placidly. I waited for him to ask what was funny but figured he was probably reading me while I tried to fight through his psychic wall. For all I knew he could know every secret I ever held.

Right on cue with the fear of Vlaine finding out my deep secrets, dream man walked out of the locker room and through the basketball court and out of the building. It was impossible not to stare, I was fascinated with the fact that he was there and in real life. I wanted to talk to him and find out why I had seen him for more than half of my life.

"What is your obsession with Draxe? I know all the girls have the hots for him, but at least they usually show a little self control when they drool over him."

"You would not understand," I shook my head. "I'm not staring because he's handsome." *I'm staring because he's my dream man*, I thought to myself.

"Your dream man?" Vlaine guffawed.

"You weren't supposed to hear that," I growled.

I was getting so agitated that I put both my hands on his face and played back the dream in my head hoping that he could see it if I tried to plant the images in his head. For added measure I flashed the images as I saw it the first time and woke up in my frilly pink child room, then a couple more times throughout the years.

"Hmmm," Vlaine clicked his tongue to the roof of his mouth. "Why the hell have you been dreaming about my brother?" He looked up pondering his own question.

"Your brother?" my mouth dropped.

"Yup," he grinned, "we're twins. Too bad for him, I stole the good looks and personality."

"Oh, but you're so humble!" I scrunched my nose and giggled.

"So you agree?"

"Vlaine, this isn't helping my issue with not being able to read you."

Just clear your mind and try again. Be patient, it takes a lot of practice to be able to find a crack in a wall.

The next three hours were spent practicing my telepathy. I still could not manage to read him, but he remained patient with me throughout the entire session. After four hours of practicing I was exhausted. If my brain could have taken a nap with my body functioning I would have gladly done it.

Before he ran upstairs to the track Vlaine asked me to walk back to the dorms once the class was complete. I ignored his request and decided to look around the locker room. Aside from Vlaine, Draxe, and I there had been no other students in the building for nearly half of the day, none at all that I knew of.

My footfalls against the tile floor echoed throughout the immaculate empty room. Rows of lockers divided a changing room from close to a dozen shower stalls. The changing area was tucked inside a small open area with a television, vanity, and some sitting furniture.

With a complete lack of students visiting the gymnasium, I was giddy with the idea of making the locker room my secret studying spot. There was a locker there that I had already claimed as my own. With an accomplished smile I turned on my heel and headed for the exit. Just as I was about to push the locker door open I heard voices coming from the men's locker room. The first voice I heard was one I didn't recognize, but the second was definitely Vlaine.

"Does Dad have you spying or are you curious to see the replicator for yourself?" Vlaine sounded angry.

"I was just going for a run," the other voice was defensive.

"If Dad wants to know how her skills are going he can check in on her himself. He can't be so busy plotting with the other academies that he has to send you to check up on me."

"Dude, calm down. Dad didn't send me."

"What were you doing?" Vlaine was exasperated.

Muffled words were followed by "curious."

A loud slam, the sound of someone hitting a locker, echoed through the wall. I jumped out of the room quickly before they found out I was eavesdropping.

It had to be Vlaine and Draxe seeing how they were the only people I knew to be in the building aside from myself. Also, they were twins so they clearly shared a father. I did not understand why Vlaine was so angry about Draxe being in the gymnasium. Why would he be suspicious of his father sending Draxe to spy on our seminar anyhow? Even more curious was the insight to there being other academies. Glaston Academy had seemed pretty exclusive before, but it would make sense for there to be more institutions for people with particular abilities.

My senses were heightened as I walked down the path back to the residence hall; it felt as if someone was watching me. As the eerie feeling began to grow I picked up my pace and jogged back quickly to the main school grounds. The stables were a tempting pit stop but I continued back to my dorm, exhausted from my skill seminar.

The room was empty so I took the opportunity to pack a bag of clothes, shower products, and some snacks for my locker. Once I finished packing my secret kit I tucked it underneath my bed, ready for the next day.

Homework proved to be too daunting with my exhaustion and after half an hour of effort I rolled onto my back and looked up at the ceiling. It may have been an infantile preference, but I missed the plastic glowing stars from my bedroom at home. Steph and Nicholas helped me decorate with them when we were in elementary school and I kept them there as little mementos.

I decided my ceiling needed at least one star. I cut a misshapen one from a hot pink paper. "You're a puerile one," I laughed to myself as I stuck it directly above my pillow. I felt satisfied that a symbolic comfort of home was close, and I soon fell asleep.

The next morning I awoke to a knock on the door. Liz was already in the shower completing her daily speed round. Groaning, I shuffled to the door and opened it to find Vlaine standing there adorning a well fitting black tee shirt, jeans, and black boots. His hair was still wet from his shower and he smelled like morning dew. I, on the other hand, was in a baby pink camisole and boxer shorts. Embarrassed I crossed my arms in front of me trying to cover as much of my body as I could.

"How much of my conversation did you hear yesterday?" His eyes were cold and emotionless.

If I had any intelligence at all I would have been afraid of him, but for some reason I had no fear of Vlaine's terrifying glare. "Good morning Vlaine, I slept well, thank you for asking! So strange because all I could think this morning was how I wanted someone to come and knock on the door so I could answer half naked."

"I don't have time for your crap," he grabbed

my wrist, "how much of the conversation with my brother did you hear?" He squeezed my wrist tightly, "I'll know if you're lying."

I yanked my arm back and shoved him away from the doorway. "Don't grab me. I did not hear much, just something about your dad and other academies. Nothing that I could make sense of if I cared enough about it to give it a second thought."

He seemed satisfied with my answer and a small bit of warmth melted the ice cold stare he was giving me. In one fluid movement he turned on his heel and walked away.

Truthfully, I was extremely curious and his morning visit made me even more interested. I wanted to know why he would think his father would send Draxe to spy on me. Who was his father? How many more academies were there and where? Also, what was the deal with Vlaine being so nice when we were in class but so off-putting whenever we were in public? Was it just some method of keeping his intimidating persona when around other students?

Leaning my back against the wall I shook my head, trying to clear it of all the unanswered questions. No matter how much they were bothering me I needed to push aside to focus on school work and, of course, taking care not to die at the hands of Professor Horicon.

Liz came out of the bathroom unaware that we had gotten a visit from the dreaded Vlaine. She nodded her head towards the lavatory letting me know the shower was all mine. Pushing myself off the wall, I skipped to pick out an outfit for the day then walked into the wall of steam to prepare for the day.

"We need to create a schedule and decide who does which section of the report," Liz clutched onto her notebook and walked at an inhuman speed.

Water beads falling from the ends of wet roped tendrils formed a large oval on the back of my shirt as I jogged to keep up with Liz. Quickly, I put together a schedule for the project then pulled out the notes and draft that I had already completed for it.

A girl with a round face and a black pixie cut sat at the table just as I was pushing the work towards Liz. "Can I work with you two? The professor said that some groups could have three people if need be."

"That's fine with me, if it is okay with Liz. The way I see it, the more eyes there are to edit the reference section, the better. I'm Abrielle, by the way." I put my hand out to shake hers.

"Tracy," she cocked her head to the side and smiled, ignoring my outstretched hand.

I hated when people cocked their head to the side like a puppy, it made me instantaneously lose trust in them.

Liz was scanning through my notes and ignored Tracy's presence. "This looks incredible, Abrielle. Oh my goodness, we are going to have this done tonight!" As the stress and fear washed away, I saw Liz smile for the first time.

Satisfied that Liz was happy, I excused myself. "I'll see you tonight to go over it some more. See you in class, Tracy."

I left the girls to help Susan prepare breakfast for the morning. Liz had gotten us to the kitchen so early that I was able to see the vast amount of work Susan put into getting the school fed.

"Well aren't you a dear," Susan's rosy cheeks turned two shades redder as she smiled at me gratefully and tossed an extra daisy patterned apron towards me.

Standing on the opposite side of the kitchen watching the students take their seats was like viewing a movie. Everyone had their own patterns and little cliques. As I observed them I was slowly beginning to visualize what their abilities could be and identify each person's own buzzing sound. The telepathy noise was easy to identify, innate even, but each person had their own noise.

I watched Adele walk in and tuned in to see if I could discover what a pyro sounded like. Tuning everything out and focusing on only her I could hear the whirring of an electric oven. *Fitting*, I chuckled to myself.

"Here you go honey," Susan's voice interrupted my meditation.

I turned expecting her to be speaking to me, but she was handing both Vlaine and Draxe breakfast sandwiches.

"Morning Abrielle," Vlaine nodded and smiled.

"Hi." I was so irritated with how he acted just an hour prior that my inflection sounded more like a forceful question.

"Want to split it?" He tilted the sandwich towards me.

I was perplexed by his ability to jump emotions so quickly. "No, I'm good. Thanks."

"Suit yourself," he shrugged, "see you in class, Abbs."

He and Draxe walked off together and for the first time I could see the striking similarities between the two. Draxe was the approachable all-American jock and Vlaine was the daredevil no one wanted to mess with.

"You either get an iron maiden or Christmas morning with that one," Susan had caught me scowling at Vlaine's back, "but you won't find a more loyal man in existence."

"I just wish he would stick with one personality," I admitted.

She tucked her hands into her apron pockets and pulled out a small glass container filled with a yogurt parfait and handed it to me. "That boy has no problem letting a person know if he does not like them. He'll open up to you sooner or later. Now go on and enjoy some breakfast, I have it from here."

"Thank you Susan," gingerly I took the yogurt from her and went off to my classroom.

Sitting through classes waiting for the time to pass until I could go to my skill seminar was like a mild form of torture. The minutes ticked by slowly and even more so when I sat next to Vlaine. It felt like there was an inside joke between the two of us that neither one acknowledged, knowing that he would be teaching me a class two hours after one we sat in together; a silent understanding.

Vlaine was one of those students that sat back without anything in front of them and just absorbed all the information given; whereas I was the type of person who needed to write everything down but was easily distracted by anything around me. My biggest distraction was the enigma sitting beside me that was Vlaine. His mood swings, notorious history, and connection to my dream man made him all the more intriguing.

"Hey Abrielle," Will caught my arm as I was running back to the dormitory to grab my study provisions backpack.

"Hey Will, what's up?" I spoke quickly trying not to let him know that I was out of breath.

"Want to help me out with Cinnamon tonight?" White teeth gleamed through his expectant smile.

"Yes," my eyes glowed with excitement. "See you then," I tapped his arm before continuing to the dorm.

I was in the gymnasium building before Vlaine giving me the perfect opportunity to hide my bag in the locker room. Once I had it stashed away I set the mats out and cleared my mind for my skill session.

I was determined to get through Vlaine's wall but an hour was far too short to crack his barrier. Though I could not read him, I was louder with my telepathic voice. By the end of class he asked if I wanted to continue for an extra hour that evening for extra credit so I answered by touching his hand and showing him the draft I wrote, my conversation with Liz and Tracy, and the short discussion I had with Will.

"Very well," he stood up and put his hand out to help me up, "the weather is perfect outside, let's set up the targets out there."

"You're my TA for archery too?" I reached for his hand and hopped up to follow him to the field.

"I'm already here with you. Rather than screwing up a class that had already started I volunteered for the job."

How noble, I picked up a bow and quiver and took my stance.

Do you have that? It seemed we would be talking via telepathy during my activity course.

I'm no stranger to a recurve. I pulled the string back to my anchor point and shot an arrow just outside of the bull's eye.

Click, slide, and poing. Clicking the nock onto the nocking point, sliding the wood shaft against the arrow rest, and releasing the arrow played a therapeutic melody. Having an entire field to myself for target practice was incredibly liberating, but it proved that I was purposefully being secluded from the other students.

I slung the quiver and bow over my shoulder and helped Vlaine bring the target back inside. "How exactly do I get graded in two classes that I have alone? I was told that grades are dependent upon the other students."

"As the assistant I decide how much effort you are putting into your work. If I think you are going above and beyond then you may get a B. If I'm in a bad mood you will fail."

I rolled my eyes at his terseness then smiled. *See you tomorrow, Professor Vlaine.*

Liz and I finished the project before Tracy even got to the dorm. She apologized for being late but I could feel the insincerity in her words. I brushed it off and told her to look over the paper and make sure that everything was as the professor specified. Once the extra set of eyes approved the paper I left the two to gossip while I met up with Will.

Will was in an especially talkative mood. We brushed Cinnamon while he told me all about his childhood and how he came to find out about his gift. He then went on to describe the friends he sat with at breakfast. They each had a different gift which shattered my theory of how they could all be friends.

"What do you know about Draxe?" I spoke quickly once one of Will's stories had ended because I was sure that I would not get another chance to ask about Draxe that night.

"Who?" He had stopped brushing.

"Draxe, Vlaine's brother."

Anticipation grew with each passing moment that he thought about my question. "Nothing actually, I never really see the guy. I have just heard that he has the same skills as Vlaine." He peeked his head around Cinnamon and gave me a devilish smile, "I think he's single."

"Have you seen him, Will? He is the closest thing to a God on Earth. Ugh, he is perfection."

"Wow girl, you have some psycho stalker in you. I can see it coming out." He let out a hearty laugh.

I gave a quick wink in response.

12

It was finally Friday and everything about my day was wonderful. I tapped my foot impatiently waiting for Ecology to end so I could get to the gymnasium and try to work on reading Vlaine. I decided that today would be the day I found a crack in his wall. Afterwards I would enjoy my first weekend at college. I was hoping people let their hair down and actually had fun once the weekend came.

Just as the class was about to end Tracy threw her hand in the air.

"Yes, Tracy?" The professor raised a brow seemingly impatient.

"Liz and I already finished our project and we were wondering if you could take a look at it for us."

My mouth was agape and the color drained from my face. *I* had done that project. *I* had done most of the work with some of Liz's help. I looked over to Liz to see if she would defend me. Her back was rigid, but she remained silent.

Catty bitch. It was so unfair. I looked over at

Vlaine who was sitting in the seat beside me as if to ask what I should do. I wanted to speak to him telepathically, but the rules made it clear that practicing skills were strictly forbidden unless it was during the seminar or the weekend. He did not look at me, just continued to draw something in his notebook.

"Liz!" I ran to catch up with her. "What the hell? I did most of that project. You could have said something."

All she could do was shrug and give me an apologetic look.

"No, Liz, don't give me that pathetic look. You're too strong to back down from anyone. If you wanted to you could have said something. Looks like that's the last time I help you out."

I felt bad for attacking Liz like that but my first taste of betrayal at Glaston Academy was unexpectedly sour.

I huffed once I was outside the school. *1…2…3…* I gave myself three seconds to get angry at Tracy. It was not making my project get done any faster. *1…2…3…* Three more seconds to erase the negativity from my mind. I imagined the stress and irritation being washed away. The next four hours would be dedicated to me and I did not need to step into that building with any negative thoughts.

The mere moment that I felt the stress lift I heard stone dust crunching behind me and turned to see Tracy walking towards me. I put my head back and rolled my eyes. *She's petty, don't let her bother you.* I thought as loudly as I could to no one in particular.

She stood in front of me, her arms by her side and leg out in a superior posture. "Welcome to Glaston Academy," she sneered, then turned on her heel and swaggered back into the school.

"Lazy looked so much better on you than vindictive," I muttered before I broke into a jog down the road.

Vlaine was waiting on a mat flipping through a large leather-bound book. When he saw me walk in he tucked the book away and flashed a complacent smile. Though part of me wanted to vent about the Tracy incident, I was glad it was never mentioned and the rest of the day was spent focusing on flexing my telepathic muscle.

Only a week into working on my skill and I could communicate mentally with Vlaine more easily than I spoke. We worked on breaking down his wall but he eventually grew tired and thought that I should work on reading someone else. At first the intrusive practice of reading someone without their permission felt rather disgusting, but he was prepared with a list of people who had offered their minds to telepaths for an extra five points. By the time I got to the seventh person on the list, thoughts and memories were coming much easier to me and my confidence was building.

Sprawling across the couch in the locker room I finished a second project for ecology and all the homework due Monday so I could enjoy a study-free weekend.

I found Will walking Cinnamon back into the stables. "You were right," I shrugged my shoulders and helped him remove her saddle. "I learned the first lesson you tried to teach me and I learned it the hard way."

"You showed too much kindness and drive. Together those can be a lethal combination here." Will was somber.

"Lethal?" With such a strong word, he surely had to be exaggerating.

He did not say anything, just continued to brush the horse. His dour mood was unnerving. "I'm usually going blind in here with the shimmering of your pearly whites, Will. Are you okay?"

"Yup." He dropped his brush and walked out of the stables.

My chest ached. Will was usually so pleasant and happy, but seeing him so despondent made me feel helpless. I continued brushing Cinnamon hoping that he would come back in and start laughing like he had pulled a joke, but he never returned.

13

Professor Horicon's was shouting. All I could hear was jumbled roars. I stepped away from him, trying to put as much space as possible between us in his small office. I backed against the wall and he grabbed the flesh of my arm angrily. The next thing I knew I was in a dark room with a narrow winding staircase to my side. I could smell the ocean and hear waves. A lighthouse? Professor Horicon had something in his hand. I ran up the stairs. He was going to kill me. My legs ached and I used my arms as padding as I bumped against the railing trying to get up the steps as quickly as I could.

Icy air stung my face as I opened the door at the top of the steps. There was nowhere to go. I was trapped and Professor Horicon was going to kill me. He emerged from the door, his eyes were black. He ran towards me and I backed up. The lighthouse was old, pieces of the railing were missing. When I backed up there was nothing there to catch me. A short memory of Samantha's warning flashed in my mind. This is how I die. I fell, fell into darkness. Suddenly I opened my eyes. The perfect nose, chiseled cheeks, soft lips. I was looking up at Draxe. "Are you okay?" His eyes searched mine.

I awoke drenched in my own sweat. Across the darkness Liz was still sleeping softly. Leaning over the edge of my bed I searched for the neon numbers on the clock that read 4:37. I put my head back down for a moment and stared up at the pink makeshift star, but impatience won and I jumped out of bed to pull on a pair of jeans and a sweatshirt. I needed to find Vlaine and figure out what it meant now that I had just seen a new part of the vision.

Glaston was not like a regular school, there was no one restricting quiet hours or stopping girls from staying in the boys dorm, the students were just too high strung to do anything wrong. Having a residential assistant would have been welcoming; walking down the eerie dimly lit halls gave me the sense of being in a horror movie. I felt like the first character in the film, soon to be assaulted by an axe wielding maniac.

As quietly as possible I tiptoed up to the third floor to see if I could sense Vlaine in one of the dorms. My hope was that if he was sleeping there was no way he could have a barrier up. I felt like I was being quite invasive but figuring out the meaning of my vision felt far too imperative to worry about propriety.

Leaning against the far corner I closed my eyes and sensed each room. I had never read someone while they were sleeping before and the experience was far more bizarre than I could have possibly expected. I could view people's dreams through what seemed like a foggy mirror. The urge to try and wipe the condensation off the mirror was strong, but I was afraid they would be able to sense me if I interfered too much.

I went through each dorm but could not sense Vlaine in any of them. I gave up and went down to the kitchen. I fumbled about in the dark searching for the switch before giving up and allowing my eyes to adjust so I could retrieve a cup of coffee to take back to the common area and wait for Vlaine to wake up.

I curled my feet under myself and reclined on the couch pondering the reason for my vision. Aside from the fact that Professor Horicon clearly wanted me dead, there must have been something dire and life changing.

Snuggled on the couch in the dimly lit room I came close to drifting asleep. Just as my head began to become heavy I saw a figure outside the window in the distance. The stables! How could I have not thought of checking them? I tossed my empty coffee cup in the trash and jogged out to see who was outside.

Dew was beginning to form on the grass and the sky was slowly changing from a crisp navy to cerulean. I could feel someone close, but I had no idea who it was.

"Hello," I called out to whoever's silhouette I had seen.

My footsteps were quiet, my ears tuned in for any movement. *Now this is where the axe wielding maniac would definitely be. Good job, Abrielle.* I snorted softly to myself.

"I don't have an axe," a voice came from a couple stalls away.

"Oh good," I snorted, "any other tools useful for murder before I come closer?"

"One of the equine variety," he answered with a light laugh.

I turned to find the face matching the voice and found a diffident smile and pensive brows wrapped in a beneficent posture.

"Draxe?" His name left my lips strained and out of breath.

He eyed me up and down. "Can I help you with something?"

Yes, you can tell me why you've been haunting my dreams for the past decade. I thought to myself. "Couldn't sleep?"

"I like to take Buttercup out first thing in the morning." He pulled the saddle strap taut around the horse's midsection.

Chuckling, "I don't think I have ever heard of a horse with an original name. Cinnamon, Buttercup, Daisy... what about something like Minerva or Poseidon?" I paused for a moment and sucked in a breath, "so, is it normal to have visions about something, but only one thing over and over again?"

"What kind of visions?" His voice was so smooth and deep, it was warmth flowing along my earlobes.

"Well for a long time it was just a couple

seconds of the vision and it comes in the form of a dream but last night it was a few minutes. I guess it's bad because I think I die or should die, almost die? I am not really sure what happens but whatever it is, it is dire."

He thought for a moment, his bottom lip pulling down into a masculine pout. "I have heard of people having visions, but not repeatedly about the same thing. I guess I could ask my dad about it if you want me to."

Draxe was incredibly genuine and personable. We had never spoken before, but he was the only person at Glaston Academy that did not seem to want to throw me off the side of a cliff. I truly liked Will, but even he had his moments when I knew it was best to keep him at a distance.

"Your dad?" The way he had said it, it was as if I should have known exactly of whom he was speaking.

"Yeah, he's Headmaster Josnic." Tossing me a sideways smirk, "He looks young, but he knows his stuff."

I could not hide my surprise at the new revelation: the Josnic family was the most feared one at Glaston Academy. "Whoa! Your dad is the headmaster? Is that why everyone is so scared of Vlaine?"

"No," he snorted and shook his head, "they're scared of Vlaine because my brother isn't afraid of anything. He has no weaknesses and will not hesitate to use his abilities. That terrifies them." He began leading the horse outside then pulled the saddle taut once again and hopped onto Buttercup.

"I did not imagine you to be much of a horse rider," my mouth failed to stop the words I was thinking from exiting.

Dimples shown when he looked over with an amused smile, "My mother had a thing for horses so my father bought her a handful of them. When he turned our old house into Glaston he decided to use them in the curriculum." Buttercup neighed and Draxe gave her a quick pat. "I'll ask my dad and if there's anything significant about what you described I'll let you know."

"Thank you," I waved and turned back into the stables.

I was giddy. The man of my dreams, quite literally, just spoke to me. My heart was racing, hands were shaking, and I felt like I could run a marathon and climb a mountain in succession with a smile. Cinnamon let out a whinny as I walked by. I stroked her muzzle then decided to continue my search for Vlaine.

A light fog lay on the field as the colors of dawn began to fade. I was still elated, but the morning landscape serenely dulled my excitement to a placid enthusiasm. My euphoric daze was cut short when I heard a bloodcurdling scream come from the dorms.

My legs were running before my mind had time to process what was happening. I burst through the door into the common area to see a circle of students formed around someone. A stream of blood was pooling on the floor and my hands began to tingle and get hot. I was ready to heal whoever it was.

"What happened?" I asked pushing through.

As I made it through the growing swarm of students I saw Tracy lying on the floor convulsing in pain with her arm split into two. Flesh was torn into bits that made what was once her arm a nearly indiscernible mass.

"What happened?" I repeated louder.

"She was practicing telekinesis. Something went wrong, it backfired," someone stammered frantically.

"Okay," I inhaled gathering all the peacefulness I could muster, "shhhh," I imagined blowing the tranquility into her. Her convulsing slowed minimally.

"Guys, give me a little space, please." My voice was calm but urgent.

The circle of students backed away a few feet, but they were still around me. Closing my eyes I recalled the giddy and exuberant feeling I just had when I spoke to Draxe. I directed the positive energy towards her and began my work.

There was a lot to do and a short time before she would bleed out. Just as I had done with the squirrel, I imagined every cell being repaired, moving up to the tissue level. The bone, blood, muscle, skin, all the cells in her arm were healing in my mind. Inhaling, I mustered every bit of energy and happiness I could find to put into healing her entire body.

"And a little bit of love for added measure," I imagined Tracy being content, her heart filling with happiness.

Please don't be dead, I squeezed my eyes even more tightly before slowly opening them to view my progress. I looked down to see Tracy staring up at me bewildered. A deep gash remained near her elbow, but the majority of her arm was healed.

"Can someone get her some water?" I finally looked up at the crowd of students. They were still, watching timidly as if something was about to explode. "Guys," I snapped my fingers, "your friend just almost died. Can someone grab her some water and maybe some antibacterial cream and a bandage?"

Finally a girl in the back of the room scampered outside towards the main building. I pulled my sweatshirt off and placed it under Tracy's head to give her more comfort. I wanted to finish healing the gash that remained on her arm but I was shaking and lightheaded from the immense amount of work I had just done.

I put my hand gently on Tracy's shoulder as she began to wriggle around. "Don't you move," I warned her, "lie down for a while. You just lost a lot of blood. I'll get you some juice in a minute and you can sip on that while we get you bandaged up."

"Why?" she croaked then cleared her throat. "Why are you…"

"Humanity," I shrugged.

The door of the building flew open and the students moved backwards in unison.

"What seems to be the problem here," the floor vibrated from the booming voice of the headmaster. It was the first time that I felt afraid of the man. He was dressed in his normal formal attire, hair slicked back, but a look of angry determination was shadowed by an unclean shave.

The headmaster grabbed my arm roughly then grabbed Tracy's. "Whoever else was here when the incident occurred, step forward."

A mousy girl with large glasses stepped forward holding her arm out. He took a moment to read each of us before grunting, "It appears my presence was unnecessary." He then turned to me and straightened his back, "Abrielle, come to my office."

"Yes sir," I stood up slowly. "Someone get her juice and bandage her up." My voice was shaky. I had to jog to catch up with him, but kept a few feet of distance.

I sat down in his office feeling strange as he stood with his back to me. "If anyone is to find out how Tracy was hurt the consequences will be dire."

My brows furrowed in confusion. "I was told she was practicing and it backfired."

"You may not know now, but you will in time. If anyone finds out how she was hurt you will be expelled from this school. Do you understand?"

"Yes sir." I felt tiny. I knew now why people feared him. He had a way of sucking the air out of your lungs just by speaking.

"In lieu of recent events," he turned around and his entire demeanor had changed, "you are awarded fifty extra credit points to put towards whatever class you choose. Congratulations Abrielle. Enjoy the rest of your day."

"Thank you Headmaster Josnic. Have a good weekend."

After the story Will had told me I was curious if Vlaine had anything to do with Tracy's accident, but I could not imagine that he would really do that. However irascible Vlaine could be, I always felt safe around him. There was obviously something I was missing, but my first priority would be to finish helping Tracy, then I could worry about whatever caused her accident.

When I returned to the common area of the residence hall my peers were looking at me as if I was some dangerous object about to explode, keeping their distance but watching me intently. I had left Headmaster Josnic's office, gossip about the interaction would ensue for days to come I was sure.

"How is the patient?" I asked the mousy girl who was still fumbling about with medical tape.

Tracy's eyes were swollen from crying and I felt a small pang of guilt for some reason. The girl stammered and could not seem to find any words or the ability to cut tape.

"Let me see, before I have to heal another wound," I laughed lightly taking the medical supplies from her.

"I would have let you die," Tracy's voice was low and remorseful.

"Well thank goodness I am the one with the healing power then," I fought the urge to poke her wound.

"Monday you're going to get your first test grade back. Just wait and see how you feel about everyone else after then. You can't be a saint and compete with everyone at the same time."

"What is the big deal? So three failed classes and you owe a disgusting sum of money to Glaston Academy. Most students here have the ability to rob a chain of banks and get away with it. Heck, if I really needed to I could get into someone's mind and work some magic."

"You don't get it," she scoffed and rolled her eyes, "it is not the money we are worried about. It is what happens if we aren't deemed useful anymore. The best and brightest get given an incredible job where we actually get to use our gifts and the losers are never heard from again."

"Wow, please describe to me the reservoir reserved for losers submitted for genocide. What is with you people, really? I am exhausted of these half told horror stories." I stood up and placed her arm down gently. "There, you're all bandaged up. If you want me to heal that the rest of the way you need to wait until I get some food in my stomach. Otherwise, try and be careful. I think you're under an insane amount of stress and it makes you pretty awful to be around, but I would rather have you here than … well… you know."

She pulled her lips into a taut line and looked away with a forced brazen expression. I was too exhausted to allow Tracy to annoy me. I patted her arm quickly then retreated to the residence hall kitchen.

Sitting quietly in the room was Vlaine. "Oh good," I sighed making my way to him, "I was looking for you earlier."

"Oh?" he raised a brow.

"Yes, do you have a few minutes to discuss something with me?" I clutched my hands together so he could not see them shaking fiercely from the morning events.

He leaned back in his seat and folded his hands behind his head. "I'm here right now and I have a few minutes."

"Great!" I grabbed a muffin then sat next to

him. "So what does this mean," I placed my hand on his arm and re-watched the dream in my head.

"It means you have some sort of twisted damsel in distress thing going for my brother."

"Vlaine," I scolded, "be serious."

"I am serious. I think you're talking to the wrong brother about this."

"What, do you want me to just walk up to Draxe and say, 'oh hey, I've been dreaming about you since I was a kid. Here let me show you so I can get your professional opinion on yourself?'"

"That sounds like a crazy stalker way to go about the discussion, but if that works for you, sure."

"Vlaine," I growled, "you're so frustrating, like, ninety percent of the time.

"Anything else?" His hands were still folded behind his head and his arms were flexed revealing a small portion of a tattoo underneath his arm.

I tore my gaze from the ink adorning his perfectly sculpted arm. "Yes. Do you have a partner for the ecology project? The professor said we need to work in pairs." Since Tracy had already turned in the paper I had done claiming it as her own I would need a new partner.

"Oh look, a few minutes are up. I've got to go." He leaned forward and continued eating his breakfast.

"Thank you for your time Prince Josnic," I

curtsied, annoyed with the lack of help he provided with my questions.

"Later, Abbs," he simpered, seeming pleased with himself.

"Infuriating man," I mumbled as I left the kitchen.

14

I spent the rest of the weekend in the gymnasium studying, practicing, and writing letters to home. It was my own personal playground where I was free to do whatever I pleased. Though there were a few points when I felt someone was watching me, I never saw anyone enter the building. I was not sure if the other students did not know about it, or if they simply did not want to take the time to venture to the place. Either way, I was content having my own oasis.

Writing the letters to home reminded me how much I missed Steph and Nicholas. I wanted to confide in them and tell them everything about Glaston Academy, but that would simply sound insane. I finished the letters by writing a bland and generic one to my mother, which curbed the home sickness I had been feeling.

Sunday evening, just as I was about to head back to the dormitories, I took out the archery equipment and began practicing inside the gymnasium. Listening and feeling the melodic click and slide sounds, I practiced shooting my arrows with intuition alone. I had hoped with each recoil of the string I would be able to tell where the arrow had gone, but that was not the case.

Though I was not able to decipher where my arrows had gone, my concentration and intuition was sharper. "Hey Vlaine," I called out. His entrance had been silent, but I could feel his presence.

"Evening, Abrielle," his footfalls drew nearer.

I turned to face him to find that he was carrying fold-up chairs into the gym. "Preparing for tomorrow's class," he lifted them so I would know what he was talking about.

"Excellent," I continued on with my archery practice.

Vlaine set the chairs down in the spot where we practiced my telepathy and walked to my side. "You should have told me you were practicing." His jaw widened into a smile and deep dimples appeared, "I am your professor after all."

"I would have called, but I don't have a phone," I shrugged in a sardonic manner.

"Anytime you need me, just try calling out to me telepathically. I should be able to hear you." His hand cupped my elbow gently and reassuringly, "anytime you want to practice, let me know."

I pondered the thought for a moment, thinking of how truly convenient that could be. I was still irritated by his mercurial nature and put up a passive-aggressive wall between us. I shot another arrow before retrieving them and putting away the equipment.

"I'll give it a try next time," I finally nodded.

He tucked his fingertips into his pockets and he rocked back on his heels, his dimples growing deeper. "Want me to walk you back to the school?"

My stubborn side wanted to say no, only because I was irritated with how he was this morning but the other part of me, the secret part, wanted to spend more time with him. "Sure," I nodded in a supercilious manner, "I need to get my stuff out of the locker room."

Vlaine was holding the door open, waiting for me to join him. I smiled in a thankful response and he took my books for me.

"What a gentleman," I murmured.

"A trait I picked up from pretending to be this kid Nicholas," he smirked.

"Touchy subject, Vlaine," my voice was querulous.

"Sorry," he grinned mischievously.

"How often were you Nicholas?" I had never actually asked him, but it was something that bothered me frequently.

His pace slowed and he looked me directly in the eye, "the night of the concert, a short time at the party, and twice at school."

It gave me great relief to find that I knew when he was pretending to be Nicholas every time with the exception of one instance. An even greater sense of reprieve came from finding out that he hadn't been impersonating Nicholas as often as I had originally assumed.

"Is it weird, pretending to be other people? Is it something you like to do?"

Our footsteps slowed and fell into a rhythm then his brows rose for a moment as he pondered how to answer my question. "I only use it if I have to. It seems like everyone else obsesses over looking or acting like another person, but to me it's just a lot of work with no reward." He laughed, "And being Nicholas was a pain in the ass."

"How so," I chuckled, "he's the easiest person to read and his personality is so simple."

Nicholas had the most static personality in my mind. He was overly affectionate and charming, like the youngest sibling that constantly needs attention. Perhaps it was because I grew up with him, but I thought out of anyone I knew he would be the simplest person to emulate.

His straight brows curved into a thoughtful curve. "I don't think you ever dug too deep into his mind." He held his hands up cautiously, "I mean that respectfully, but I think you trusted him so much that you never dug any deeper than his surface."

I scoffed, "my Nicholas?"

"He has such a mild exterior, but the man is actually really complicated. Even if he seemed stoic and fluid, every move he made was actually incredibly calculated."

"Okay," I tried to understand, "give me an example."

"I couldn't understand how he was best friends with you and Steph and could be so…" he made a repulsive face, "affectionate." Shaking his head, "he made this effort to treat you two exceptionally respectfully so you would always expect that same treatment from any guys you dated."

I stopped walking and stared at Vlaine, contemplating what he had just told me. Could I have missed such a large part of someone that I considered my best friend since elementary school? Nicholas always made sure to take my backpack, open doors, and was never repulsively sexual like most teenage men. He had always been the perfect gentleman to Steph and me, but never crossed the line from friendship into relationship.

"Wow," I shook my head dubiously, "so all the time there was a deeper part to Nicholas than the carefree heartthrob?" I chewed on my lower lip trying to figure out what age Nicholas could have possibly decided that he would play that role in Steph's and my life.

"Yeah," he snickered, "he's a pretty good guy." His lips twisted in contemplation. "I guess there was some dude, Liam or something, and he stomped on both Steph and your heart. He asked his mother what to do and she told him that no one can ever be told to do something, but led to the direction they should go. Ever since then he has been trying to lead you both in the right direction."

I recalled the memory Vlaine was referring to. "Steph and I were thirteen when Liam dated both Steph and me at the same time, thinking it would be funny or something. I mean, it was thirteen so 'dating' meant a phone call each night, but it took Steph and I nearly two weeks to figure it out and we were both devastated."

We continued walking and I could not shake the idea of Nicholas spending our entire friendship showing us how we were meant to be treated. Vlaine walked me to my dorm and before turning away he gave me a wistful glance and began to say something, but quickly snapped his mouth shut. He turned his body and said goodnight before leaving.

"See you tomorrow, Vlaine," I whispered.

Monday began terribly. The physics professor arrived half an hour early and my need to get there an hour early allowed him time to discuss the test we had on Friday. Though I received the third highest grade in the class, the highest graded student was only worthy of a B+. The rest of the students were graded accordingly leaving me with a C. My stomach dropped at the news. Physics was supposed to be my specialty. Part of me wanted to crumple the paper up and burn it. Instead I thanked the professor for explaining the grading policy and tucked the test neatly into my book.

My head was hidden in the crook of my elbow on my desk as the students gathered into Ecology. All I wanted to do was crawl back into bed and hide from the world.

The sound of heels clattering, trying to regain balance caught my attention. I glanced up to see Tracy standing on her desk. "Professor B. I would like to make an announcement."

Professor B. watched looking exceptionally nervous. Tracy squared her shoulders and shouted, "I am a terrible human being that should choke on my own tongue. Last week Abrielle finished the entire project in one night and I took the credit because I am a spineless bitch and I willingly accept a failure in this class. Thank you." She jumped down from her desk and strode out of the room.

The professor was speechless and I could feel my face enflamed with embarrassment as students looked over at me questioningly. A moment later the professor cleared his throat, "was Tracy accurate with her confession?"

"Um," I squirmed feeling my face get even redder, "well, it is true that I did most of the project, but Liz helped too. I would disagree with everything else she said though."

Vlaine strolled into the classroom and looked at me, "what's wrong Abbs? Did you dip your face in a bucket of red food dye?" He leaned back, hands crossed behind his head, arms flexing, and a large grin on his face.

Tracy had a change of heart and declared her wrong doing with taking credit on the project. And stop flexing like that, it's distracting. I thought to myself. "I'll tell you later," I whispered. "Wait," I gasped as Tracy strolled into the classroom as if nothing had just happened, "did you have something to do with that little occurrence earlier?"

"What occurrence?" His face softened into innocence, "I was in the kitchen. Whatever happened?"

My jaw dropped, "it was you! You pulled a Nicholas, but on Tracy!" I whispered leaning towards him.

"No, Abrielle," he shook his head "that would be wrong. My incredible gifts are only to be used during ISE or on weekends."

That was unexpectedly kind. "Thank you," I mouthed.

He squared his gently clefted chin towards me and gave a lopsided grin, "anytime, Abbs."

Betrayal and aggravation had been all I felt for Vlaine when I first met him. He was off-putting, intimidating, and powerful, but was the only person that I completely trusted at Glaston Academy. Our lessons together were my favorite part of the day and the patience he had with me was beyond anything I could muster for another individual.

Two weeks had gone by quickly and I had made no progress with breaking Vlaine's wall. He wanted me to work on healing but the only way I could do that was by fixing something that was injured. He figured that a diseased animal would be similar and he would bring in tumor ridden rodents for me to try and cure. It was nearly impossible to tell if I was making any difference with the tumors just because of the immense amount of work that went into trying to reverse the damage as well as decrease the size. Accomplishment came with knowing that I was putting the animals in a more comfortable state while I was working on them.

People seemed to have a new respect for me after seeing my healing powers in action and I was no longer treated like a person harboring a terrible and contagious pestilence. It was refreshing and empowering to have gained that bit of respect from the high strung group of students so quickly. Humans have short memories, and I was sure that within a week or so I would be back at the bottom of the social ladder.

Liz, in her constant imperturbable state, kept her distance but broke each night with a sincere "goodnight Abrielle." Will and I would meet each evening to brush the horses. Our nights were usually in silence, but every so often he would tell me a story about some Glaston memory. Sometimes I would try telling him a bit about my past but whenever I did he was silent, seemingly absorbing the information but never responding.

One morning I woke up exuberant and

vigorous. I sauntered into the gymnasium, sat on the floor, intertwined my fingers with Vlaine's, and began trying to break the wall.

"Wait," I jumped towards him, "I have an idea. Lay your head on my lap."

"That's really sweet Abrielle, but I just don't think I'm ready. I mean you never even took me out to dinner. You didn't even notice my new haircut." He ran his hand through his hair.

I rolled my eyes, "just do it and trust me."

Hesitantly he rolled onto his back and rested his head on my lap. Fighting the tingling sensation that danced through my stomach, I placed a hand on his forehead and another on his chest. Inhaling, I willed him to be calm and content. His shoulders fell; it was working, at least a small amount.

My hands grew hot and my body buzzed as I began healing him, checking for anything that could be wrong. Mentally I massaged his muscles, cleansed his tissues, and calmed his mind. As the seconds passed Vlaine's body melted into a relaxed state. Once his breathing found a gentle but steady rhythm I moved to his brain. Starting from the dura mater and working my way into his lobes I healed and read at the same time.

Patience was a virtue as I combed through every cell. An image of the headmaster and a group of men at a table flashed in my mind. Vlaine and Draxe were in a room full of men dressed in the same dapper attire as the headmaster. They were discussing some corporation whilst in the background were various names and skills written on a whiteboard under the words "think tank."

I gasped, "Vlaine, I did it!"

He sat up quickly, his face nearly colliding with mine in the process. "What do you mean?"

"I did it. I found a memory. It was a bunch of men in an office, your dad was there. There were names on a board and they were discussing…"

He put his finger over his lips signaling me to be quiet.

"Vlaine," I grabbed onto his shoulders to make my point more direct, "I did it! I read you. It took me three weeks, but… be proud!"

He sat there silently thinking. I pulled him in for a hug and squeezed tightly before I let go and started skipping around the basketball court. I was exuberant, thrilled, I felt amazing. Hours of work had gone into breaking Vlaine's wall and I had finally found a crack.

After a few circles of skipping I sat back down in front of Vlaine and pushed my fingers between his and prepared to try again. Just because I was able to get one memory did not mean it was going to happen any easier.

He squeezed my hands and stood up.

"I need to keep practicing. Where are you

going?"

He sighed and pulled his phone from his pocket. "I need to do something. Let me get you a tutor for about an hour and then I'll be back once your lunch block is over."

My thrill deflated. Vlaine did not seem proud in the least that I had made such a momentous accomplishment. Anger bubbled as he walked away dialing someone. I reached into the same lobe that I had found the last memory and dug around again. The wall was up and impenetrable once again.

He was pacing on the phone and a few minutes later Draxe walked into the gymnasium. My heart fluttered as I watched him walk towards us.

"Looks like I'm taking over for a while," he smiled and opened his hand towards the spot where Vlaine and I usually sat. "Shall we?"

I looked over at Vlaine nervously as he hung up the phone. I thought I had done well, so why was he acting so strange?

Draxe is going to take over for a while. Try and have your clothes back on before half past noon. Vlaine's voice rang clearly in my head.

I looked at him and grinned, *Green looks terrible on you. I would never break your heart like that.*

Vlaine chuckled, "I'll be back in a bit. Good luck."

"Let's get started," Draxe smiled and sat down where Vlaine typically took his seat.

I took my place in front of him hesitantly and watched as he extended his hands forward. As soon as I began to put my hands towards him I retracted them. What if he could read the dreams I was having about him? I would seem like a complete freak and I would absolutely die if he could tell how infatuated I was with him.

His eyebrows furrowed, "is something wrong?"

"Yeah," I scooted my butt further away from him, "it is kind of strange to explain. I just don't want you to read me, but I know you will be able to when I put my hands in yours if you are not able to right now."

He chewed on his lip then smiled, "how about I teach you how to engage a psychic barrier? It takes a lot of time and practice to learn, but we have a few hours if you don't mind cutting lunch short."

"Yes, I would really like that," I bounced back closer to him.

"Okay Abrielle," my name sounded so nice as it flowed through his lips, "clear your mind and think about absolutely nothing."

I twisted my lips and tried as hard as I could. A black wall formed in my mind and I tried my best to simply concentrate on it. "This is really hard," I admitted.

"Like I said, it takes a long time to master this stuff. Vlaine has been working on it since he was six years old." Draxe scoffed, "you really freaked him out by finding a weakness. He was not actually expecting you to find one, he was just trying to get you to fine tune your focus."

"That's not insulting at all," I mumbled. "Okay," I inhaled deeply, "blank space. I am looking at a black wall of nothingness."

Pushing my shoulders back I closed my eyes and cleared my mind. Just as I began to relax Draxe's breath drew closer and I opened an eye to see his hand stretching out towards me.

"I am not as strong with telepathy as I am with other things. I am going to need to take your hand to try to monitor your progress."

My chest tightened. Of course I wanted him to take my hand. I wanted to touch him so badly it hurt. His eyes were sincere and as they bore into me above those perfectly chiseled cheeks my stomach did flips. The prospect of him finding out that he was in my dreams was terrifying. Although I had no control over subconscious thoughts, I still felt like he would judge me somehow.

"Um, so listen," my voice was shaky and devoid of confidence, "I understand that there is no getting around working together on telepathy without you finding something out." I shook my hands nervously.

He leaned back, "Did you do something

wrong? Did you hurt someone?"

"No, nothing like that," my defenses rose. How could anyone think I could hurt another living creature? "Do you promise not to freak out if you see something?"

"I can promise to try not to freak out." His expression was genuine and thoughtful.

"Since I was a little girl I have been having this dream," I steadied my breathing.

"Oh, right, I asked my father about that."

"Wait," I stopped him, "I need to finish this thought or I will never let you help me. Since I was a little girl I have been having this dream and in it I see you."

"What do you mean?" Draxe's interest was piqued.

I grabbed his hand, "let me show you."

The same thing I had shown Vlaine was what I shared with Draxe. His face remained serious from when I first held his hand until I finished. There was nothing degrading or demeaning in his expression and he did not run in the other direction away from the bizarre girl that has been dreaming about him for years. Quite frankly, I would have been terrified if someone had shown me something like that regarding myself, but Draxe was calm and attentive.

He brushed his knuckles against his jaw

ponderingly then leaned forward. "Do you mind if I do a bit of searching on my own?"

"I just shared the most embarrassing thing with you I could imagine. Yes, by all means my mind is open."

Draxe adjusted his seating and squeezed my hands. His eyes were shut tightly and lips pulled in a thin line. The seconds passed slowly as I waited for him to say anything regarding the visions.

Finally he broke the silence. "It is not unheard of for telepaths to see into the future. You have a connection with the mind of others and you can see into different parts of time. When you combine parts of your timeline with that of another, it creates a vision. The strange thing is the vision was reoccurring." He looked down at our intertwined hands, "my best guess is you thought about it enough to recall it often in your sleep or perhaps your subconscious did not want you to forget the image."

He further explained that he hypothesized that it was extended from actually encountering the people in the dream. What he said made sense and the relief that I felt when I found that he held no judgments was extraordinary. The only thing I wondered was why I felt so strongly about him after having the dream. Perhaps he was my savior for whatever was to come and I felt love for my rescuer.

"Have you ever had visions?" I was hopeful that perhaps he shared the same one as me.

"No," he looked down and shook his head,

"I'm not a very strong telepath. I'm not a very strong anything actually."

Glancing at his muscular physique I let out a loud laugh.

He jumped in surprise, "what?"

"Sorry," I blushed, "I may not completely understand how to decipher another person's gifts but physically you look really strong."

"I'm the headmaster's son and I failed out of Glaston. Just because I can lift a few weights doesn't mean I can amount to anything in our world."

"Our world? This is still Earth. So we happen to be at a college where the students can do things that scientists cannot explain yet. You're still superior to 99.9% of humans. You're kind, smart, strong, and you have, wait... what are your gifts?"

"Same exact ones as Vlaine," he shrugged.

"Vlaine never told me his," I thought about the two that I knew he had, but other than that he had never mentioned what his particular gifts were. Come to think of it, no one at Glaston Academy spoke about their gifts. Liz and Will told me because I had asked them. I guess they assumed because everyone else seemed to have a particular detector for these things.

Draxe chuckled, "You two spend like twenty hours a week together. I would have thought it would have come up since you guys are friends."

"Vlaine has friends?" I laughed and combed my hand through my hair nervously. "He tolerates me at best. Your brother is an incredibly patient teacher but as a student it seems pretty clear he wants nothing to do with me."

Vlaine and I certainly were not hanging out in pajamas eating pizza and watching terrible movies together, but in a school full of people terrified of the man, I trusted him completely. He was the first person I would go to if I had a problem and the one person I looked forward to seeing every day.

One of Draxe's fingers twitched and I realized my left hand was still in his and he could "see" everything I was thinking at that moment.

He sucked in a breath and straightened his back. "I know everyone here thinks that my brother is evil and a vicious murderer. For the most part they would be correct, but he doesn't skin-walk for just anyone and he definitely does not punish people for being mean to other people. In fact, he usually gets a thrill out of the backstabbing that happens here."

I shrugged. Vlaine was a topic that I was consistently baffled about. When I was in my ISE class he was wonderful. The patience he had was incredible and he did everything he could to motivate me to prefect my gifts. Outside of my skill class he was hot and cold. He pushed me away, but he did not ignore me like he did with other students. I suppose in a strange and deranged way I was friends with Vlaine.

I looked at Draxe and tried to push away any thoughts of Vlaine and soak in every second I had in this small proximity with Draxe. He smelled like grass with a slight musk, a dimple burrowed into his right cheek enhanced his all-American boy smile. He was so kind, perfectly kind. There was no reason he should have accepted my visions like he had and he treated me like a human being, unlike anyone else at Glaston. But that physique and that face, it was perfection. Oh God, I hoped he couldn't see what I was thinking.

"Anyway," I wanted to drift from any secretive thoughts I had of either brother, "let us practice my psychic shield."

He complied happily and we devoted the class to my concentration and shield. I needed to find a way to protect my thoughts, especially if Professor Horicon was able to see them. Providing a shield was uncomfortable and there seemed to be no way for other thoughts to stop popping up in my head, especially with my hands in Draxe's.

Petrichor. Just as exhaustion began to overtake me I smelled my favorite scent. How could Draxe suddenly smell like it had just rained? Melancholy washed over me and I opened my eyes.

Someone was watching me and I turned quickly to face Vlaine. As soon as I saw him looking towards me I retracted my hands from Draxe's. Why would I feel strange about that? Draxe was helping me; he was my designated substitute so there was no need for me to withdraw my hands so quickly.

"Draxe was teaching me how to put up a psychic barrier." I smiled.

Vlaine stood there tapping his thumb to his ring finger. "Abrielle you get to go home early today. I'll take your initiative into account and the early day will not affect your grade. I will see you tomorrow."

"Two hours early?" I stood up and walked to Vlaine.

"Yes," he nodded, "two hours to get a head start on some homework. Go make some good impressions Abbs." Vlaine then turned to face his brother and gave Draxe a distinct look that made it clear the conversation they were about to have was between them, and only them.

I did not want to leave the gymnasium. The building was my secret hideout from the rest of the school. It was the one building no one seemed to use aside from me. At least I was the only person there after ten in the morning. For all I knew between nightfall and dawn an orangutan led circus put on a spectacular for hundreds, but during the afternoon it was mine and I felt like I was being shunned out of the one place that felt comfortable for me.

"I'm going to take a shower," I lied to the twins standing in close proximity to me, "I'll let you two talk."

"Abbs," Vlaine shook his head, "I can read you." He lifted his shoulders as if I was ridiculous to think I could get away with any sort of white lie. "Just go back to the dorms. It is not that big of a deal."

I rolled my eyes and walked out of the building. Back at the main building peers were still in classes, others were studying, and a few were sitting on the grass in the field between the buildings. I was headed back to the dorm but decided to lie out in the sun on the field and study. Just as I got comfortable I realized I never did find out what Draxe and Vlaine's gifts were. I shrugged to myself and planned to ask the following day.

The sun began to sink and the skies became darker. I was nearly done with everything I had due for the week but there was a question I could not quite solve in physics. With any luck the professor would be in his office still, though it was most likely he had gone home for the day hours ago.

I decided to try my luck with finding the professor. As I walked into the building I became too aware of the silence. There were no students around, and no voices that I could hear, and no professors I could see. I made my footsteps as silent as possible and continued down the hallway. Once I reached the end of the second hallways I heard voices and one of them sounded distinctly like Professor B.

I listened intently trying to find the source of the voices. The silence of the school helped me to find a small crack in the wall from which the voices were emanating. I stepped back and studied the crack. At first I thought it was a fault in the design of the building, but the old mansion had no faults. "Old mansion," I whispered to myself as the possibility of a secret door dawned on me. Most old mansions had secret rooms. I had even seen the headmaster disappear into one before. The clue to open the door had to be around there somewhere.

On the wall were blocks of pearlescent wallpaper sectioned off by hardwood. On each section was a painting of some sort. The painting I was staring at was a duplicate of Vincent Van Gogh's *Portrait of Dr. Gachet*. It was upright and perfectly lined; there was nothing to show that there had been movement of any sort of either the painting or the panel it hung on. My eyes searched the top of the wall and the bottom. As I searched the edges of the wall something caught my gaze. On the side of one of the lengths of hardwood outlining the panel was what seemed to be a piece of the wood that had been drilled. Lightly, I pressed my finger against the imperfect area of wood. I was pressing on a button that had very little give. I pressed harder and as I did so the panel popped open ever so slightly revealing a wall behind it.

I looked around to be sure that there was no one near me. When I was sure there was no one in sight or earshot I opened the panel to the wall behind it. The wall had a small sliding door. Slowly I pushed the door to the side to reveal a staircase. Before closing the wall and panel behind me I made sure that there was a way to get out before closing myself into a secret passage. There was a handle on the inside of both and I felt comfortable enough to continue on.

What was I doing? I did not sneak around places, especially ones that were so obviously not meant for students. The better part of my brain told me to turn around and pretend that I had never found the secret space, but the other half wanted nothing more than to explore.

As I silently ascended the staircase the voices were getting louder. I knew three of them, it was Professor B., Professor Horicon, and the headmaster. I was close enough to the top of the stairs to see a room open at the mouth of the steps.

"I think it is in our best interest to contact the headmaster at Valdor," Professor B. was pacing.

The eloquent voice of Headmaster Josnic replied, "There is no need to contact Peter at this time."

Professor B. rebutted, "Peter asked us to report to him the moment anything interesting happened. I would say cracking Vlaine months ahead of our projected date is something of interest."

They were talking about me. Why was there some secret meeting about me? I inched closer to make sure I did not miss a word of the conversation.

It was Professor Horicon who spoke next. "I propose you have Draxe take the classes over. He is softer than Vlaine but his devotion to you is unwavering. He will teach her and not ask questions. Continue teaching her to build walls to psychic attacks both with telepathy and empathy."

"Vlaine will continue with the lessons," Headmaster Josnic said flatly. "How are her grades?"

Professor Horicon and Professor B. began

speaking at the same time but Professor B. yielded and allowed Professor Horicon to speak. "She usually scores between first and third in all her assignments and completes all work ahead of time. Macroeconomics is her weakest class and literature is her best. Overall her grade point average is a 3.6 but it has only been a couple weeks. It would have been significantly lower if your son hadn't pulled that stunt when Tracy Stillsburn tried to take credit for the assignment." He sounded more disgusted with each word.

"Barry, do you concur with Leonard?" the headmaster's voice was devoid of any emotions.

"Yes. Her homework, papers and test scores are highly satisfactory and all the work is above and beyond what is expected, especially from a student that still technically has not graduated high school yet. She shows great interest in her school work and is extremely motivated to succeed. In my opinion she is well on her way into the tank."

"Barry, we are ready for my sons to be part of this conversation. Please retrieve them."

As quickly and quietly as possible I descended the stairs and searched for the handle to exit the room. I should have taken note where the handle was in relation to the stairs. The seconds seemed like hours as I tapped my hand against the wall looking for a way out. I could hear footsteps on the stairs getting closer. I was out of time and my only option was to hide behind the stairs as Professor B. left and try to sneak out after him.

I watched as he pulled the handle and snuck out of the room cautiously. Counting down from thirty, I wanted to leave enough time to slink out without him in sight but not enough so he would be returning as I escaped. The panel gave a small creak as I slipped out of the room. Professor B. was turning the corner at the far end of the hall but did not seem to notice me.

Ever the indefatigable student, Liz was lying on her bed flipping through flash cards. Typically I was just as eager to study, but all I wanted in that moment was a friend. Steph would have known what to say about the strange meeting I had just spied on and for a brief moment I wished so hard she could be there that I had to push the thought out of my head for fear that it could come into fruition. Who knew what the consequences would be if Steph somehow did show up in the dorm? Was that even possible?

I shook my head and decided to find something to preoccupy my mind. "I'm going to go watch T.V. downstairs. Would you like to join?" I invited Liz in the rare event that she actually wanted to do something aside from studying.

She held up her flash cards as proof, "test tomorrow, I've got to study." Liz was curt as always.

"Do you want me to quiz you?" I did not particularly want to help her, but I knew the panic of getting ready for a test.

She shook her head and continued flipping through her study aids. With that I turned on my heel and headed downstairs to claim one of the couches and enjoy some mindless programs. After half an hour of getting sucked into some reality television show that had absolutely no premise I heard the light tapping of footsteps. I did not feel threatened, and ignored the steps. A moment later Liz sat down at the other end of the couch and we sat in silence for a few minutes.

"You have really pretty hair," her voice was a strange balance of terse and kind.

She was trying to be a friend! "Thank you," I smiled, "I love yours. I just don't have the bone structure for pulling off a styled bob."

It was true, Liz had high cheekbones that sloped down to a slender chin and her natural blonde hair perfectly curved along her delicate jaw line. My eyes were squished whenever I smiled by high cheekbones and a round face that begged to be lengthened by hair that flowed at least halfway down my back.

I nudged the remote to her and told her I was up for watching anything that was not thought provoking. With a smile she put the remote control on the table beside her. We watched television together in silence, the same contented peace that Will and I shared. If anything, I would leave Glaston Academy with the understanding that communication came in countless forms and words did not have to be spoken to seal a friendship.

15

I dropped my books at the door of the gymnasium and walked towards Vlaine with a purpose. "Look," I thrust my hands on my hips, "I worked hard to be able to find a crack and then you get all loopy weird when I am able to do it. I'm going to find a crack again but first you are going to teach me how to put up a psychic barrier. I can put up a wall so that I do not get thoughts from other people; I have been doing that for too long. Now I need to make sure no one can get mine. Teach me teacher, and don't flake out on me again."

His stony expression cracked into a smile. "Whatever you say, Abbs."

"Wait," before you give me any instructions I want to try something first."

Vlaine nodded his head in compliance. I sat down and cleared my mind as best I could. I imagined the black wall that I had put into my mind the day prior with Draxe. Once I cleared my mind totally and completely I imagined a glass barrier around my brain. Next I put an imaginary brick wall around it and sealed it with a nice black cloth.

"Okay," I nodded, "give it a try and then critique me."

Intrigued, he sat next to me and concentrated on reading me. A minute or so later he put his hand on my arm then informed me that I had the right idea, but I went about it a bit wrong. Though it was harder for him to get into my mind, he was still able to and that made me nervous because it was only a matter of time before he found out that I knew about the secret room and the meeting that had taken place in there.

Tuesday and Thursday seminar classes were too short to allow the significant accomplishment of anything. While I practiced archery Vlaine and I would communicate telepathically allowing me to work on my distance telepathy. If the conversation ever became dull he would pull out an extra bow and begin a competition between us, one that he would always win since he was the closest thing to a super human I had ever met.

I was not ready to go back to the dorm after class and found myself wandering through the woods around the school. I followed one of the horse trails that twisted the farthest from campus. Adventuring through the secluded forest of upstate New York was emotionally affirming. If the students were not so high strung, Glaston Academy would be a truly magical place.

Walking in solitude was always my favorite

way to let my imagination take off. I played with the idea of a team of do-gooders. Of the students of whom I knew their abilities, we could make a kick-ass team of pseudo-superheroes. Liz had invisibility, Adele could start fires, Tracy had telekinesis, Kyle had an affinity to animals, and Will had telepathy. I wasn't sure of the complete list of Vlaine and Draxe's gifts, but manipulation and emulating someone were enough on their own.

When I returned to the school something was off. I could sense a difference in the energy around the campus. Memories of Tracy's mangled arm flashed in my head. I quieted my mind to try and hone in on what exactly I was feeling. There was a tangible level of angst around the school. I found Liz to see if she knew what was going on and after a pointed look she told me there was a new student.

I jumped in the air with excitement; I would not longer be the new meat at Glaston Academy. I skipped my way to the stables to find Will knowing he would share the excitement with me. Cinnamon gave a loud whinny when I entered the stables, but Will was nowhere in sight. After searching the dorms, common area, and school for him I gave up and sprawled out on a couch to watch television.

Halfway through a gore-filled movie I heard soft steps behind me. I turned and smiled a "hello" expecting to see Liz, but it was another student. I put the remote on the table and anticipated being ignored but to my surprise he was cordial.

"Hello," he put his hand out to shake mine,

"I'm Erik."

"Abrielle," I smiled, taking his hand in return.

"Do you mind if I sit here?" Playful mischief was hidden in his hazel eyes.

"Not at all," I moved my legs underneath my body.

Erik's dark hair was longer than Liz's, but perfectly kempt as if he just left a modeling shoot. He was handsome, but not in an overstated way. His thin nose widened slightly at the base just a few centimeters above full proportionate lips. Something about him felt familiar, like I had met him before but I could not quite place him.

"Do I smell bad or something?" He mused, running a hand through his soft waves.

"What?" I was confused, but then I noticed how far I was leaning away from him. "Oh, no, you smell good, like the ocean." Could I possibly sound more socially inept? "Sorry, I'm just accustomed to being treated like a diseased rat around here. If anyone looks at me it's with repulsion."

"Why? Aren't you a healer? We had a healer at my school and everyone flocked to her." He leaned back and stretched his arm out against the back of the couch. "You always want to make friends with someone that can save your life before a doctor can."

"Healer or not, I'm the new student. Wait, your school?" I turned my entire body to face him and tucked my legs underneath myself. "What do you mean?"

"I just transferred here," he flashed a charming smile. "I'm from Glaston's sister school over in Pennsylvania."

"Glaston has a sister school?" Was this supposed to be common knowledge?

"Yeah," he laughed sliding his hand through his long locks once again. "There are a few. You really are new, aren't you? Or do they just not talk about the other schools here? There is one in Pennsylvania, Alaska, Oregon, New Mexico, and Scotland."

Did everyone else know about the other schools or was everyone so tight-lipped here that we did not even know about the place we were attending? "Like I said, diseased rat," I pointed to myself.

"They're missing out." He brushed his knuckles against my cheek, "Looks like you finally have a friend at Glaston."

My first instinct was to shudder away from his touch, but as soon as his fingers brushed against my skin a sensation of relaxation washed over my body. His touch was warm and comforting, like I had just been hugged by a best friend. I was instantly at ease with Erik and I felt like I could tell him anything.

Erik and I spent hours conversing that night. I learned that Valdor Academy was the first and main school of the affiliated colleges for gifted students.

Erik was inducted into Valdor when he was seventeen just like me, though he did not explain what his particular gift was. The school in Scotland was opened second because of the numerous gifted people in Europe. The other ones were opened in accordance to try and obtain the most intelligent students with admirable gifts from different parts of the country. Each school had their own set of rules and standards dictated by the headmaster of that particular institution.

I was tempted to ask him about the "think tank" but I did not want to tread on territory that could get me in trouble. Though Will was hot and cold with our friendship, I would heed his advice not to trust anyone. Erik and I talked until early morning and I awoke from the sound of movement. I was lying on the couch, my head propped on Erik's hip. He was sound asleep leaning against the opposite arm of the couch.

That night was the first night when I felt like I was actually an autonomous college student. I figured the "best years of my life" would be spent staying up late, cramming for examinations, and testing the limits of my liver with friends that I made along the way. Roughly a month into college and I finally scored my late night chat session with a friend I had so longed for.

I sat up slowly trying not to wake Erik, but failed in my attempt. "Morning princess," he smiled and rubbed his neck.

"Stiff neck?" I nodded at the massaging

motion he was making. "Here," I scooted closer to him, "I can fix that in no time." Forgetting about the school rules, I allowed my healing to go to work and half a minute later his shoulders relaxed.

"See, healers are the best people to be friends with." He stood up and stretched. "Where are you off to? Classes don't start for another three hours."

"I need to take a shower, get breakfast, and then show up disgustingly early to my physics class."

"What, do we have a test or something?"

We? "I just get to every class early to study, do homework, or write letters back home. Do you have physics this morning?"

"Yeah," he yanked a piece of paper from his pocket that was folded up. "I have physics, ecology, robotics, ISE, and weight training today. Tomorrow I have ISE then macro."

"Wow," I jumped over to him and looked at the paper. "We have three classes together. Come on up to my dorm once you're showered and I'll give you the syllabi for our classes so you know what to expect. Mine is room 217, I'll be ready in eight minutes." I began to jog away.

"Want me to bring breakfast to your room and we can get you to show up on time for the class instead of a day early?"

"Whoa Erik," I laughed, "Looks like you are going to be a bad influence on me. Yes, that sounds good."

Twenty minutes later Erik knocked on my door, a paper bag filled with fruit and bagels was in one hand and a tray of coffee was in the other. "I come bearing gifts," he grinned and walked into the room.

I twirled my finger in my hair, "coffee? You sure know how to make a girl swoon." I pulled out the syllabi that I took copies of for him. I had highlighted the due dates of papers and projects in each class. "I am not sure what your strengths are but macro is mostly notes. We have one homework assignment each week that is due via email and there is a quiz or test in physics each week. Ecology is easy as long as you trust your partner not to stab you in the back." There was a tint of resentment in my voice. Erik rested his chin on my shoulder as I explained the classes and professors to him.

"Looks like I made friends with the right person," he sipped his coffee and looked over the paperwork. "Our headmaster, Peter, is a total hippie. He does not care too much about what grades we get as long as we try. Glaston seems like it has a stick up its ass." Taking a bite out of his bagel he muttered, "Must be why it has more kids in the tank."

"What?" I jumped up and looked at him.

"I said that Glaston seems to have a stick up its ass."

"No," I shook my head vigorously, "what did you say after that?"

"It must be why so many kids flunk out. You guys have the lowest graduation percentage of any of the schools." He pronounced every syllable clearly.

"That is not what you said," I sighed and ran my hand through my long hair.

"Has anyone ever told you how pretty your hair is?" he walked forward twirled a lock with one hand and ran the other along my face as he did the night before.

Instant tingles traveled from my face to my toes. I did not care about what he said anymore, I just wanted him to keep touching me. *Abrielle.* A voice in my head shook off the trance. Whose voice was that? It was not Erik's voice I heard and I did not sense the telepathy buzz from him. Whoever it was knocked me from a strange stupor that Erik's touch had given me.

I shook my head, "sorry for staring." I giggled uncomfortably, "I left two lifelong friends behind and it is just so good to be making a new one." Standing up I straightened out the grey sweater dress I put on that morning and grabbed my books. "Thank you so much for breakfast and coffee, but I am going to get some last minute studying done for physics just in case he has a pop quiz or something."

Erik arched his brow and stood up. "I'll accompany you." He took the books from my hand and led me to the class.

Throughout physics he passed me notes and made gestures just to make me laugh. It was fun being infantile in a school that took itself all too seriously.

He was the friend I was missing, the friend I was craving. The instantaneous comfort and joking was so similar to the friendship that I had with Nicholas, it was soothing and nostalgic in equal measure.

We walked to ecology together and he sat down in the seat next to me. "Wait," I put my hand out, "that's Vlaine's seat. This one to the right of me is open."

"Vlaine, as in Vlaine Josnic?" a devilish grin spread across his face.

"Yes," I spoke hesitantly wondering how he knew Vlaine. "Don't tell me you are afraid of Vlaine too." Erik's expression was taunting.

"I'm not" I pushed my hair back and crossed my arms across my chest, "I'm the only one at this school that doesn't seem to be afraid of him."

"I guess you are one of two now." He had a look of determination and defiance that made me uneasy.

His excitement with angering Vlaine made me uncomfortable and I would not be part of getting Vlaine angry. I took out a study game I had made myself for the class and began connecting terms and definitions on the page to distance myself from the situation. A few minutes after sitting down Vlaine walked in and stood by Erik.

"I know that you're well aware that is my damn seat," Vlaine growled at Erik.

My stomach twisted in a knot watching the interaction. I knew Vlaine's history well enough to know that he was not all talk but I knew very little about Erik, aside from the fact that he was quickly climbing the ranks to being my closest friend at Glaston.

"There's one open on the other side of this pretty little healer." Erik's voice was taunting.

I froze with my mouth slightly agape. Why was Erik doing this? Why would he taunt Vlaine when he had such a notorious reputation? I looked up nervously at Vlaine whose face was serious and angry.

"So what you're saying," Vlaine's voice was icy, "is that we sandwich this 'pretty little healer' between two assholes?" Just then Vlaine and Erik did a weird handshake and a short guy-friend pat on the back. "How the hell are ya?" Vlaine dropped his books on the desk.

"Just transferred here man, already making friends," Erik nodded his head in my direction. My face grew hot as embarrassment burned my cheeks. "Can you believe it? Guess I screwed up too many times for Valdor to keep me but your old man thought I was worth another shot."

"Awesome, glad to have you here," Vlaine gripped Erik's forearm in another strange handshake. "But seriously, Erik, this is my seat. Sit on the other side of Abrielle."

Erik held his hands up in a surrendering motion, grabbed his things, and switched to the seat beside me. They began talking again and I quickly stopped them, "do I need to switch seats with Erik so you two can continue your bromance?"

Both men laughed at the same time and fell into a silence as other students entered the room. Once class was over I got up abruptly assuming that I was in the way of the two men from conversing. I backed up and straightened out my books.

"Where's your next class?" Erik was focusing solely on me.

"Not anywhere close to this building, I usually have to jog there just to get to the class on time." I began walking towards the door. Vlaine was gathering his items slower than usual, no doubt listening to the conversation.

"I have old man Leonard teaching my ISE class, I can spare a few extra minutes if you want me to walk you there."

"Don't be late on your first day, maybe another time." I stopped walking and looked at Erik, "no idea who Leonard is, but have fun at your skill seminar. I'll see you around."

"Abrielle," his melodic voice stopped me in my tracks, "want to study again tonight?"

"Sure," I nodded, "I'll meet you at the common area later."

16

For the rest of that week I would brush Cinnamon while waiting for Will to meet me, but I hadn't seen him since before I became friends with Erik. After brushing the horse I would meet up with Erik and we would study until we fell asleep. Will's absence was unsettling and on Saturday morning I made it a point to investigate his absence. After searching for a few hours I gave in and asked Liz who took a couple seconds to shrug her shoulders before continuing on with her studies. Eventually I found Vlaine in the kitchen and I sat down with him.

"What's up Abbs?" he took a bite from an apricot and continued reading a newspaper without ever glancing my way.

"Have you seen Will at all? I've been looking for him and haven't seen him in almost a week."

"I think he got the boot from Glaston." His words were uninterested.

"What do you mean? He was kicked out?"

He shrugged and turned the page in his

newspaper.

"Do you have any idea how to get in touch with him? Who will take care of Cinnamon?"

"Looks like you've been taking care of Cinnamon without him." He turned another page without looking up.

I took his chin gently in my hand and forced him to look up at me. My stomach flopped and I shuddered at the contact. Vlaine was watching me patiently. Mentally, I kicked myself and tried to make words form without thinking about how my body was buzzing from touching him.

"Is there any way you could find out what happened to Will? There are so few people I actually interact with here and it would really suck to lose one of them."

His hand gently took mine and pulled it away from his face, "of course Abbs."

My hand was still in his and I was taken aback by his willingness to comply. My heart was beating faster by the second. Just in time to break the lock between Vlaine and my eyes, Erik sat at the table.

"Hey Abrielle, Vlaine, what's going on?" Erik took a bite of a breakfast sandwich and rubbed his hands together noisily.

I retracted my hand from Vlaine's and smiled. "Hey."

Vlaine was still watching me. My eyes fluttered nervously between the two.

"So Erik," I straightened my back and calmed my mind, "did you still want to practice today?"

"What are you practicing?" Vlaine looked back down at his newspaper.

"Her skills," Erik winked and tapped his fingers together roguishly.

Vlaine looked at me pointedly, "is that not something you should be practicing with your professor?"

"Oh trust me," I cocked my head at him, "I would love to but my professor wants nothing to do with me outside of class."

"Abrielle, when have you ever asked to get help outside of the class?" He slapped the newspaper down, making a loud thwacking sound. "Maybe your grade would improve if you made some effort to do some extra work."

My jaw dropped in shock. "Vlaine, you…" I was a volume lower than yelling. I sucked in a breath and lowered my voice. "I would love to discuss this with you outside and away from earshot of other people."

"Nah, I'm good." He looked back down at his paper.

Only Vlaine could go from giving me tingles

just by touching me to making me want to punch something.

"This," I flipped my hand in the air, "this is why I cannot get help from my professor after class. Every single time I try to speak or ask questions I get shut off before I am even finished. And if I am doing so bad why do you have to stop a lesson and go have a meeting about how I did something you didn't even think I was going to be capable of doing. You're just," I stood up quickly, "you're mean." I pointed my finger at him. "You're just mean. You make me trust you then you're hot and cold just like everyone else."

1…2…3… I breathed in, allowing myself to feel angry. He was still looking down, seemingly unaffected while my lips were quivering with anger. That was the part that killed me, how apathetic he was towards my outburst. *1…2…3…* I took another deep breath to try and rid myself of the miserable feeling welling up inside my chest. Both methods were equally ineffective. I could feel the stinging in my nose that was slowly working its way up to tears.

I put on my best face to act like I was over the small incident with Vlaine and I smiled at Erik. "I'm going to meet you at the building. It's down the road about a quarter mile and you'll see a small path leading from the road and into the woods."

I walked out of the kitchen with grace and poise. I would not let Vlaine know that he upset me. Everything except for the budding friendship of Erik sucked at Glaston. I hadn't spoken to my mom, Steph, or Nicholas since I got there despite the letters

I had sent out each week, no one aside from Erik liked me, I finally found my dream man only to come up with more questions, and there was a group of professors talking about me like I was a sheepdog about to be sent off to a dog show.

I replayed the conversation in my head and slapped myself in the forehead when I realized that I had mentioned a meeting about breaking his wall. I began running to the gymnasium, as if I could outrun the past few minutes. Tears began to slide down my face, I ran faster.

Bursting through the gymnasium door through to the locker room I splashed cold water on my eyes and looked up. They were slightly puffy, but my face was red from running so it would calm at the same rate as my cheeks would. After a few more minutes in the locker room I was presentable, my cheeks were slightly rosy and my eyes were glistening but not swollen. I walked into the gym and walked towards the opposite end of the room where Vlaine and I usually sat. I looked over to our usual seat like a bitter memory and tossed the thoughts of Vlaine aside.

Sitting upright, I calmed my mind and focused on listening to everything around me. I reached to listen to the thoughts of students who were still asleep in their dorms. Midway through watching Liz's dream through that steamy window I heard the door open. Slowly I backed out of the dream and opened my eyes. Vlaine was sitting across from me, a line of sweat formed at his hairline. He interlocked his fingers in mine as we did whenever we would begin class.

"When do you want to practice?" His eyes were searching mine and he was sincere, thoughtful.

Right now, I thought to myself, *all the time. It's the only thing I look forward to.* I cleared my throat, "are you free tomorrow?"

"I've got a meeting tomorrow morning but I'll be free after ten," his thumb rubbed my knuckles.

"Great," I pulled my hands from his, "I will meet you here around ten thirty tomorrow. Thank you for your time Mr. Josnic."

I closed my eyes and repositioned my seating to continue searching the other students. It took half a minute for the guilt to force my eyes open so I could apologize to Vlaine for being so cold but when I opened them he was nowhere in sight. I hadn't even heard the door open but it was no surprise, Vlaine was elusive.

Erik strode in a few minutes later wearing a roguish smile. He sauntered over to me and kneeled down.

"Sorry about that," I flicked my wrists, "Vlaine can get under my skin like you could not imagine."

He laughed, "I've known Vlaine for a long time. He seems to have that affect on the womenfolk."

"Oh really?" I arched my brow, "because no one here talks to him. In fact, I have never seen a girl talk to him before."

He tapped his finger to his head, "you only see what Vlaine wants you to see. He is a manipulator, remember?"

Anger erupted throughout my entire body. Not only did I trust Vlaine, but I could feel that Erik was lying. I knew when Vlaine was manipulating me, but the rest of the school avoiding him was not something that was implanted into my head at all times. I had no idea why Erik would lie about something like that, but it only proved to worsen my already dour mood.

"He would have no reason to manipulate that into my head, Erik. It's not like something like that would play into his favor.

"Of course it would," he laughed, "you're a healer, you live to save lives and make the underdog happy." He inched closer, "what wouldn't you do to make an outsider happy?"

My brows furrowed at his invasive truth towards my character. Of course I had a soft spot for anyone that was in any sort of pain, be it physical, emotional, or what have you. There was only one way I was going to prove to myself that Erik was being deceitful, and it was through telepathy. I pushed myself into his mind as well and rapidly as I could. He had a block but it was not nearly as strong as Vlaine's. I knew how to go around it and find the fracture.

Just as I was about to go into explore his mind he put his hand on my face. Erik's thumb rubbed the outline of my ear. Instantly I melted; the comfortable warm sensation spread from my face down the rest of my body. I had to break eye contact with him to avoid drooling on myself

"That was really good." His voice was soothing, "it took you six minutes to break into my barrier by being angry." His thumb rubbed my cheek softly and hand traveled softly down my face to my arm and to my hand. "Try breaking the barrier by being calm."

I was mad for six minutes? That was impossible, I was never mad that long. I stood up abruptly and rubbed my hand on my forehead.

"Thank you for offering to practice with me," I smiled, "but my mind is not in it. I guess the whole Vlaine situation bothered me more than I thought."

He raised his hand to touch my face and I slapped it away. There was something strange about how his contact affected me. "You are so sweet," I tried to sound sincere, "but my boyfriend back home would get so mad if he knew you kept touching me like this."

"Your boyfriend?" His expression made it obvious he did not believe me.

I was such a terrible liar, but I knew I could show him a memory to help make my lie seem more believable. I imagined the first day of school when I was pretending to be Nicholas's girlfriend. The date was on the blackboard in the background. I touched him and showed him ten seconds of the memory, long enough to let him see the interaction but not long enough to catch on to the fact that it was faked.

"I see," Erik squinted disapprovingly.

"Yeah," I backed up, "sorry for wasting your time. See you tonight!"

I ran out of the gymnasium and to the stables as quickly as I could. The one person I was becoming friends with was playing some sort of game with my mind. Whenever he touched me I felt so serene and calm. It had to be his ability, but I could not understand why he would want to force me to be comfortable.

I wished I had a phone so I could talk to Steph. If I told her that some guy I had just become friends with was trying to control or influence me in any sort of way she would tell me to steer clear of him and would send Nicholas after him. She would also say something to the effect of "sweetie, that's what your fist is for." Just thinking about how Steph would toss her hair back and instruct me to deal with Erik made me feel better.

Cinnamon was restless in her stall and I wanted desperately to ride her and allow her some exercise. Just as I began to pick her hooves I heard a voice behind me.

"You want me to teach you?"

I jumped and turned to face Draxe. "What?"

He leaned against the door of the stall, "do you want me to teach you how to ride?"

"Maybe another day, I just want to be alone right now."

What was I saying? My dream man just offered to teach me how to ride a horse that I had wanted to ride since the moment I saw her. In defense, my interactions with men that day were all terrible and I did not want to find out how things could go wrong with Draxe.

I needed a girl's night. I jumped at the realization that I was not a prisoner, I was a college student. I did not need to stay at the school and I did not need to attend every class. In fact, none of my classes had an attendance policy.

I leaned against the other side of the door, inches away from Draxe. "Actually, do you have a cell phone that gets reception here?"

For a moment he looked panicked, but quickly replaced the expression with a demure smile. "Yeah, but it's in my room. You can use it when I get back with Buttercup."

"Thank you!" I hopped up with excitement.

"No problem," he tapped his hand on the stall and walked away.

Cinnamon nuzzled my arm and I turned to see she was nearly out of water. As I walked to get her some more I saw Draxe entering the school. I filled up the bucket and gave him the benefit of the doubt assuming he needed to use the restroom or something.

"He's a guy," I exclaimed loudly. There was no reason for him to use the restroom.

Draxe was nowhere in sight when I searched for him in the school so I made a beeline to the *Portrait of Dr. Gachet* to listen if they had gone to the secret room. After hearing nothing for a few moments I slipped back downstairs then heard muffled voices on the first floor.

The noises were coming from the same room my literature class was in. I put my back up against the wall, controlled my breathing, and listened. The first one to speak was Draxe.

"She wants to call Steph and I told her she could use my phone. You're going to have to play best girlfriend for a day."

"No," Vlaine's voice was angry, "I'm not babysitting Abrielle today."

"So what, you are going to just let her hang out with her friend?"

My stomach clenched from hearing Draxe's accusing and bitter tone. What was wrong with me hanging out with Steph?

"Yeah, why wouldn't I? She's not going to say anything about the school." Vlaine's voice was quiet and defensive.

"That's not the problem and you know it. The other schools know we have a replicator here. What if one of them sends a scout while she's out playing teenager?"

"Have you not seen the new addition to the school Draxe? Open your friggin' eyes, they already have. Have you not noticed Erik's here from Valdor?"

"He is not a scout. They would have had to start the transfer application months in advance."

Vlaine growled in aggravation. "Oh, you don't think they have a telepath there that saw something just like Abbs did when she saw you?"

Draxe snorted. "You're getting paranoid, brother."

"You're naïve as shit, Draxe," Vlaine gritted. "I'm the paranoid one, but you want me to play Steph for a day because she wants to see her friend. I'm not going to deceive her like that, not again. She would know the second she saw me anyway. This is just ridiculous and if you're so concerned, then you do it."

"You are useless. I'm going to ask permission from dad." Draxe was annoyed, "guess I will act the part of the best friend that you already know everything about."

A clatter happened and Vlaine whisper-yelled, "leave dad out of it. He's going to send her to the tank the second he has a chance. If you make him think something is wrong he'll do it."

I was done snooping; I needed to know what was going on. I rounded the wall and entered the room. "Want to tell 'her' what the tank is?"

Vlaine was clutching Draxe's shirt but let go once I entered the room.

"Damn it," he muttered and rubbed his temples.

"Vlaine, do you want to go for a walk?" My voice was calm, much calmer than I felt.

He glanced sideways at Draxe. "Yeah," he threw his hands up in defeat, "let's go for a walk."

That was easy, I thought to myself and followed him outside to the horse trails.

"What is the tank?" I wasted no time getting to the point.

"The 'think tank' is where Glaston's best and brightest go to be used for practical things. You know where your gifts can actually get utilized for some worthy purpose. I know you are on the list and they want you once you prove you're a replicator."

"So the tank is where the smartest and most talented kids go. Is that a good thing or a bad thing?"

"It's good I guess," he shrugged, "but then your life is dictated by people who think they know what is good for you rather than you making decisions for yourself. You'll be told you are using your skills for something and will just have to take their word that they are telling the truth."

I laughed, "That sounds inevitable, doesn't it? I mean, that's what an occupation is anyhow. It sounds like a great job for those of us that don't have an issue with authority."

He shrugged and kicked a rock. "It's a catch 22. There are really three ways to go. Be a professor at one of the academies, go into the tank, or run away from Glaston and hope you never get found or that anyone cares to find you."

"Why is it such a big deal that you have a replicator? Are there bad guys or something and you want my supposed replication for assistance?" I sounded ridiculous asking that.

He smiled, amused. "I think the idea is to keep tabs on you to make sure you don't become the bad guy."

"There are other schools that apparently want to spy on me or something. How would keeping all this from me make me trust Glaston or want to be on their side?" There was an obvious edge to my voice. It felt terrible knowing people were talking about me and my future but not including me.

"Abbs I don't really prefer you to be on Glaston's side, but the headmaster does. I just care that you're safe."

I ignored his statement and continued on with my questions. "What are your gifts?"

I must have surprised him with the question because his eyebrows rose momentarily. "Manipulation, telepathy, and flight."

"You cannot fly," I giggled, but was unsure if he was telling the truth.

"No I can't," he laughed, "but I can do this strange kind of explosive energy wave, thing. It's cool, but pretty devastating."

"So what does manipulation cover?"

"I can manipulate minds, other people's powers, and my own appearance."

"How many times have you manipulated my mind?" I wanted to know the answer, but was afraid of what he would say.

"None, I have just changed my appearance so I could scout you at your old school." He looked at me nervously.

"What was the purpose of going to the concert with me?"

Dimples made a debut as a nostalgic smile spread. "Remember that boy that was playing the guitar? Well he was a plant. I wanted to see how you were at scouting gifts other than telepathy. I also wanted to get into your mind a bit more to see what kind of person you were."

I smiled thinking about the talented child and how incredible his gift was to witness. Vlaine wrapped his hand around my wrist gently. I stopped walking and looked at him wondering what he was doing.

"I wanted to know what you were thinking," he answered my thought.

"You can tell without touching me." I lifted my shoulders confused. I was the one that needed skin contact, not him.

"I couldn't right then. What were you thinking?"

"I was thinking that the way the boy communicated was beautiful." That was bizarre, what had I done differently to block his way into my thoughts? "Are you going to the tank?"

He laughed and shook his head, "I'm lucky if I become a professor. My reputation is not deemed worthy at the tank."

I stopped walking and turned to Vlaine. Now that I had his full attention I was going to ask him the thing weighing heaviest on my mind. "Vlaine," my voice was hardly a whisper, "why does Professor Horicon want to kill me? Is it because I'm a replicator?"

I hated that Vlaine and Draxe knew about my vision but nothing had been done about it and it was never really mentioned. Their father had undoubtedly been informed, yet Professor Horicon was still teaching at Glaston. I deserved to know more than I was being told and furthermore I deserved to feel safe.

Vlaine's face was solemn and he took both my hands in his. "I'm not going to let anything happen to you. My dad and I have been keeping track of his thoughts and plans."

He pulled me into a tight hug and my body went rigid before melting into his embrace. It felt so nice being wrapped in his arms.

"If he touches you, I swear I will make his mind a prison," he spoke into my hair.

I shivered. Vlaine could actually do that with his mental manipulation gift and he could make it the most harrowing experience imaginable. I should have been frightened by him, but his protectiveness was empowering.

"I trust you," I squeezed him appreciatively. "Thank you for keeping me safe, Vlaine."

He rubbed my back soothingly and the more he embraced me the more I wanted to stay in his arms. I pulled away quickly trying to shake the pleasant tingly feeling that was coursing through my body.

We walked the rest of the trails in silence. Just before we got to the clearing of the campus he bumped his shoulder into mine. "I've got a surprise for you. I'm going to take care of something then I will be at your dorm in twenty minutes to get you. Wear something that says 'I'm a college student now.' See you in twenty, Abbs." He winked and jogged off.

When I got back to my dorm to change Erik

was standing outside the door. He looked so trustworthy leaning against the door with his male model hair and pout.

"Yes?" I asked hesitantly.

"I'm sorry for manipulating you." He was pouting and his eyes were soft and genuine. "I'm so used to using it that it is just habit now." He followed me into my dorm as he spoke. "I know that's not an excuse, but I wanted to let you know I really am sorry for pushing you away like that."

I squinted at him, annoyed. "So what is that whole face touching thing?"

"It has a calming effect on people. It is how I get things to go my way. It can either be friendly or have a trace of pheromones."

I felt disgusted. Clearing my throat, "you use it to 'get your way.' That's pretty sickening."

"The pheromones are a last resort. I didn't use those on you." He stood in front of me, blocking my way to the closet.

I put my hands on my hips and contemplated shoving him out of the way. "Look, you were the first actual friend I made here. I don't really want to lose my first Glaston friend. Let's make a deal, you don't do that touchy manipulation crap and I will give you a second chance. You cannot possibly say no to being friends with a healer." I arched my brow, stuck my foot out, and crossed my arms over my chest.

"Yes," he clapped his hands together, "let's watch a movie tonight. Anything you want. I'll bring the popcorn."

"Sounds good," I nodded and pushed by him and grabbed a mature looking outfit. Erik was standing there still. "I need to get changed," I nodded towards the door waiting for him to leave.

"Go ahead," he leaned against my bed.

"Erik," I gritted to which he put his hands up and apologized and left the dorm.

Being friends with Erik again was a huge relief. He had told me the truth when I asked and promised not to manipulate me again. I did not fully trust him, but I wanted a friend so badly I would put my common sense aside.

I was ready and Vlaine knocked on my door after twenty minutes as promised. He led me down to the stone dust path that led to a sleek black motorcycle in the driveway. Handing me a helmet he nodded for me to put it on.

"You would have a motorcycle," I shook my head nonchalantly, trying to hide the excited butterflies flittering about my stomach. Riding on the back of a motorcycle with a hot guy was about to get checked off my bucket list.

"Hold on to my waist tightly and use your telepathy if you need to talk."

I scooted close to him and wrapped my arms

around his waist, probably too tightly. I had never been on a motorcycle before and the exhilaration hardly outweighed the apprehension. After driving southeast for forty-five minutes he led me towards a booth at the far end of a diner off the highway.

Someone was already in the booth he was heading for, curls were bouncing around with each movement. I knew those curls. My heart jumped and I squealed and ran to the booth. Steph looked up at me with a sly grin and I toppled her over with a tight hug.

Steph hugged me back laughing, "I was wondering when I was going to hear from you. I figured by now you had made all sorts of college friends and forgot about me."

"Ugh," I sat down across from her, "nearly everyone at Glaston is horrid and the classes are ridiculously time consuming. So what have I missed from back at home? Have you gotten any of my letters?"

"Same old, same old," she pulled out a compact mirror and checked her reflection. "Our Nicholas went on a date with Molly. I haven't gotten any letters yet, but according to what I heard from your mom you basically got dropped off in the middle of a forest and your carrier pigeons may have gotten lost."

"Isn't that the truth," I rolled my eyes. "What about you? Do you have any new boyfriends to speak of?"

Vlaine slid into the booth next to me and nodded a polite hello. She leaned closer to the table and sucked her cheeks into an impish smile. "No, no boyfriend still." She was doing the gorgeous Steph smile that could make anyone swoon and directing it at Vlaine. She pulled a few curls forward and looked at me, "what about you?"

"Nope, there is really no time for relationships at Glaston." I gave her a begging look hoping that she would figure out that I wanted her to stop trying to pull Vlaine in with her megawatt smile.

Please, not Vlaine, stop giving him that look. Don't complicate my life more than it already is, I thought to her. She would never hear my thoughts, but I hoped that perhaps she would simply catch on from knowing me for so long. I wanted to keep the bizarre friendship that I had with Vlaine without any girl drama getting in the way. All I could see from any relationship between the two was her contacting me to find out what he was doing, where he was, and to put me in the middle of whatever fights they had.

I was intentionally thinking loudly, but it was meant for Steph, but I hadn't considered Vlaine would catch on. *I've got you,* Vlaine's voice was crisp in my mind.

"Unless," he put his arm around me, "he happens to be your professor's assistant." He winked at me and kissed my temple quickly but gently.

I stifled a laugh and nudged him, "you being my professor was supposed to be a secret." *Oh my*

God Vlaine, nice kiss on the temple, that was like an aunt kissing her niece she hasn't seen in a month. Steph's eyes were darting between Vlaine and me.

Vlaine grinned, "I have to run an errand. I'll give you girls some time to catch up. See you soon Abbs." He kissed my nose and I cachinnated.

He had certainly halted Steph's advances, but was so awkwardly funny with his attempt at faking a relationship. I watched him walk out of the diner and back to his motorcycle before returning my gaze to Steph.

"You two are cute together," she gave me a lopsided grin.

"I needed to see you," I pouted, "I have no girls around to hang out with. My roommate is so taciturn. I'm just having a hard time adjusting I suppose."

"Maybe she is jealous of you. Don't think I didn't catch on to you changing the subject." She squinted judgingly at me.

After dodging the subject again she decided to catch me up on the latest gossip at my old high school. I filled her in on the people at Glaston without actually giving her any details. An hour and a half later Vlaine came back in to hurry the conversation up on account of the impending storm.

I hugged Steph tightly wishing I could take her back to Glaston with me. She gave Vlaine another longing glance before blowing me a kiss and getting into her car. I shook my head and smiled. Being resisted by Vlaine was one of the very few times I had witnessed her not getting what she wanted. It would be a short-lived disappointment, I was sure by the time she got home there would be a new interest that would swoon for her.

17

"Would you say we are good friends?" Erik looked at me thoughtfully.

I thought about the past several weeks that had gone by. Erik and I would spend most of our nights watching television or studying together. I held him at a distance because of the trust I had lost knowing he had been trying to manipulate me and our friendship for some unknown reason. My lack of trust made me relieved on the random nights that Liz would join us. Though she was nearly silent the entire time, she gave me a bit of comfort.

"Yes," I peeked above my notebook at him. He was not a telepath and would not know what I was thinking, "you and Vlaine are my best friends here."

"I want to talk to you about something." He turned on the couch to face me completely.

I turned to him and put my notebook down noting the seriousness in his voice. "What is it?"

He sighed, inched closer to me, and

whispered, "I am going to try and transfer back to Valdor." Rubbing his palms on his face he added, "Glaston is a little too uptight for me."

"Oh," my breathing hitched, "really?" Erik was part of my daily routine and he was my closest friend. In a strange way it felt like he was breaking up with me. I wanted him close to me, not at another school.

"What are you doing this weekend for Thanksgiving break?" He quickly broke the silence.

I could feel he was about to offer an alternative to the stressful and awkward dinner I had planned with my mother so I lied in hope of something better coming along. "I am not sure yet, why?"

His hand went towards my face and I slapped it away quickly. "Sorry, force of habit," he looked down and away. "Come to Valdor with me. You would love it there and, hey, you might even want to transfer too. The headmaster is so easygoing, he is basically a tree hugging hippie that loves everyone. There is no silence between people and everyone is friends with one another. Sure there are cliques, but it's a small old school so it is bound to happen."

He sold the idea well and it could not hurt just to go for the weekend and see a sister school of Glaston. "Okay, I'll go for a road trip with you."

"Good," he puffed his chest triumphantly, "you are going to love it."

Though my weak psychic barrier was up, the moment I walked into the gymnasium Vlaine knew that I would be at Valdor that weekend.

"When are you getting back?" he growled while pacing back and forth.

I felt tiny under his gaze of scrutiny. "We're leaving Wednesday night and returning early Sunday morning."

"You're going to be in a car with him for eight hours, sixteen hours altogether." He was still pacing. "What about seeing your family for Thanksgiving? What about the animals?"

"Why are you acting so paranoid? Erik is your friend. The animals are going to have to go on without me just like all other animals had to for the past however long."

Vlaine and I had been working on my psychic wall during the week and on weekends he would take me to animal hospitals as a "veterinary student" where I would work on healing the animals. Oftentimes he would alter the perceptions of the people there so it did not look like I was performing miracles. With each visit I would walk away with stronger healing abilities and the accomplishment of saving the lives of animals.

"It's not Erik," he stopped pacing and walked close to me, "it's Valdor. I just do not want you going to Valdor. I have been there many times and the looks are just as deceiving as a pheromone pumping emotion manipulator."

"Wow, no, it sounds like you and Erik are best friends. I heard no hints of repugnance there." I crossed my arms, "I appreciate that you are worried I will fall in love with Valdor and put in for a school transfer and Glaston could lose its healer and replicator, but if you are so goddamn worried why don't you ask Erik if you can go so you can make sure Valdor doesn't suck me in with its charms." I pursed my lips. "Actually, please don't ask Erik. I don't really want you to go."

He looked at me like I had slapped him. I was excited about getting away and seeing another school full of students with gifts and abilities like Glaston.

His face quickly turned to a stony expression. "Let us get to working on your replication."

I shrugged and sat down. It was the first time we were focusing on my replication skill, something I did not think I could actually do. It was going to be a long four or five hours. I lay back on the gym floor and folded my hands under my head.

"I want you to think for a moment before answering these questions." He pulled a gym mat over to us and sat on it. "What do you think of Liz's ability to turn invisible? What about Rayna's ability to adapt to extreme temperatures? What about my ability to create an energy wave?"

I smiled. I did not need to think about it, but I allowed the ideas of the student's abilities to swirl in my head. "They're beautiful, they are all beautiful. I think it is incredible and there are so many ways they can be used for making the world better."

"Which one do you find the most 'beautiful'?"

That was a difficult one to answer. I thought of how incredible it was that Liz could be invisible, the amazing places I would travel to if I had Rayna's tolerance to temperatures, and the possibilities of a powerful wave that could emanate from my very hands. I thought back to the remarkable way the child communicated through the guitar; how he turned foreign words into music notes he understood and then would answer back with more plucks of the strings.

"What was that?" Vlaine sat up excitedly. "I couldn't read you."

"I was thinking about that guitar boy again." I looked over at Vlaine and smiled.

"Keep thinking about him. Replay that night in your mind." He rested his hand on my shoulder and I allowed myself to reminisce. "Nothing! I could see and hear nothing." He paced and then excitedly took out his phone, "hold on a sec."

He rambled something into the phone and a few minutes later Draxe walked into the room holding a beautiful Martin acoustic guitar. I sat up and tried to figure out what was happening. Draxe handed me the instrument and sat down on the mat next to Vlaine.

"Hold the guitar, close your eyes, think about the boy, and listen to my words when I begin to talk."

I took the guitar hesitantly and arched my brow. I thought his idea was pointless, but he had gone from being angry to exuberant in a matter of minutes. The last thing I wanted to do was put him back in a foul mood.

I sat up, balanced the instrument on my lap, and closed my eyes. Sucking in a deep breath, I blanked my mind. Blowing the air out of my lungs, I thought about the young boy. I searched every detail of my memory and studied everything about him. I was deep in the memory when I heard Vlaine ask me once again what I thought about the boy's gift. I smiled and began to answer, "Incredible." Instead of hearing words leave my mouth I felt my fingers move and heard the guitar.

My eyes shot open and I looked at Vlaine. I put the guitar down and I asked Vlaine to repeat his questions. His words were German, I could not understand them. One more try. I picked up the guitar and closed my eyes, mind wandering to the boy. This time Vlaine asked what I thought about the fact that I could heal animals. I answered it was my favorite gift, once again I felt my fingers on the guitar.

"Yes!" Vlaine jumped up excitedly, "you did it!"

I looked up to see Draxe recording the entire event and Vlaine was doing a touchdown dance. I was confused. The only thing that seemed different to me was when I felt my fingers on the guitar when I tried to answer.

Draxe offered the recording to me and I watched. The first time Vlaine spoke clear German my fingers plucked away translating the words. My answer was silent, just notes played on the guitar. The second question was spoken in Russian. My fingers plucked when I heard the question and when I answered. I had truly replicated the gift of the boy I was thinking about. My jaw dropped in disbelief of the video I was watching. I had barely recognized what I had done, but seeing the video of it happening was breathtaking.

"I did that?" I gasped.

A look of pride was spread across Draxe's face and he nodded to my question.

I still had no idea how I managed to do that. "I want to try again, with something else this time."

Vlaine finally stopped jumping around and looked over at me thoughtfully. Draxe tucked his phone into his pocket, "Abrielle, you did that just by thinking about someone else's gift?"

"I was remembering how amazed I was by the boy's ability. I thought it was incredible and I focused mostly on that."

"You focus on your amazement of someone else's gift and you can emulate it?" Draxe was searching his mind for something.

"That must have been why I could not read you when you were thinking about the boy." Vlaine rubbed his knuckles against the small bit of stubble growing on his jaw.

Draxe leaned in, "what else do you think is amazing?" I could not tell if he was trying to assist or was genuinely curious.

"I have only seen a small handful of things. I have never seen Adele or Liz at work, but I bet their talents would be equally as beautiful as a translation through music."

Vlaine nodded at Draxe, "go pick up Liz and bring her here. She's with Professor Quail right now. Quail will understand."

I snorted. "Do you make it your business to keep track of Liz?"

He looked up at me and gave a lopsided grin. "I make it my business to know everything about the people you spend time with."

"Excuse me," my face contorted with both confusion and disgust. "You're keeping tabs on me?"

"Word got out that you are a replicator. I want to make sure no one kidnaps you."

My moment of feeling powerful and proud diminished in a mere moment. He had already told me the think tank wanted me because of my replication abilities, but his need to keep track of me made me feel like our entire friendship was a farce. "I don't think you will ever understand how demeaning that sounded, Vlaine. In fact, you made me sound like a pawn."

"You are valuable to anyone because of your intelligence; even more so because of your gifts, but add replication to the mix and you could be used to fight wars. The hope was to keep your replication gift a secret between Glaston and Valdor. It's a bit of a long story and Draxe will be back in a few minutes with Liz. I promise I will tell you in time, but sorry for sounding so obtuse."

I walked away and into the locker room to splash water onto my face and rid myself of the anger and hurt boiling inside of me.

Just as I turned the faucet on Vlaine turned me around gently. "If it pisses you off knowing that your whereabouts and friends are my top priority then be pissed." His hand reached out towards my face but he retracted it suddenly. "I just want to keep you safe, Abrielle." A look of determination appeared, "I'm going to keep you safe."

How could he make me mad one minute then make my insides feel like they were melting? I splashed water on my face and gave myself three seconds to be flustered and another three to calm down.

Draxe and Liz were standing in the gymnasium waiting for me. "Hi Abrielle," her lip twitched into a smile that vanished as quickly as it appeared. "They said you need to see me in action."

"Yes, please. That is if you do not mind, of course." I felt awkward asking her to show me her gift. It was so personal that I was not sure if she was going to comply.

"No problem at all." Her expression was gentle.

I watched her standing in front of me and suddenly she was gone. A moment later I felt a tap on my shoulder with a simultaneous giggle.

"Incredible!" my jaw dropped. "That is absolutely amazing Liz, spectacular."

I closed my eyes and thought of how incredible her gift was. When I opened them I saw no looks of astonishment. Liz was back to being visible. Instinctively I walked over to her, thinking of how incredible her gift was, and I lightly touched her hand.

"Oh my God!" she screamed. "What the heck! Did she just steal my skill?"

I jumped backwards in shock. Vlaine looked at me and back to Liz. "Liz," he began sternly, "she did not steal your ability. We need your utmost discretion because this can be very dangerous for Abrielle." He paused and looked at me, "I'm guessing that you needed to touch her because you were having difficulty emulating her invisibility. Sort of like how skin to skin contact creates an easier telepathy conduit, perhaps it is the same for particular gifts."

"Liz," Draxe's smooth voice began, "why don't you go ahead and do your thing so you can prove to all of us, yourself included, that you still have your invisibility."

She complied, and sure enough she was able to disappear. "So you are a replication," she walked around me in a circle as if I was some strange specimen. She looked at Vlaine and Draxe, "Jeremiah is going to want her." Pain was in her voice.

"Yeah," Vlaine nodded somberly, "he already knows about her."

"Who? What? Why don't I know anything that is ever going on?"

"Jeremiah recruits gifted individuals with rare talents," Liz spoke bitterly. "He wants them for nothing but financial reasons and does not care how he gets a hold of them. He is an awful person." Her voice was so solemn, I wanted to hug her and heal her emotions.

Thus began a discussion that led me to find out how Liz ended up at the school and some of the dangers of people knowing that I had the gift of replication. Jeremiah had scouts that came into a bit of luck when they saw Liz disappear one day. He went to her with an emotional manipulator, similar to Erik, and persuaded her to go to his company. It was a place where gifted people were tortured into doing Jeremiah's bidding. Headmaster Josnic had his own team in place to try and save as many people as he could from Jeremiah's lair.

"He's ruthless," Liz's eyes welled up, "you have no idea."

There were no words I could offer her to express my gratitude for sharing her dark past or for showing me her gift. "Thank you," was all I could whisper.

Both Vlaine and Draxe walked me back to my dormitory, which seemed more suspicious to me than if I had returned as I normally did.

Before leaving Vlaine squeezed my hand, "You were incredible today." He turned to Draxe, then back to me, "I am so proud of you, Abrielle."

"Yeah," Draxe added, "most replicators don't know they are one and even then it takes months to learn how to do it. Good job."

"Well, they obviously don't have an incredible teacher like I do," I winked playfully.

Vlaine's cheekbones rose in a smile he tried to hide, "Later, Abbs."

Draxe and Vlaine turned around at the same time and I watched the two walk away together, enthralled by the twins. They looked so similar in some ways but Vlaine's gait was fierce and confident while Draxe strolled through like a famous athlete. I was fascinated by Draxe's appearances in my subconscious throughout my life, but absolutely captivated by Vlaine's rough exterior. They were an intriguing mystery to me and I could not help the giddy feeling that arose from knowing the devastating loyalty they had for me.

18

I had a suitcase full of clothes and a gym bag full of drinks and snacks. The idea of a road trip was becoming more and more exciting by the moment. Like a gentleman, Erik picked up my belongings and brought them to his car.

"Are you ready?" he started the car engine excitedly and brushed strands of his male-model hair out of his eyes.

I nodded and began searching the radio stations for good road trip music. "Let's do this," I laughed with enthusiasm.

Eight and a half hours later we entered the gates of Valdor Academy. Erik pulled into a small parking lot on the side of a glorious white brick building. I stepped out and a cold gust of air saturated with the smell of the sea whipped my long hair into small tangles around my face. The school was breathtaking and the sound of waves lapping against rocks in the distance called for me to explore the shore.

"I called the headmaster ahead of time and he said we could stay in the barn. I know how that sounds," he held his hands up in a stopping motion, "but it is like a small inn. You will have to see it to understand."

I followed him to the barn that he was talking about. Sure enough the inside was made into a guest house. The bottom floor had a kitchen, living room, and dining room. A bay window hung along the back of the barn where the other doors once were. Ocean décor lined the loft along with a large bed that was located directly above the kitchen.

I looked around nervously not seeing another bed. On cue with my thought process Erik nudged my arm, "we've fallen asleep watching movies so many times I figured that sharing a bed was not such a big deal." The color drained from my face and then he laughed, "I am just kidding. The couch is a pullout and there is a fold up cot in the closet over there. You can have the actual bed."

I shook my head, "you can have the bed and I'll take the couch." I walked over to the kitchen to put the snacks away that I had brought for the car ride. As I looked out the bay window the sandwiches in my hand fell to the floor. At the end of a jetty by the shore was the lighthouse I had seen in my vision.

"What's wrong?" Erik was quickly by my side. I tried to form words but I could find nothing to explain my reaction. His thumb traced my cheekbone softly, "shhh," he soothed, "you're safe."

Tingles of his soothing manipulation tickled my cheek. Part of me knew that I should not trust him, that I should find a way to get back home but the larger part of me was content and yearned for him to keep touching me. I would be spending the next four days alone with him and in the first few minutes of being at Valdor Erik had already manipulated me into being calm.

"Let's go check out the school," Erik smiled, never breaking contact with me.

I said nothing, just followed him as he held my hand and led the way. It was beginning to get dark already as the winter ate the hours of sunlight. The lighthouse stood in the distance as a constant reminder of what my fate would be if I was to remain anywhere near Valdor Academy. What did Professor Horicon have to do with everything? Erik's thumb rubbed my palm gently, keeping any despondent feelings at bay.

The front doors of Valdor opened to a display of beautiful architectural works and modern art that rivaled museum exhibits. The entrance itself was not nearly as stuffy as Glaston Academy and had a much more welcoming vibe. Glaston had always seemed like a strange boarding school, but Valdor actually looked and felt like a real university.

He walked me through the halls and finally upstairs to the laboratories. Specimens, skeletons, and all sorts of scientific displays made my chest flutter with excitement. On the professors desk in the first lab was an exploded skull model. I wandered over to it, tempted to touch it.

"I wish Glaston had a Beauchene Skull, or proper labs for that matter." I pouted.

There were only two laboratories at Glaston and they were shared between all the science courses. It was bizarre that we had a schedule of when we were allowed to use the laboratory for a class or demonstration.

Erik nodded and led me outside to the beach. "Valdor does not waste much time on core classes like exercise or literature. We get to choose our major, just like a typical college."

"What happens when we graduate? The schools seem pretty tight-lipped. What does our diploma say?" It was something I had wondered but never got around to asking about.

"We have contacts at a handful of major universities. Depending upon your GPA when you graduate you can practically have your pick from a couple top schools. You show up on their records and everything so if you ever need to send transcripts they will have them at the school." He smiled, proud as if it was his idea.

"That is so illegal," I shook my head.

"What would you rather? Grow up where there is no institution that assists you with your gifts and just pretend like they do not exist forever?" He was defensive and for the first time since I had met him, he seemed angry.

His defensiveness made me flustered. "No," I shrugged, "I did not mean that I disagree with how they do it. I just hope that the schools never get into any sort of trouble for this stuff."

"They won't," he said gruffly and continued down the beach.

When we were done touring the entire campus of Valdor it was dark and the safety of the barn was enticing. Erik had kept contact with me at all times, but I would have still fallen in love with the school even without any manipulation.

"You were right," I smiled as he began preparing dinner, "I absolutely love this school."

Grinning, "I thought so Abrielle, now you know why I want to come back here." Stuffing some chicken into the oven he turned, "you should really think about putting in for a transfer. Glaston has nothing but snotty backstabbing people, terrible rules, and a complete lack of university necessities."

"I'll think about it," I smiled. "I'm going to get into pajamas," I walked off to the suitcases and rummaged through them.

While Erik was busy with getting dinner prepared I searched through the items for a phone. There was none in the barn and I could not find a cell phone in any of Erik's things. I still wasn't able to afford my own phone with no job, something I was regretting greatly at that moment. Finally I gave up and figured that it was probably beginning to look a bit too suspicious if it took me more than five minutes to find my pajamas.

I went into the bathroom to change and focused on getting any sort of thoughts to Vlaine.

Vlaine, I thought as loudly as I could imagining the words traveling across the distance and flowing into his head, *Vlaine I think I need you. Erik used his emotional manipulation on me today and I don't know why. I found the lighthouse from my vision, it is at Valdor. Please figure out some way to help me out.*

I listened but received nothing back. Later that night while I was falling asleep I tried calling out to Vlaine once more. Still, I received nothing in return.

The next morning I woke with a start when I heard someone banging on the door. I sat up nervously and stared at the door. Before I had the chance to get up from the couch Erik was already at the door.

Erik opened it and standing there was Vlaine and Steph. I jumped up and ran to the door and hugged Steph while tossing Vlaine a thankful glance.

"Happy Thanksgiving," I choked out while I squeezed her tightly.

Her body was rigid and she took my hands. "I… I need you to come with me."

"Of course," I searched her eyes for a clue as to what she was about to say.

"I went to the school last night to look for you," her eyes were welling up, "my dad had a heart attack." A sob erupted, "I just need you to be there when I go see him."

"Of course," I squeezed her again, "let me grab my stuff and I'll be right there." I looked at Vlaine, "Thank you so much for taking her to me. I'll be right there."

"You drove eight hours?" Erik asked accusingly as I was walking to the luggage.

"Dad's plane," Vlaine answered quickly.

I was dressed and ready to go in five minutes. I turned to Erik and hugged him. "Thank you so much for bringing me here. I absolutely love the school. I'm sorry for leaving so abruptly. I'll see you on Monday!"

He gave a curt nod and closed the door quickly. Vlaine, Steph, and I walked through the campus to where a small plane was landed in a clearing. Vlaine took my luggage and led me into the plane.

"Your dad has a plane?" I wanted to be surprised, but somehow I was not.

"Yeah, flying is a hobby of his."

I followed Steph to her seat and sat across the aisle from her. She was usually so poised, it was strange seeing her so upset. As soon as the plane took off she stood up, stretched out and in an instant

Steph was Draxe.

"Oh," I exhaled the realization, "I forgot you two both can do that appearance emulation thing." Shaking my head I ran over to Vlaine and hugged him tightly, "thank you so much for coming. I was not sure if you were going to hear me."

He looked over to Draxe nervously then back at me, "no problem at all, Abbs."

"What?" I looked at Draxe who was stifling a laugh.

"This was a kidnapping mission, not a rescue one." Draxe was full on belly laughing. "He thought you were going to be furious."

"No, as soon as we got here he did that hand on my face thing when I saw the lighthouse. I tried to communicate to you telepathically but I have no idea how close I have to be to someone to do that."

"What did he say exactly when he touched you?" Vlaine looked concerned.

"I don't remember his exact words but he told me I was safe then showed me the school which, by the way, is incredible." My gaze darted from one brother to another, "the lighthouse at Valdor is the lighthouse that was from my vision. I know for sure. I had the vision again last week." They looked at each other not knowing what to say to me. "How far can I communicate?"

"Telepathy isn't a distance thing," Vlaine

began, "it grows stronger the more you use it and the further away you are. I am not really sure why I couldn't hear you." He stood up and began walking to the cockpit. "We're going to make a pit stop on the way back if that is okay."

Halfway back to Glaston Academy we stopped at a farm that one of the headmaster's friends owned to pick up Thanksgiving provisions. Vlaine remained quiet for most of the flight home, but Draxe was surprisingly chatty. We talked about books, hobbies, gifts, and he even promised to teach me how to ride Cinnamon before dinner would be served. I was tempted to try and read Vlaine, but my gut told me to leave him to his silence.

19

"Why exactly is everyone afraid of your dad?" Cinnamon was trotting steadily beneath me and Draxe was beside me on Buttercup.

"His temper is notorious and he's a lot like my brother in the regard that he does nothing to control it. He really cares about helping people develop their gifts and making their lives easier than his was, but he also has a set of different laws in his mind than are for regular humans."

"What do you mean by that?"

"If he truly feels that someone is a threat to the integrity of Glaston then he will not hesitate to use whatever method he feels at the time is necessary. That can mean anything from taking points from your final grade away to execution." He stated everything matter-of-factly and without much emotion.

The sky was crisp, the trees were bare, but the ride was beautiful. It was a strange way to hear that my headmaster was not above killing students as a form of punishment. It seemed that Draxe giving me this information would be better suited for a scary basement with the sound of water dripping rather than horseback riding through the woods.

Draxe chuckled, "I heard the kids freaked out when you saved Tracy and my dad called you to his office."

I nodded and gave Cinnamon a quick pat, "yeah, they looked at me like I was off to the gallows. Now I know why."

He led us off that path and through thick grasses until we got to a hidden trail. He looked over at me and winked, "my secret path."

"Draxe," my voice cracked with nerves, "how did Tracy get hurt?"

He slowed Buttercup down nearly to a halt. "You realize you're like Vlaine's best friend. He gets along with you, me, and Aiden, and only us. He was friends with Erik when he was a kid, but now it's just us." I followed along losing track momentarily trying to figure out who Aiden was. "He knew how much effort you put into that project and when he found out Tracy took all the credit he got pretty pissed. She has telekinesis and he manipulated her gift so that the power that she could have directed elsewhere just made a sort of explosion in its source. Her arm got shredded as a result." Draxe sighed and shrugged, "He really doesn't like people screwing over his friends."

"She could have died," my voice was hoarse.

A devious smile formed, "wasn't it convenient that there happened to be a healer awake and nearby?"

I gave him a sour look and concentrated on Cinnamon and her dainty trot. I was livid at myself for feeling comforted by Vlaine protecting me, rather than angry at him for hurting her.

We got back to the stables just in time to see Vlaine walking over. He shouted to Draxe that dinner was ready and walked back towards the school.

"I'll take care of the horses," I grabbed for Buttercup's reigns.

"You're having Thanksgiving with us." Draxe got down from Buttercup and started walking her to her stable.

"I am? Like, with your family?"

"Yeah," He laughed and shook his head as if I had said something ridiculous, "why else would the kidnapping happen this morning and not tomorrow or late tonight?"

"Rescue mission," I winked, "but are you sure your dad is going to be okay with that?" The conversation we had just had regarding his father's reputation did not make me feel like enjoying an obscene amount of side dishes.

"Didn't you hear what I just said?" His voice was lighthearted and his smile was endearing, "our dad let us use his plane to go get you. That little ten person Cessna is my dad's baby. I mean, he loves that thing more than he loves me. He knew about the plan and was even the one who suggested you join us for Thanksgiving."

As I set Cinnamon up in her stable I felt fear creep over my body. I was actually afraid of seeing Headmaster Josnic. He was always so formal and reserved, but his actions thus far that day had been so personable. What would I wear at a holiday meal with someone that was always in three piece suit? Would I ignore the fact that his sons had taken his plane to get me from Valdor, or would it be open to discussion? Thanksgiving quickly became more complicated than I had expected.

Susan, the headmaster, Vlaine, and Draxe were discussing a football game when I walked into the kitchen. It was strange seeing the headmaster there conversing with his sons. I eyed Susan wondering why she was here on a holiday.

"Hello," I smiled politely to everyone, "happy Thanksgiving."

"Happy Thanksgiving Abrielle," the headmaster spoke eloquently, "I must excuse myself. I have an emergency meeting to attend in the city."

"What a terrible way to spend a holiday," I frowned, "I hope that your meeting goes well."

"Thank you Abrielle," he straightened his tie, "terrific work in your Individual Skill Enhancement Seminar." He turned to Vlaine and Draxe, "boys, I'll see you both later."

I was sure that was the most intimate moment I would ever witness between Headmaster Josnic and his sons. They said goodbye to him and continued to help Susan with setting up the table. The usual small tables were stashed away and replaced with a large dining table.

"Looks terrific, Aunt Sue," Draxe flashed a smile while taking the turkey from her.

"You're their aunt?" I gasped, intrigued.

Susan made an exaggerated nod. "Their mother Evelyn was my sister. Once their father became the headmaster he let me work here as the librarian. That only lasted until he tried my roast dinner. After that he switched me to the cook. I've been feeding the pupils of Glaston for the past fifteen years."

I helped them bring dishes to the table and hid my eyes from Susan out of embarrassment, "I'm sorry, but this is going to be forward. Do you also have a gift?"

"No," she shook her head, "I'm just a regular old woman with a talent for baking. Osiris knows I can keep a secret and after I first saw our Draxe here throw an impressive amount of force from his hands at the age of four he let me in on the little family secret."

"What about the rest of your family?" I was trying to get around from asking about Vlaine and Draxe's mother. I had never heard them mention her and I figured for that reason I was treading on touchy territory.

"My children are spending time with their families. Glaston Academy seems to give everyone the goose pimples and they shy away from visiting unless absolutely necessary." Susan's smile turned her ruddy cheeks to a soft red.

I watched the reaction from the twins hoping they would give more information than what their aunt had provided. Draxe seemed to catch on to what I was asking. "We have an older sister Bridget who is blissfully unaware about any of this stuff. She is the oldest and was born without gifts and wouldn't know if someone had one if they rolled a fireball in front of her face. Our older brother Jackson is at the Think Tank and doesn't seem to ever leave there. We might get a phone call from him once in a blue moon, but that's it."

"You have siblings?" I smiled in surprise. "So strange that your sister did not get anything but the three boys of the family got abilities."

"Our mother did not have any gifts and we are not quite sure if they are genetic, but if it is I'd say it's dominant." He paused for a moment and gave Vlaine a solicitous glance, "our mom passed away when we were only three. It was pancreatic cancer."

"I am so sorry to hear that," I hated not knowing the right thing to say in these situations.

"It was a long time ago," Draxe gave a half smile. "As a result, one of the initiatives at the Think Tank is using gifts to heal terminal illnesses." A hopeful grin took the place of the half smile.

"That is a wonderful endeavor," I added to suppress any silence.

"Speaking of which," Susan's bubbly demeanor was back, "when did you first find out that you were a healer?

"Just a few months ago, really. Whenever I saw animals that were hurt I knew I could calm them down and I figured I was just helping them to calm enough to limp away. I guess I was healing them all this time. I never tried it with a human before the accident here."

Susan was serving herself and passing around the bowls filled with vegetables. "Vlaine had told me about the kitten you found nearly froze to death by your old high school. I was so moved by how gentle you were."

My heart caught in my throat. I knew the kitten she was talking about, it was last February and the only person who was there was a random student that had been running track that day. The thought to ask Vlaine when he first began scouting me had never occurred. I had just assumed it was at the beginning of this school year.

I looked over at Vlaine who was staring at his plate. "When?" I cleared my throat, "when did you start watching me? How many people were you before you were Nicholas?"

"Oh I'm sorry to upset you dear," concern

splashed across Susan's face.

"No Susan, no worries, but I am curious now."

"I saw you just by chance last December when you went to the *Nutcracker*. I started scouting at your school a month later." He pushed his fork around his plate nervously. "At first I kept you at a distance until I knew who your best friends were and saw how you interacted with them. I didn't... I wasn't Nicholas until school started." He had dodged my question.

"That is unnerving," I smiled uncomfortably. "We are going to have to revisit this conversation some other time."

"It took him long enough to find you," Susan laughed awkwardly. Vlaine's face grew pale.

"Excuse me?" The fake smile was starting to hurt my face.

"Oh, sorry dear, I thought he would have told you by now. He saw you in a vision, that's how they found you." She gave me an endearing smile and stuffed a forkful of potato into her mouth.

So much for being able to keep secrets, it seemed that Susan had a knack for flapping her lips. Either she was terrible at being discrete or she was giving up this information for a reason.

"Well imagine how supportive such information would have been when I revealed my darkest secret to Vlaine." I glared at Vlaine who was avoiding eye contact with me. "Yet another thing we will have to revisit."

"Nope," Draxe dropped his fork and put his hands up in surrender, "I like food way too much to sit in an awkward silence. Vlaine just tell her so we can clear this up before auntie's pecan pie is ready."

Vlaine looked up at me finally and sighed, "a few years ago I saw a vision of you running from someone. Liz, who I did not know at the time, touched you and gave you her invisibility while you were running from the man. That is how I knew you had replication. None of us were actually able to sense it from you. Honestly, I recognized your face before I even picked up that you had any abilities."

"What did you feel when you saw the vision?" I thought of how strong my emotions were when I had the visions with Draxe in it. I was hoping that I was not crazy for feeling as strongly as I did whenever I woke up.

"I wanted to do everything in my power to protect you," he looked sincere and grave as if he was feeling it while he was looking at me. In a true Vlaine fashion, he changed the subject and his expression quickly before too many of his thoughts or feelings were revealed. "You were a pain in the ass to get a read on from far away. I could never tell what the relationship between you and Nicholas was."

"Oh please," I guffawed, "you should have known just by being in the same state that we were just friends, but best friends."

"I didn't think that was possible," he shrugged.

"Girls and guys can be just friends," I giggled and pointed my fork at him, "look at us, for instance."

"Thank goodness he found you," Susan lifted her glass of Chardonnay, "it is truly a miracle to have a healer at Glaston Academy."

"Thank you Susan." The sweet smile on her round face told me that she truly wanted me there. I felt more at home with that feeling than I ever had with my mother.

That is an excessively melancholy thought, Vlaine's voice sang in my head.

No, I winked at him, *it's hopeful.*

"Enough of that," Susan cleared her throat, "I may not have any special abilities like you children, but I know when a conversation is happening and I am left out of it. Audible voices will be used at this table."

"Sorry, Auntie Susan," Vlaine apologized in a sing-song manner.

Thanksgiving was comfortable like I had been accepted into the Josnic family. Before the sun had set Susan retired for the evening and the twins and I had our fill of delicious food. With the entire school to ourselves, Vlaine, Draxe, and I thought it would be amusing to use our freedom to stay up all night watching scary movies. Draxe was snoring just a few minutes shy of midnight.

"Those are my brother's hushed screams from the pure terror of this riveting film."

I snorted, "at least he can sleep. I am going to be forced to be awake all night for fear that there's a serial killer in my closet."

"There is," Vlaine whispered, "I can hear him."

"Stop!" I laughed and nudged his arm with my elbow.

He crouched down and lowered his voice. "You would be safer camping outside tonight. I can hear him thinking about how he's going to use his kit of torture devices on you."

My eyes glowed with an infantile idea, "let's camp in here tonight."

"In the common room of the dorm hall?" He laughed and shook his head.

"Yes," I wiggled excitedly, "go get a tent and we'll set up like we're really camping." It was the sort of ridiculous thing that Steph, Nicholas, and had done frequently.

"Okay," he caved in to my request, "we have one hidden somewhere. Go grab your pillows and blankets and I'll get the tent."

"Wait," my face flushed with embarrassment, "there's really no one in my room, right?"

He gave my shoulder a consoling rub, "Stay here and protect Draxe, I'll go get your stuff.

20

"You realize that camping works better when you're outside?" Draxe was poking his head inside the tent flap.

I sat up quickly but Vlaine remained asleep, curled on his side on the far side of the tent. We had stayed up until three in the morning telling fake ghost stories before switching to a game of truth or dare. The game lasted two questions until it turned into a deep discussion about how we came to find out about our gifts and how our families had dealt with it. I tried not to be envious that Vlaine had support, but I was unspeakably grateful that I was in a place full of people like me.

"We were make-believe camping," I laughed. "He gave in to my crazy side."

"Spontaneous," Vlaine corrected me with his eyes still closed.

I shrugged and giggled.

Draxe rubbed his eyes, "sorry I fell asleep so early."

"We didn't make it all night anyhow, but we can try again tonight if you want."

"If there is food in the mix, count me in. I'm going to take a shower. See you tonight," he zipped the tent flap.

"Thank you for giving into my spontaneity," I nudged Vlaine.

"Next time we're bringing a mattress. I may be stuck in this position." Vlaine groaned.

I put my hands on his arm gently and healed any aches he may have had. "You just have to ask if you're ever uncomfortable."

He stretched and sat up. His pride would never allow him to ask for assistance, nor would it let me know that I had actually helped him at all.

"Can you heal yourself?" his forehead scrunched with concern.

"I have never tried," I answered thoughtfully.

"I'm going to take a shower then a nap so we can try to pull this all-nighter thing again. See you tonight Abbs."

He stood up and my stomach did a flip when I noticed his disheveled hair. I let my eyes wander to the tattoo peeking out from underneath his shirt. Once he was far enough from the tent I mentally kicked myself. I had always thought Vlaine was attractive, but until that morning I kept him labeled strictly platonic in mind. I was notorious for blurring friendship lines and I was doing it again because Vlaine was the only guy friend I trusted. I shook my head at my own thoughts and stood up to go get breakfast.

After a shower I walked down to the kitchen. A few minutes after I began eating Vlaine walked in. I stopped chewing and ogled how perfectly his jeans and sweater fit him. *Oh no,* I thought to myself. If I stayed in the room Vlaine would know what I was thinking, he would know I was checking him out.

"Coffee?" he looked over at me and held up an extra cup.

"I'm good," I shook my head.

He shrugged, his lopsided grin turned into a full one. My eyes wandered from his smile to his arms; his sweater hugged them providing a satisfying outline to his muscles.

"See you tonight," I jumped up and rushed out of the kitchen before he caught any thoughts that I was having.

"What is wrong with you, Abrielle?" I muttered to myself once I was back in my room. I surrounded myself completely with study material. In an attempt to purge all thoughts of Vlaine from my brain I managed to finish all the papers due for the rest of the semester. All I had to worry about until winter break was studying.

In the middle of studying macroeconomics

my door opened suddenly. "I could have been naked," I arched a brow at Vlaine.

"I could hear macro crap and I figured there was a ninety percent chance you were naked." He shook his head disapprovingly, "I was wrong."

"Ew," I threw a pillow at him, "stop reading my thoughts."

"Stop thinking so loud," he tossed it back at me.

"Vlaine," I looked at him seriously, "please stop reading me."

"Abrielle," he mocked my seriousness, "learn to put up a wall." He beamed and folded his arms, "the campground is ready. Take a break from studying and let's try for an all-nighter again. Draxe brought the pecan pie and I brought chips."

"Be right there," I harrumphed.

I picked up a handful of note cards to pull out in case my mind started to drift to thoughts of Vlaine. Worst case scenario, I would just excuse myself to go study. For some ridiculously illogical reason, the idea of Vlaine finding out that I was developing a crush on him was far more mortifying than Draxe seeing my reoccurring vision of him. At least I had no control over my vision, but I needed to find a way to keep my emotions at bay.

Whenever I started to develop a crush on Nicholas I would push my feelings onto another target and quickly because I knew that if Nicholas was single it would not be for long. The only other person I could push my feelings onto was Draxe or Erik. I did not trust Erik and even though Draxe was exceptionally good looking, his personality was not as enticing as the moody, bad boy one that his twin had. Finding a celebrity crush was the next best thing. I crossed my fingers that the movie we would be watching had an attractive actor that I could toss my feelings at and hope they did not stray towards Vlaine.

I doubled over laughing when I walked down the stairs and saw a huge fort made out of couch cushions, chairs, blankets, and pillows in front of the television. There were three mattresses inside the makeshift fortress.

"Looks like we're roughing it tonight," I giggled as I sat down in front of the middle mattress.

That night and the following one we used the fort to watch movies and hang out. A strong friendship had cemented between Vlaine, Draxe, and me over those few nights and I was seeing them differently. They were closer than I realized and played off one another in such a way that hilarity constantly ensued. It was a harsh call back to reality when the students began to trickle back in throughout that Sunday. I did not want to deal with the stresses of Glaston; I wanted to stay hidden in our childish fortress.

Monday morning I awoke startled by my vision. I was always afraid to fall back asleep after them and I decided going for a walk would be a good way to clear my head. It was still dark out, but I wanted to go to the stables and check on Cinnamon.

When I returned to the dormitory I could feel the energy buzzing around the place and it was more chaotic than usual. "What is going on?" I asked a quiet girl that lived diagonally across the hall from me.

"You feel it too?" she pushed her glasses up on the brim of her nose.

I nodded, "it feels awful." I searched around for the source.

"I think it's outside now. Tennis courts?" she nodded her head in the direction of her best guess. We began walking towards the area.

The sun was just beginning to rise; red hues glowed above the frosted grass. Our footsteps crunched as we walked towards the tennis courts. I could see two figures in the distance and jogged closer to see what was happening. I was just a few yards away when I saw Vlaine lift his hands. A strange wavy air was in front of them, as if they were the pavement on a hot summer day.

Vlaine pushed his hands forward forcefully and a ball of the wavy air sped towards Erik and once it reached him he was thrown backwards. I could feel the reverberations from the blast and I was knocked onto my rear. A horrible scream erupted from my throat before I was able to process the event.

I ran to Erik's side. The side of his head was bleeding, his ears were bleeding, there was blood everywhere.

"I can heal you, I can heal you," I sobbed as I forced my shaking hands towards him.

"You need permission," the girl grabbed my arm. I looked up to see tears spill over. She was shaking just as badly as I was.

"Vlaine," my voice shook, "give me permission to heal him." I could not meet his gaze.

"Don't!" Vlaine growled through gritted teeth. "Do not touch him, Abrielle."

"He's going to die," I screamed, finally looking at him.

"Good," he spat.

"No. No. I'm going to save him," I stood up and began to run towards the school. Vlaine grabbed my arm to stop me. "Don't touch me," I pushed his hand away and continued running to the school. I felt so betrayed. I had trusted Vlaine completely but just witnessed him try to kill someone he once called a friend.

"Hello," I screamed into the hallways. "Hello, I need a professor." I was running as quickly as I could, trying to find anyone.

A hand grabbed my shoulder from behind me. I turned quickly to face Professor Horicon. "Professor, I need you to give me permission to heal someone." My words were barely audible from my sobbing.

Professor Horicon grabbed my arm tightly and we were suddenly in his office. I shook my head, *I'm in shock.* It was the only explanation for me not knowing how we got into his office. I begged him for permission once again to heal someone.

Professor Horicon was irate. "Your little stunt screwed up the plans."

He continued screaming at me, but I could hardly understand what he was saying. I had seen this before, I knew this situation. I had seen it in my dreams so many times and I was finally here. I backed up away from the venomous Professor Horicon and he closed the space and grabbed my arm. Suddenly we were in that room, inside the lighthouse at Valdor.

"Teleportation," I tripped backwards in shock. Professor Horicon's ability was teleportation and that was how I had gotten to the lighthouse.

He stopped yelling and was holding my arm steadily. "Calm down, he will be here soon." He glared at me with odium.

"Who?" My body was shaking so terribly that I didn't think I could run away without collapsing. "I need to heal Erik," I pleaded.

"Jeremiah, of course." His voice was slimy, if words could ever have a texture.

My stomach dropped. Liz was terrified of this man. If a girl with invisibility was terrified of someone then I certainly needed to find a way out of there. *Teleportation.* If I could calm myself enough to find the gift beautiful and extraordinary I could replicate it. That was why I needed to run up the stairs. To allow myself enough time to focus on the beauty of the gift.

Turning on my heel I broke from his grasp and ran up the stairs of the lighthouse. I thought of how incredible it would be to travel the world. The incredible ability to go anywhere in a single moment was certainly an incredible thought: Paris, the pyramids, pink sands. Why was I thinking in alliteration?

I burst through the door of the lighthouse and thought about the stables. A pile of hay sitting outside the stables seemed like a soft enough target for my first attempt at teleportation mimicking. I squeezed my eyes and imagined it. I closed my eyes and I was still on top of the lighthouse. Once more I clenched my fists and tried to teleport but it was too difficult. I would need to contact the source of my replication, just like how I needed to touch Liz to be invisible.

Professor Horicon came barreling through the door and towards me. In his frenzy he grabbed me but I stumbled backwards over the edge of the lighthouse where the railing was broken.

The moment of contact was precise. I felt my body fall through the air but it fell onto the hay. A guttural cry rang through my ears. I tried to look around but realized my mouth was the source of the sound. Pain was radiating from every point of my body. Footsteps ran towards my side and I saw Draxe look over me.

True concern was in his eyes. His hand went towards me but quickly retracted. "Are you okay?"

There it was. All these years of seeing him ask me that question and it finally happened. His appearance was as flawless as I had seen it so many times before and just as I felt in the dreams I wanted so badly to touch him. I wanted to hug him and share my excitement that the vision had finally happened. I tried to reach for him but I could not move my arm. Panic set in as my limbs failed to work. All I could do in that moment was blink and make horrifying noises.

"I'll be right back with help," Draxe's eyes were filled with fear. "Just hold on Abrielle, I'll be right back."

It felt like hours, though only seconds had gone by when I heard Draxe yelling, "Dad! Dad I need your help."

I tried to calm myself but the more I thought about what was happening the more panicked I became. I was paralyzed. The teleportation had saved me from getting killed upon impact, but I still fell far enough to get paralyzed from my fall onto the hay.

How is it fair that I cannot move my body, but I can feel the pain? I thought to myself while the tormented moans continued to escape my throat.

"Oh God, Abrielle," Vlaine's voice was close by.

I tried to move away from him as an image of him killing Erik came into my mind. I was assuming Erik was dead by now. There was no way he could have been alive after all that blood loss.

"Listen to me Abbs," Vlaine's voice was shaking, "you're going to be just fine. My dad can heal you and I can make you think that you're not feeling any pain. I am going to manipulate your mind so you don't feel anything, okay?" His voice smoothed into a calming one.

A few seconds later the pain lessened significantly. I could still feel it radiating from every part of my body but it had subsided enough for the horrible moans to cease.

Why? I thought to him because I could not speak. *Why would you do that to Erik?*

"He was spying for Jeremiah. I thought he was just a scout for Valdor, but he was one of Jeremiah's spies. He was going to kidnap you." His hand touched mine lightly.

Is he dead?

"No, not yet at least. He is in a coma for sure, but last I saw he was still breathing."

For some reason I felt at peace with that answer. I did not care what condition Erik was in at the moment as long as I knew he was alive.

My vision finally happened. Professor Horicon was working with Jeremiah too. Teleportation really is a beautiful thing.

"Abrielle," a smooth deep voice spoke by my side. "I am going to put my hand on yours. I can replicate just like you so I am going to use your healing gift on you."

Headmaster Josnic's hand was hot against my skin. I knew he was trying to heal me, but I could feel nothing being mended. A huff escaped his mouth after a few minutes of having no results.

I calm the animals first. Once I know they are calm I picture every cell in the body getting healed. It takes a lot of concentration, but it's effective. I thought out loud to anyone that would listen.

"Did you hear her, Dad?" Vlaine whispered harshly. "Calm her and yourself, then imagine the body being healed starting from cells and working your way up to the full tissue. Take your time, she sure has to. I saw her work for the better part of an hour on a dog that got hit by a car."

The headmaster grunted in response.

"You're going to be okay, Abrielle." Vlaine put his hand on mine gently, "I promise."

Those were the last words I heard before I passed out.

21

Consciousness crept slowly through turbid images. I could hear groans but my eyelids were too heavy to open. More moans echoed in my ears.

"Oh thank God," I could hear Liz's annoyed voice.

My eyelids fluttered in response. As the light from the room filtered into my vision I recognized the noises belonged to me. A breath caught in my throat as a whimper battled with words to find which one would slip through my lips first. A strangled bark resulted making me jump at the sound my own body had made.

A hand tightened around mine and pressure dissipated from my shoulder as a face came into my peripheral vision. My body ached and turning my head sent a deep burn into my throat. Fingers swept the side of my face and blurred features hovered above mine. I squeezed my eyes trying to clear what I was seeing. The fingers were caressing the top of my head. It was soothing and I had to fight the calmness not to fall asleep.

"Where am I?" I croaked after much effort.

"In your room," Liz grumbled irritated, "now that you're awake maybe your sentinel can finally leave." I could hear rustling, but my eyelids were too heavy to open. "I'm heading to class. Call me if you need anything." The corners of my lips tilted up at her hidden kindness.

"Stop," I coughed and fought for strength to speak, "stop the stroking, it is making me fall asleep."

The hand stopped in place allowing my alertness to grow. I fluttered my lids and my vision finally cleared. Vlaine was looking down at me.

"Are you okay?" he was leaning over me. Wisps of dark hair fell into concerned eyes.

I began to laugh at the complexity of the situation. The vision of Draxe leaning over me had come into fruition. Now the twin of the man I had seen in the vision was leaning over me completing the vision in the same manner.

The laughing turned into a sob. There were so many emotions just swirling with confusion. "How long… what day is it?"

"Tuesday," Vlaine seemed worried and began caressing my hair again.

"I was asleep for a day?" I wanted to sit up and see if the headmaster was able to heal me, but fear was winning over curiosity.

"You've been recovering for a week and a day." His touch was gentle and cautious as if I was a Fabergé egg.

"Wow" was all I could muster. I had never been asleep for more than twelve hours before then.

"You were thrashing a bit but I think that my dad was able to help you. Maybe not completely, but the sleeping probably helped with the remainder of the healing. Hopefully."

"I'm afraid to try and sit up," I whispered ashamed.

"I'll help you." He tucked a piece of hair behind my ear then grabbed a pillow from the floor and put it against the wall. Warm hands wrapped around my waist as he hoisted me up against the pillow.

"1…2…3…" I sucked in a sob. "3...2...1..."

"What was that?" His brows were furrowed trying to understand what I was doing.

"It's something I do when I don't like what I am feeling. If I am mad I let myself be mad for three seconds. Then I give myself another three to get over it. Same with any other negative emotion; be it anger, worry, jealousy, so on and so forth. Right then I was petrified, but it was not helping me figure out if I can move. Then I gave myself three more seconds to become strong no matter what happens."

"You're amazing," he breathed.

I blushed and tried to calm the butterflies swimming about my stomach. Vlaine's face was only a few inches from mine and the sheer proximity was causing electric pulses to flow through my body.

I decided I would try wiggling my toes first. They moved on command. Next I would try my entire leg. I shook my leg followed by the wriggling of my fingers and arms. Finally I pushed myself up higher on the bed with my fists.

"I can move," I laughed relieved. "He did it, he healed me."

"I'm going to go let him know." Vlaine's entire demeanor changed from a caring friend to that of an instructor.

"Vlaine, wait." I called out before he left the room. He stopped and turned to face me and I pushed myself up from the bed slowly then closed the space between us. I wrapped my arms around his neck and squeezed him tightly. "Thank you so much for staying with me and thank you for being there when I woke up."

His arms wrapped around my waist tightly in return. "Go ahead and jump in the shower and get ready if you can. We are going to have a meeting shortly and you'll need to be there."

I was actually being invited to a meeting that concerned me? Falling from a lighthouse and transporting to a pile of hay to become paralyzed and on the edge of death had done wonders for my own sovereignty.

"Considering how slow I am moving I will be ready in half an hour. Where will the meeting be?"

"Meet me outside the *Portrait of Dr. Gachet*, I know you know where that is." Vlaine flashed a devilish grin and sauntered off.

Every movement came with great effort and difficulty but I was ready within half an hour as promised. Students parted and moved out of my way as I made my way out of the building and to the school. *Just call me Moses*, I thought as every student parted like the Red Sea.

Vlaine and Draxe were huddled next to the painting, their dour expressions matching that of Dr. Gachet. Whatever they were discussing was so solemn and personal it felt insolent for me to intrude. Even the silence felt intrusive to the moment. In unison they looked up at me and motioned me to move closer. Cautiously I did as they gestured, still feeling as if I was intruding. They both gave a quick look around before opening the door to the secret room.

Before that day I had walked up the stairs as an eavesdropper but somehow being invited felt just as immorally inquisitive. Nevertheless I followed the two men into the secret room holding onto the hope that the fruition of the vision meant there would be no more brushes with death.

Sitting upright with hands folded properly on

one another was the headmaster. Vlaine and Draxe sat in the chairs on either side of their father. The Josnic family truly was beguilingly affable. I sat in the seat directly across the headmaster and the discomfort I felt when I first entered the classrooms came back with the possibility I was sitting in the wrong seat. What a silly thing to worry about.

"Good afternoon Miss Abbott." The headmaster's voice was smooth and had a hint of a foreign accent. "Egregious events have warranted my attention and immediate action. You seem to be at the center of these nefarious incidents." He paused for a moment, still as a monument then continued. "Your gifts have gained the attention of certain bellicose individuals." He stood up and walked towards a wall with a whiteboard then turned to me. "Far be it for me to be contumelious, if you wish to join their efforts I will grant you pardon just this once."

"No sir," I spoke clearly and without hesitation. "I don't know what these people want, but I know that I don't want to help them get it." I really had no idea what I would be used for and why. In fact, the entire situation was confusing.

"Very well," the headmaster cleared his throat. "A vile man that goes by the name Jeremiah has been known to infiltrate the sister schools of Glaston Academy. He had spies here, one of them being my trusted friend Leonard Horicon. I haven't the slightest idea how many other spies are here, but I will need assistance finding them and finding out what they plan to do with their accumulation of students."

"Recent events, sir?" There was clearly more to the story than Professor Horicon teleporting me to the lighthouse at Valdor Academy.

"A few other events have occurred while you were in your coma, none of which you should concern yourself with." Silence hung between us as I fought myself to be polite. I was about to protest for answers to what exactly he meant by a few events, but he halted my thoughts with a gentle question. "Do you wish to help me?"

I rubbed my hands together nervously. I did not want to enter into some reconnaissance without understanding the depth to which I would be used. "I would love to help, Headmaster Josnic. What can I do?"

In graceful yet rapid movements the headmaster wrote a list of names on the board. "The names of the individuals we feel suspicious of will be written on this wall. In the meantime I would like you to focus solely on strengthening your abilities. I will grant you absence from your classes but you will be expected to complete all assignments and examinations on time. Fortunately, we have winter break coming soon and hopefully you can resume classes normally once the next semester begins."

I sat in silence for a few moments as anger began to rise. "Headmaster Josnic," I began.

"Please, in this room we are partners. Call me Osiris."

Though he meant it to be respectful, it only angered me further. "Osiris, I feel that it is incredibly repugnant to ask for my assistance but not tell me what events have led to my assistance being necessary."

"Very well," Osiris opened a panel in the wall and removed a folder placed it in front of me. "In the past week thirteen of Glaston Academy's students have gone missing and two were killed in an altercation. Given the nature of the abilities these students had, trust me when I tell you it was no normal quarrel."

I opened the folder to view the files and pictures of the missing students. A paperclip held a small stack of photographs together. Mangled body parts were strewn about from an apparent explosion. Bile rose as I studied the repulsive images.

"How did the students go missing?"

"We were attacked," Vlaine spoke this time. "A group of men came onto the property at night and just went through the dorm rooms attacking people. Either the thirteen students they took were planned or they took them looking for you."

I could feel my face twisted in disgust. "Where was I when this happened?" Sleeping and useless was the answer.

"We had you underneath the school. There is a small infirmary under there and we kept you hidden until just a few days ago."

"Liz is still here." My four words held innumerable questions.

Osiris offered me the best answer to my question. "Yes, your room was one of the first ones they breached. She heard the commotion in time to become undetectable. It was particularly upsetting for her when she recognized some of the intruders."

"What does he want with these students?"

"Power, success, financial gain, unlimited resources, world domination, you name it." Draxe shrugged and looked at his father. "We've all thought about how much easier life would be if we could use our particular talents for financial gain. Imagine a team of us with different gifts put together."

"Then," Vlaine added remorsefully, "imagine a replicator on your team."

"So this Jeremiah character is looking to nab me as a special weapon? Why not you, Osiris? You have the same gift as me and I am sure yours is much more developed than mine."

"Jeremiah and I worked at the Hagan Think Tank together. I know his radical tactics and he is well aware of my position. Because my skills are more developed, he would not be able to sway me in such a way that I would side with him. You, on the other hand, are just a child; easily threatened and easily swayed."

I ignored his condescending statement regarding my age, though it was not easy. "Hagan

Think Tank?"

"A group of gifted individuals created our own little research base in Hagan, New Mexico about seventy years ago. My father was one of the men to create the organization. It exists solely to improve, study, and further understand our abilities. The Hagan Think Tank does this in a respectable manner and we set down strict moral principles. It has its very own governing system, as do most businesses."

"The academies were created as a stepping stone for the think tank." Draxe stood up and went over to the white board and added Liz to the list of individuals. "Students work at one of the schools afterwards, others move on and get normal jobs, but the best and most trusted ones are offered a position at the tank."

"Why is Liz on the list?" She may have been a particularly moody individual, but I hardly thought she was capable of anything nefarious.

"She was captured by Jeremiah before. Just because she acted scared does not necessarily mean she is. She could be as deep as Horicon for all we know."

Draxe had a point. There was no telling what actually happened when Liz was held captive by Jeremiah.

"Okay," I pushed the folder of missing students towards Osiris, "is there anything else we need to cover in this meeting or shall I go on looking out for suspicious activity, working on my gifts, and trying to not get captured by unknown assailants that could be any particular individual at this school or otherwise?"

"I know it's not a lot to go on," Vlaine's voice was kind and calming, "but it is really important that we keep you safe. We are not completely sure what Jeremiah intends to do with you or any other students but we do know that he's a contemptible man that enjoys seeing people suffer."

Osiris shot a dubious glance at Vlaine. The brief moment when the expression replaced his typical placated was unsettling. "Abrielle, please allow me some time to speak with my sons. Go ahead and begin working on your assignments, one of them will be with you shortly."

I fell onto my bed in an exaggerated manner and something hard jutted into my rib. "Ow," I grunted rolling to the side to see what I had landed on. Lying there on my bed was a box wrapped in blue paper. Though my fall hadn't dented the box, a corner of the wrapping had been torn. My name was written in cursive on the box, but there was no indication of who had left it there. It was certainly out of the ordinary. Should I open it or ask one of the Josnic men before doing so?

Liz walked into my room in the middle of my contemplation. I asked her if she knew where the box came from and she shrugged in response and plopped onto her bed, not giving me a second glance. Her exterior was solid, but she was still just a girl beneath that tough shell.

"I'm so sorry Liz, I heard what happened. I cannot imagine how awful reliving those terrible experiences must have been." I truly felt horrible that anything could have happened to anyone at the school because someone was trying to get to me. I tucked my legs underneath my body and softened my voice, "I don't know what I can do to help, but if there is anything I can do please let me know."

She dropped her books on the floor and turned towards me. "What would you have done to help if you were lying in that bed, even if you were all healed? There was nothing you could have done because you wouldn't have known what was happening. You being away saved my life."

Her words stung, but they were true. I would have most likely froze and been in a confused panic. "You're right," I shrugged, "but tell me what to do if it happens again so I know you'll be safe."

Her eyes became glossy as they began their thousand yard stare. "I heard his voice," she finally whispered, "I thought it was a nightmare but I heard his voice and I turned invisible right away."

"Jeremiah?" I clarified.

"No," she shook her head, "Slade, his right hand man." Her eyes met mine and fear had taken them over. "Once you hear his voice you never forget it. Under the bed, in the closet, any of those hiding places are suicide positions. They turned over the beds, tables, everything. I heard them in time to run into the hallway. I crouched invisible in the corner by the stairs and hoped they wouldn't get close enough to hear me breathing. Hiding in plain sight is the best way sometimes."

I stood up and sat next to her on the bed. Liz was never personal, but my empathetic side yearned to comfort her. She did nothing to push me away so I remained sitting by her side as she continued.

We sat facing each other cross-legged on her bed. "Slade and four of his friends just started barging in the rooms whipping things around. That was when I saw Professor Horicon and three other professors run up the stairs." She began to rub her hands together nervously, "I thought they were there to help, but they weren't. Other people must have thought the same thing at first because six people were snatched by Professor Horicon. Poof," she snapped her fingers, "he would disappear then reappear moments later." She slid off her bed and started pacing, "and I just stood there in the corner invisible and doing nothing."

"Liz," I stood and shook my head, "there was nothing you could have done. They would have captured you or worse."

She straightened her back and composed herself. "Anyway, the entire thing was over in a matter of minutes. A few days ago you were placed in our dorm room and Vlaine stayed by your side for the entirety. He slept on the floor and even used our shower."

She had changed the subject to sway my

attention to Vlaine and it had worked. I wanted to know every detail of what happened while I was healing. A fluttery and giddy feeling swirled throughout my chest thinking about how he had remained by my side for days.

Dwelling on my feelings for Vlaine and trying to find hope that he felt the same way in a memory that caused Liz pain was selfish. "I am amazed by your strength, Liz, I would have been frozen in a moment like that for sure. I hope you realize how strong you are." She said nothing, just moved away from me and back to the comfort of her bed. "I'm not sure how well I could protect anyone right now, but maybe I could see if I can learn to replicate that energy wave thing that Vlaine can do." I gasped, "Erik!" I had been so distracted with everything else going on that I had completely forgotten about him. "Is he okay? What happened to him?"

"He was a spy, Abrielle. Don't get so attached to bad people just because you want to save the world." She flipped her short blonde hair in a haughty manner then began painting her nails. "He was recovering slowly whilst under the supervision of Susan and a nurse that she happens to be friends with. Naïve little thing, she was. Anyway, after you fell from the sky like the little angel you are and your pack of sentries realized you were going to live they gave him one heck of an interrogation and he admitted to transferring just to send back information."

It felt like she had pressed me with a branding rod. "You know Liz, I'm sorry for whatever has made you so incredibly and practically insufferably astringent. I have been nothing but kind to you and in return you have this way of offering me a microgram of kindness and then burying it with thirteen ounces of bitch." I leaned against the wall and slid along it slowly onto the floor. "Whatever is going on is bigger than Glaston's infamous backstabbing routine and you know by now I don't take the bait for that. I have been polite to you so please cut the sardonic shtick and just try being a little nicer. If it is absolutely impossible then I'll get transferred to another dorm posthaste."

She continued painting her nails, her shoulders were tucked underneath her ears as if she were crouched. I stared at her quietly waiting for her to tell me to switch dorm rooms. She finished her nails and by then her shoulders had slouched back into their normal position.

"You know, Draxe was my first crush here at Glaston." Her cheeks turned bright red and I thought for sure she was going to break eye contact. "I still have a little thing for him. It kind of sucks watching him pine over you."

The hard-as-stone Liz was jealous and had a crush on someone? "He is incredibly gorgeous," I giggled.

"Model gorgeous," she fanned herself with her hand.

"He is so handsome and is just as kind as he is attractive." I rested my jaw on my hands, "but I really only have eyes for his brother."

She gasped and sat on the floor in front of me. "You have a crush on Vlaine?"

"Yup," I blushed, "and if it puts you at ease at all I am positive that Draxe does not have any feelings for me. If he's in a close proximity for an extended amount of time it's because I am just an assignment for the Josnic boys. They are supposed to watch me or whatever."

"You talk in your sleep sometimes." Liz rested her hands on her knees and her mouth twitched as if she was about to say something else.

"I had no idea, sorry about that." If anyone would know that I spoke in my sleep it would have been Steph, but she had never said anything about it. I knew that sometimes I would yell or groan when I was having a nightmare, but that was all. Was it a new thing?

"Yeah, sometimes you say Draxe's name in your sleep."

I understood why she was jealous, why she thought I had stolen her crush. "Oh my goodness, you were hearing my vision. Give me your hand, I'll show you." To my surprise she extended her arm towards me. I held it and envisioned what I had seen thousands of times and then the newer one that had ultimately led to my short lived paralysis.

Her eyes grew wide. "You've been seeing his face since you were little?"

"Yes, and to be honest I think I fell in love with

him for most of my childhood because it always felt like he was rescuing me from whatever had scared me so much. When I saw him for the first time here I practically swooned. Draxe is incredibly handsome and very kind, but Vlaine is the one that gives me that heart-beating-in-my-throat and stomach butterfly feelings."

She glanced up at me from underneath her lashes, "Vlaine is super hot in that tortured and rugged bad-boy type of way."

I tucked my face in my hands in embarrassment over my first vocal acknowledgement of my crush on Vlaine. She started giggling and bumped my shoulder, "I cannot believe we are both head over heels for the Josnic twins."

I had finally broken the shell of Liz and I had made a friend. It felt incredible.

A knock at the door halted our giggling. "It's me," Vlaine called from the other side of the door before opening it. Liz gave me a sultry grin and a quick wink before going back to her bed to continue studying.

"Good," I stood up and grabbed the wrapped box from the bed, "do you know what this is?"

"Looks like a gift, Abbs," he smirked.

"Vlaine," I arched my brow feigning annoyance, "do you know where it came from? If I open it am I going to blow up?"

"There is only one way to find out. I'm just going to step out in the corridor here while you give it a try."

"Okay, so obviously you know where it came from because you're being a pain in the butt." Delicately I removed the paper. Inside the box was the newest model cellular telephone. "A phone?" I looked up at Vlaine confused.

"With everything going on I wanted to make sure you had a way to get in touch with someone at all times."

It was incredibly sweet but I had no way to pay the bills for the phone. I searched for words of gratitude but he was already reading me.

"Don't worry, your full boat here at Glaston Academy will pay the bills. It's your phone."

"Thank you so much." I had gotten accustomed to being without any ties to the outside world but the new phone was a sense of freedom and responsibility that I had been missing. I could not wait to call Steph, Nicholas, and my mother. The numbers for Vlaine, Draxe, Osiris, Susan, and the school were already programmed in the phone.

"You're going to hate this," Vlaine sat next to me on my bed and sucked in his cheeks, "my dad wants me or Draxe to keep an eye on you twenty-four by seven."

"Don't you guys already do that?"

He chuckled and leaned against the wall, "I guess we do, but he wants us glued to your side in the event that there is another intrusion."

My face was flushed and I glanced towards Liz who was holding back a grin. It sounded like mine and Liz's dreams were coming into fruition.

"I understand," I nodded, trying to hide my smile.

"Thanks for being so accepting," he brushed his thumb against his bottom lip and my eyes lingered there before he began speaking again. "Draxe is going to take the first shift. I'll see you tomorrow about mid-morning."

Liz was smirking now and I was trying not to laugh. "Thank you again for the phone," I held it up and grinned approvingly. "I will see you tomorrow." He nodded and was nearly out the door before I called to him, "wait!" I walked to him and hugged him quickly, "it means a lot that you stayed with me the entire time I was healing. Thank you for taking care of me."

He looked over to Liz who just shrugged as if she was apathetic about breaking some unspoken vow. He did not respond, just simply closed the door lightly behind him as he left. The moment that he closed the door Liz burst out laughing.

"Oh my God, this is going to be priceless." She cleared her throat and put her shell back in place. "Those boys had better respect the sanctity of my study time because if there is so much as a sneeze when I am studying for finals there will be hell to pay."

I shook my head and laughed. Was this what a friendship with Liz was going to be like? She was like a cat, poised and distant until she was ready then for a few brief moments she was warm and affectionate only to be replaced with the hard exterior once again.

I tried to separate myself from Draxe and Liz as much as I could by tweaking and perfecting the work I had already finished for the semester. It was in vain, they hardly spoke anyhow. Draxe seemed enthralled in whatever he was reading and taking notes on and Liz was studying. I knew that Draxe was no longer a student so I asked what he was doing to which he flashed a charming smile and explained he was trying to become a professor at one of the schools. It made sense that being the son of a headmaster would gain him favoritism but it was also comforting to know that the warnings that students gave one another were closer to a freshman tale than the truth.

Draxe fell asleep on a cot at the other end of the room and I turned my light off shortly after. Half an hour passed and Liz followed suit. I turned to her and smiled, "thank you for being nice."

Rolling on her side to face me she whispered, "If it is any consolation I was happy when you woke up." In a peculiar way it was Liz admitting that she liked me before I explained that I had no romantic feelings for Draxe and before I complained about her bitchy tendencies. "Goodnight, Abrielle."

22

"Grab my hand," Liz shouted spreading her fingers out reaching for mine. We were running through the residence hall trying to get to the fire escape door out back. I grabbed her hand as she said then she turned invisible. I concentrated on doing the same and seconds later I replicated her gift. Explosions were rattling the floor beneath us and chaos enveloped me in fear. My knees gave out on one of the explosions but Liz's strong grasp kept me from falling to the floor.

"Almost there," she tugged my arm.

Just as we were about to open the door it flung open from the other side. I froze in panic staring at the man who could not see me. Liz pulled me quickly against the wall and I tried to calm my breathing. I couldn't hear Liz, I couldn't smell her, but I could feel her hand tightly grasping mine.

The man walked slowly into the building, assessing the chaos that had ensued from the explosions. A gentle tug on my hand told me to side step slightly and I did as Liz guided. I watched the man walk in a slow circle around the room and I played back the moments in my head. When he opened the door I knew I had exhaled sharply and I was out of breath. I smelled like mint and tea tree oil, Liz used only unscented *products. Why hadn't I thought of this before? I could be invisible, but not undetectable.*

Another man came to the side of the stranger and they both turned and walked straight towards me. Liz's hand was shaking and I held my breath. Was I still invisible? I was too frightened to move. The man reached his hand out and touched my face gently.

"There you are," he grinned.

I let go of Liz's hand so she would not be discovered as well. His expression never faltered as I became visible once again.

"Liz, Liz run," I screamed sitting up in my bed. Scurrying and a shattering sound preceded the room filling with light. Moments later Liz and Draxe were standing over me. I was still panting and shaking.

"What did you see, Abrielle?" Liz sat by my side and took my hand in hers comfortingly. I took Draxe's hand in my other and played the vision back. I expected her to be scared or angry but she looked rather determined instead. Draxe stood up and began pacing.

"Visions that have not happened yet can be changed, right Draxe?" Her hand was still in mine.

He shrugged looking defeated, "I can't see why not." Just then I realized that he had slept in his jeans and sweatshirt. Draxe's lack of comfortable clothing told me that either he was trying very hard to be proper or they were expecting something like my vision to happen. "Go ahead and give Vlaine a call, he should know about this right away."

I nodded and pulled my phone out from beneath my pillow. I had fallen asleep text messaging Steph and Nicholas all night. There were a few messages from both of them I texted them responses quickly before calling Vlaine.

"Morning Abbs," he answered sounding groggy. "What's up?"

A tingling feeling extravasated throughout my entire body when I heard his voice. The shock of the vision dissipated and I was able to calm my voice enough to not sound alarmed. "Is there any way you could bring over some coffee? I've got something I want to show you."

"I guess it is close enough to five to obtain some breakfast. I'll be there in a few." He answered with a sexy and raspy just-woke-up voice.

I asked Liz who the men were in the dream. The man that had touched me was Jeremiah and the man next to him was Luther. Luther was another person who could teleport and according to Liz was just as despicable as Slade. They followed orders without question and seemed to enjoy seeing people suffer just as much as Jeremiah. I felt intrusive asking what Jeremiah's ability was and Liz told me that he could influence electricity. A doubtful look must have been on my face as I wondered what he could do that was so terrible with electricity.

"Think about it Abrielle," her voice was mournful, "your heart works on its very own electrical system. The least of your problems is him stopping your heart or starting it again. He has his very own torture room designed to use his gift on people."

Draxe was still pacing when Vlaine came into the room. One glance at Draxe's demeanor and Vlaine was by my side waiting for an explanation. I took his hand and showed him the vision. He stood up and began nervous strides just as his brother had. His hands were folded on top of his head lifting his shirt enough to reveal sculpted lower abs. I shook my head from the thought and tried to focus on the situation.

Draxe asked his brother the same question Liz posed to him earlier.

Vlaine sighed then sat beside me. "We're going to have to work really hard on your replication. I haven't heard of someone changing their vision but that doesn't mean that you can't. Go ahead and get dressed. I'm going to let my dad know then I will meet you at the gym."

I took my time getting ready to meet Vlaine. The morning sun would not peak across the horizon for another hour and walking in the cold darkness was not at all appealing. I felt comfortable taking my time since the vision I had before occurred for over a decade before it happened and there was no telling how long it would be before this one came into fruition.

I gathered my assignments and dropped them off in the professor mailboxes before I left for the gym. The building was filled with an eerie silence when usually Susan would have been up and getting breakfast prepared at that time. Curiosity brought me into the kitchen where I could hear the soft clanging of pans in the back of the room.

"Susan?" I called out softly.

"Oh, good morning dear," she was wiping her hands on her daisy speckled apron. "It's bitter cold out there this morning, my car would not even start!" Her nose was still red from the wintry outdoors.

"Where do you live?" To anyone aside from Susan it would have been a rude question, but I knew that she enjoyed having someone to talk to.

"Oh just up the ways a bit. If you remember taking that turn off of the highway to get on this road there's a sharp left turn that you'll miss if you don't know it's there. My little cottage is just up that way." She tilted her head and pursed her lips in a disapproving manner. "You hold on just a minute Abrielle," she disappeared into the pantry and came back out holding a pair of thick gloves. "I know where you're heading and you'll get frostbite by the time you get there. Go ahead and return them to me once you get back."

"Thank you Susan," I took the gloves reluctantly. "I'll return them to you as soon as possible."

I jogged my way to the gymnasium and a terrible burning in my throat made it hard to breathe. My new cell phone was in my hands and I looked at it quickly to see it was only six degrees outside. I was hoping for a burst of warm air once I got inside the gym, but it felt just as cold in there.

Vlaine was walking towards me, his eyes aglow with excitement. "I have the coolest idea!" He held up a bow in one hand and a quiver filled with arrows in the other.

I had no idea where he was going with his idea. My archery class was only half of a semester and most of the time we neglected to practice because I was more than proficient and working on my skill class seemed more important most days.

"You figured that I was so impressive with a bow that you're just going to send me into Jeremiah's lair to take all the bad guys out *and* give me an A for the course."

"No, you're getting a B- in archery," he shook his head seriously before getting excited once more.

"Wait, a B-?" I crossed my arms across my chest and pursed my lips. "I was an ace and hit the target every single time. Maybe it was not a bull's-eye, but my grouping was exceptional."

"It will look like favoritism if I give you a better grade. Also, it gets weighted differently since it was a half-semester activity." Once again his face changed from serious to enthusiastic. "I was thinking, what if you could project your replication onto objects! I want to practice you using my concussive power and then once you have it down try projecting it onto the arrow so when the arrow is midflight it will send out the blast instead of your hands."

"Wow, Vlaine that would be pretty incredible. Do you think it's even feasible?"

"That's what I am hoping to find out before the end of this week."

"We are going to get me to master manipulation then," I waved my hands around like I was casting a spell as I searched for a proper word, "superimpose, for lack of a better word, it onto an inanimate object by the end of the week? Mighty presumptuous, aren't we?"

"I have faith in you Abrielle," he squeezed my arm reassuringly.

The first time I tried to emulate his gift I failed miserably. I was able to create a wave that left my hands, but it threw my body backwards instead of going forwards. He tried to stroke my ego by telling me that it would take a while to get it since my nature was more restorative than destructive. Three hours and a broken coccyx later I could push the force forward.

Susan brought us lunch and retrieved her gloves so she could go home for the day. After eating we worked on aiming the calamitous force. It was dark by the time we had returned to the residence hall. Draxe was waiting in the room and Liz was lying on her bed studying. Final exams would begin next week and I was sure that aside from literature, which was a take-home exam, I would fail them purely from being distracted.

Instead of studying for my finals, like I should

have, I practiced pulling a psychic barrier up against anyone who would try to read my mind. It was just another way a telepath could find me if I was invisible or use information against me. Draxe was on watch once again that night but he was not planning on falling asleep. I employed him to assist me with my psychic wall. Though I could just simulate the music gift if it was a dire situation, putting up a psychic blockade was an extremely difficult task.

Liz hypothesized that because of my empathic abilities I wore my feelings, and essentially my thoughts, on my sleeve. Her theory was a nice idea, but mine was that I could not be good at everything. Psychic barriers were my weakness and it seemed that it was something I would always struggle with.

The next morning I woke up frightened and yelling like I had the day before. Liz was by my side before I woke up trying to calm me down. Draxe sat across the room looking at me powerlessly, as helpless as I felt in the midst of Jeremiah and his men.

If the vision was going to be a reoccurring thing it was not fair for Liz to lose sleep when final examinations were just around the corner. I asked if there was any way I could sleep downstairs on one of the couches in the common area, but Draxe made it clear that everything had to be run by his father. Liz said that being woken up would give her more time to study but I could not tell if it was because she enjoyed having Draxe around or if she was being kind. Most likely, her statement was the product of both speculations.

Eight hours of working on replication in the gym with Vlaine allowed me the time to grasp the power to successfully aim an explosion towards a particular target as well as the ability to mimic the appearance of either Steph or Vlaine simultaneously.

I thought being able to master the reproduction to two different abilities would make me feel strong, but I only felt vulnerable. I could not understand why of all the people in the world I was the one to get this particular gift. It should have made me indestructible and powerful to be able to imitate the gifts of others; the ways I could help the planet were endless. Instead of learning to help the world I was learning to utilize the gift to save myself from some lunatic. In my eyes, that was raw weakness.

Draxe was in my room by the time I returned from practicing with Vlaine. He was quizzing Liz for finals and they were in the middle of flipping through ecology note cards. I lay on my bed and listened as they went through the cards; it was the perfect opportunity to rest and study at the same time. I folded my hands on my stomach listening to them and thought of how brilliant it would be to be invisible and hide from the worries of the world.

23

I had fallen asleep while listening to them and woke from the vision again. Draxe was by my side this time and a consoling hand was wrapped around mine. I looked to Liz's empty bed just before I heard the shower running.

"We can tell when you are about to have your vision now," Draxe's expression was more pity than sympathy.

"I wish I could control it somehow," I whined.

He patted my shoulder quickly, "the more you practice, the more confident you will feel. It's your brain that keeps playing this vision to you so maybe once you believe you can overcome your impending fate it will stop reminding you that it's coming."

Draxe had meant for it to be helpful, but it made me feel worse. I did not want to be tormented by the same vision every single morning and most of all I did not want the lives of others to be endangered because of some bizarre innate talent I was born with.

I rolled my head into my hands and tried to rub away the stress. "I just don't understand how people could have been working on the inside for Jeremiah and there was no knowledge of it or who they were. How did Osiris not know that Professor Horicon was a bad guy?"

"Abrielle," Draxe exhaled, "the abilities that these people have as a team is something you cannot wrap your head around yet. You think just because you understand how to pretend to be Vlaine for a few minutes and throw a ball of energy you can understand what a group of people who have worked in a place that have spent over seventy years dedicated to learning about these gifts can?" He stood up and straightened his clothes then looked me in the eyes. "You haven't even scratched the surface yet."

I felt like I had just been slapped. What he said may have been the truth but it stung and it made me defensive. "And the Josnic men feel that I'll be able to penetrate this surface by keeping things from me?"

Draxe raised his brow at my outburst. "Knowing everything wouldn't help you. You're already getting round-the-clock body guards and five people monitoring the thoughts of suspected infiltrators." His voice had been soft and compassionate, but the words were harsh.

"You two really are brothers, aren't you?" I gritted, annoyed by his bluntness.

I did not wait for him to respond; I just

grabbed a change of clothes and went straight to the barn. Cinnamon was sleeping, dressed in her turnout sheet. She stirred slightly when I went into her stable and exhaled loudly but remained lying down. I stacked more hay into the stable, gave her a quick pat, and then continued to the gym.

I had gotten ready in the locker-room and had time to practice before Vlaine arrived. I needed to practice appearing like him without having to touch him. I imagined all of Vlaine's features; his typical black boots, stonewashed jeans, tight fitting thermal sweatshirt, his wide strong jaw that curved softly underneath thin bowed lips, straight brooding brows, perfectly proportionate nose, and a simple short hair that always seemed to be flawlessly muddled.

"That is terrifying," Vlaine was staring at me. "Damn outré is what that is," he shook his head and walked towards me. "Walking into a room and seeing me was one of the last things I expected this morning. But, hey, you got to look like someone besides Steph."

"How did you know it was me?" I let go of my concentration and allowed my natural appearance to come back. "I could have been Draxe or one of Jeremiah's men."

"You're thoughts are too loud," he winked and handed me coffee.

Heat rose to my face as embarrassment clutched my entire torso. If he could hear me concentrating he knew what I thought of him, how I thought of him. I wanted to get out of the room and away before he read anything else. Just as I tried to think of excuses to leave he started picking up the archery equipment to bring it outside.

"You don't happen to be hiding any telekinesis in there to make this a little easier, do you?" The targets were not heavy, but they were large and awkward to carry.

"I wish," I giggled slinging a quiver full of arrows on my back, "telekinesis would be amazing." I picked up a target and began to follow him outside. "Are we trying for the arrow blasts today?"

He nodded and finished setting everything up. Once the targets were in place I picked up the bow and began concentrating.

"Wait," he walked closer to me, "start off slow. I don't want you attempting to blast a deadly weapon right away while trying to concentrate on a dozen different things."

Vlaine pressed his chest into my back and his hands slid down my arms onto my hands. His face was so close to mine the warmth tickled my cheek. Softly he spoke, "I'll do the shooting for now until you can get a feel of how this is going to work." My body was frozen into place and my breath caught in my throat. All I could concentrate on was Vlaine's body pressed into mine.

White clouds of breath left my mouth but all I could feel was the heat of his proximity. It was not fair; he had to know what he was doing to me.

"Vlaine," I breathed keeping myself still, "let me shoot a practice arrow before we work on any abilities."

"Sure," he pulled away slowly. Cold air hit my back where his body had just been. It was a necessary system shock that allowed my mind to clear enough to be able to hold the bow on my own. My body still felt tingly and I was acutely aware of his distance from me.

It was taking me too long to gather my wits so I shot off an arrow to get the feeling of the projection. I hit the top right corner of the target then shot another one just outside of the bull's-eye.

"Are you ready now?" I could hear him stepping closer.

I squeezed my eyes shut and tried to imagine something else. My mind went blank trying to think of things to focus on. Just as my mind went into a panic trying to take my mind off of Vlaine my pocket began to vibrate. *Just in the nick of time,* I thought to myself. I pulled my phone out to see that Nicholas was calling me.

"How peculiarly fortunate and slightly freaky," I laughed to myself. I held the phone up so Vlaine could see that I was getting a call.

"Making good use of the phone, I see." I was about to answer it but then he pushed my hand down gently, "you've got a psychopath heading for the school to try and abduct you. Do you think Nicholas can wait until tonight to talk to you?"

I shrugged and declined the call. "I suppose, it was probably a pocket dial anyway."

I tucked it back into my jeans. If it was important he would call again or send a text message. A moment later it buzzed and I picked it up to see I had a voicemail. A bunch of jumbled noises and static was recorded.

"Yeah," I nodded to Vlaine, "it was just a pocket dial."

I straightened my back and focused on the target. Vlaine moved closer and positioned himself as he had before.

"Ready?" he let go of my right hand so I could put it on top of his instead.

No, I thought, *nowhere close to ready.* My breathing was faster, my hands were shaky, and it felt like I would be frozen like that forever. Part of me wanted to stay there indefinitely, practically being held by Vlaine.

He moved his face, his lips just beside my ear, "you've got this. Just calm your mind and focus on replicating my gift."

His breath tickled my ear and my knees wobbled underneath me. *Focus Abrielle,* I cheered myself on, *focus on making that arrow the hand that the blast comes from.*

Vlaine pulled the string back to my anchor point and held it there for a moment allowing me to concentrate on my visualization. He counted down from three and let an arrow go. I watched the arrow move through the air, focusing on the point just before it hit the target. Another arrow flew through the air and I had the motion of Vlaine's arrows memorized. The next one I would try sending a blast from.

Vlaine released the arrow and just before it hit the target the arrow burst into hundreds of shards. My jaw dropped and I turned to face Vlaine, thrilled with my accomplishment.

"No way," he laughed in disbelief, "I thought for sure my hands were going to be blown to bits."

"Thank you for the unwavering confidence," I chuckled. "Let's keep going," I grabbed his hands and put them around me once more.

Eager, I heard him think as he held the bow sturdy in my hands once more. My face flushed when I realized how compulsive I had been.

"Sorry for being 'eager,'" I used air quotes, "I was just excited to try it again."

"What?" He leaned back and I turned to face him. Even though he had leaned away from me our noses were nearly touching. I edged backwards though his hands were still on mine.

"You said, or thought, the word 'eager' and I realized how awkward it was that I just grabbed you." His hands fell from me and he took a step back. "What?" I felt like a criminal, like I had done

.C. LYNCH

something appalling.

"I thought it to myself, but I never directed it to you. You should have had to break the wall down to have heard that." His brows were furrowed.

"Are you saying that I actually read something from you?" He gave a quick nod in response. "Yes!" I jumped up with excitement. "I actually read you and I wasn't even trying to! This may be the best day I've ever had."

I shot a victory arrow towards the target that exploded just before hitting it. "I did that *and* I read you." His expression was contemplative and I gave him a reassuring pat, "I couldn't have hurt your pride that badly. Try to be proud of me."

He shook his head then smiled, "I am, you're just catching on a lot faster than I thought you would."

"Don't worry Vlaine, I'll try not to take that too personally."

We practiced for two more hours in an equally as intimate position while I exploded arrows. The exhilarating feeling of watching the arrows explode was starting to wear off. Vlaine readjusted his head next to mine and I could feel his eyelashes flicker against my skin. Once again I was aware of how close he was to me, his chest and torso on my back, the warmth of his breath from his face being mere centimeters from mine. I focused on his breathing as he released the string. I imagined our hands being the pile of the arrow. *Boom*. The center of the target exploded. Shreds of canvas and foam were scattered about the field.

Cold air against my back startled me from my catatonia. Vlaine looked just as shocked as I did. He started laughing and tossed the bow to the ground.

"Holy crap Abbs, you did it! We have got to get dad and Draxe down here." He pulled out his phone and called his brother and told him to get Osiris and come down the field behind the gym.

Vlaine ran back inside to retrieve more targets and started setting them up. Draxe and Osiris pulled onto the field in a black pick-up truck within a matter of minutes. Excitedly, Vlaine waved them over. "We haven't done it with her shooting the arrow yet, but watch this!"

Vlaine stood against my back, slid his hands on mine, and readied the arrow.

"That's a bit intimate," Draxe scoffed.

Vlaine paid no mind, just pulled the string back. I focused on him as I had before; his proximity, the warmth from him, his smell. He smelled amazing. I shook my head of the obsessive thought and focused on our hands. His left hand covered my right and the opposite was true for the other hand. He released the string and once again I imagined our hands as the pile of the arrow. *Boom.* The center of the target exploded.

I jumped away from Vlaine and looked at Draxe and Osiris for approval. "Holy crap, Abrielle, that was awesome! Dad did you know someone could do that?" Draxe was just as excited as Vlaine and I had been.

"Abrielle, try it without the assistance of Vlaine." Osiris nodded and crossed his hands in front of him.

I picked up the bow and shot a practice arrow into a new target. I breathed deeply and completed the visualization, imagining my hand as the arrow pile. The arrow exploded into shards. Loosening my neck I pulled out another arrow. This time I would do it exactly as I had when Vlaine was holding me. Pulling back to my anchor point I imagined both of our hands as the arrow pile. "Boom," I muttered as a hole blew through the center of the target.

"Brilliant," Osiris clapped his hands together. "Marvelous work, Abrielle."

"Now we definitely can't let Jeremiah get his hands on you!" Draxe laughed as he jogged over to the exploded target.

"Before I was simply a bag of old clothes set out for charity but now, now I'm worthy of keeping, Draxe?" I walked by his side and picked up the few arrows that were still intact.

He laughed and tousled my hair, "sorry Abrielle, you know what I meant." It was an endearing little sister treatment. It made me feel accepted that neither Vlaine nor Draxe seemed to hold me at a distance in front of their father.

Osiris cleared his throat and straightened out his jacket, "we will have a meeting today at three. Until the meeting I would like you to keep practicing. Wonderful work, all of you."

Draxe caught up to him and they drove off leaving Vlaine and me to continue practicing.

I played around with my visualization and exploded three more targets before I asked Vlaine if he could help me with my barrier. Adrenaline was the only thing keeping me from dying of embarrassment knowing that he was surely able to read my every thought while practicing that morning. His stance never faltered and he never addressed those thoughts and though I should have been relieved, I was more frustrated than anything. A simple 'I'm sorry but I just don't feel the same,' or, even better, a 'we're on the same page here, Abbs' would have been beneficial.

Burning sensations tingled along my fingers and toes as the heat from the gym thawed my extremities. We went into the room with the snack bar where the light in the small space would heat the room to a more reasonable temperature than the basketball court would reach.

My barrier was weak but my concentration was growing stronger. By the end of the session the longest I could keep him out of my thoughts was just shy of two minutes. Before going to our meeting I called Nicholas back but the phone went straight to his voicemail. I sent Steph a text message asking her to let Nicholas know he pocket dialed me and I would call him later. As Vlaine and I were walking I received a message from Steph saying that Nicholas hadn't gone to school that day but she would swing by his house later to check on him.

Osiris was sitting calmly in his chair dressed in a freshly pressed grey suit. I never saw him leave the school but for all I knew Osiris took trips on a daily basis that warranted a perfectly tailored three-piece ensemble. It was strange how he was always so dapper. I wondered if it was an effort to demand respect and apprehension from the students or if he had meetings where the proper attire was business formal.

"Colleagues of mine have seen individuals known to work with Jeremiah at Blyden and Aldershaw within the past week."

My mouth dropped, "Blyden, as in Blyden High School?"

Blyden High was where I went before I attended Glaston Academy. It was where Vlaine had scouted me for months before I was inducted into Glaston.

"Yes, Abrielle, and I am sure that you can imagine the theories that my colleagues and I have developed considering these rather flagitious individuals have made appearances that were a bit obvious rather than the surreptitious methods Jeremiah is known for."

Osiris always spoke in a manner that made me feel inferior. Perhaps it was a belittling tactic to keep students fearful. "I apologize for being an abecedarian in here, but what is Aldershaw?"

"One of the schools," Draxe spoke now. "There is Glaston, Lanshaw, Aldershaw, Intervael, Valdor, and Ernvlik. They are in New York, New Mexico, Scotland, Oregon, Pennsylvania, and Alaska respectively."

I thanked him and tried to memorize what he had just told me. Professor Horicon and Erik made sure they knew I was here so why would they go to Blyden High or Scotland? I figured Scotland must have had something to do with another student they wanted. The only other person at Blyden High was Samantha, but as far as I knew she was only a telepath.

"Abrielle, dear, what can you tell me about your father?" Osiris's tone was gentle.

"Dear?" I arched my brow at his attempt to be engaging. "Please refrain from any terms of endearment, Headmaster Josnic. I appreciate your sensitivity towards the subject, but I don't need any sympathetic sobriquets." I sighed and straightened my back, "I have some pictures with Curtis from when I was a baby but he left when I was two. All I have is a name and some old photographs. Cherie Abbott is my mother and tried to fill in for the father role as best she could."

My father was a touchy subject. The pain of neglect never stopped stinging and my mother refused to speak about him. She had kept the pictures of him as keepsakes, but that was all I knew about him. Hell, she would never even tell me his last name. She was a teenager when she had me and kept her last name and gave me hers. My birth certificate was kept in her safe and she never allowed me to touch it because she was terrified I would lose it and get my identity stolen.

"Very well," Osiris stood up and walked to the panel where he had kept the folder of missing students.

"Dad, don't." Vlaine stood up abruptly. Osiris ignored Vlaine and continued with what he was doing before Vlaine's outburst. "Dad!" Vlaine walked over to his father and took a folder out of Osiris's hands and shoved it back into the drawer and closed the hidden panel.

"Come on Abbs," Vlaine walked to my side and extended his hand towards me, "this meeting is over."

Draxe stood, "Vlaine let him continue with the meeting."

"No," Vlaine growled, "this meeting can wait until after finals at least."

"What is going on? What does this have to do with my father?" I looked around at the three men in the room waiting to see who would speak first. Osiris stood with a stiff upper lip, Draxe had sympathy smeared on his face, and Vlaine looked like he was about to pull a trigger. "Draxe," I walked towards the one who would allow me to play off his sympathies, "what does this have to do with my father?"

He shrugged, "everything, maybe, or nothing, possibly."

The vagueness of Draxe's answer bore a pit in my stomach. "Osiris, please continue," I waved my hand irritated. Vlaine punched the table and stormed out of the room.

I wanted to go after Vlaine, but if I had the uncertainty of where Osiris was going with the conversation would have been too much to bear. Osiris laid a green folder in front of me and sat down. "Your father was accepted into Valdor Academy when he was nineteen. He's been a professor at Aldershaw Academy for the past decade. We suspect that Jeremiah's men were in Scotland looking for him."

"They should have known that my father isn't involved in my life."

I could not understand why they would want to go to my father but Osiris thought that my replication could be genetic. My father was known to be a healer and a telepath, but replication was rare but could be easily hidden or he could have been as unaware as I was.

The meeting ended with Osiris warning me about the dangers of Jeremiah and how the training I had done with Vlaine was vital to my safety. Jeremiah's intentions were to create a less orthodox and much more violent version of the Hagan Think Tank. Not only did he want to exploit the abilities of others for his own financial gains but he wanted to manipulate the genetic material of people with different abilities. Osiris and Jeremiah were part of a particular genetic engineering sector of the research and development team at Hagan and Jeremiah had his own ideas that violated the principles of the think tank. Needless to say, a replicator like me would be the key to his research.

Osiris said that the sector was closed down when Jeremiah's intentions were known and their friendship caused them both to lose their jobs. Jeremiah was debarred but Osiris was allowed a teaching position and he soon became a headmaster. I was still curious as to why Jeremiah would not just attack and grab Osiris for his replication abilities but he provided no answer to my query.

Just as the meeting was ending he asked Draxe to step outside so Osiris and I could speak privately. "I apologize for unscrupulous concerns," he paced near the panel of hidden folders, "Vlaine is exceptionally strong but I am concerned about the affect your relationship will have on his safety."

At first I was taken aback by his claim because I had assumed he meant a non-platonic relationship until I realized he was worried because Vlaine fought for his friends and when Jeremiah came for me he would undoubtedly fight to protect me.

"I understand your concern seeing how devastatingly loyal and protective he is when his friends are concerned, but the only consolation I can offer is that Vlaine is not in my vision."

I left the room and did not wait for a reply. The more I thought about what he said, the more it bothered me. Once I was back in the hallway I pulled out my phone to call Vlaine but he turned the corner just as I was about to dial his number.

His hands were balled into fists and he was walking straight towards me. "I didn't want you to find out like that," his stance was still defensive but it was clear now that it was not me he was angry with.

"What, about my father? I don't care about that right now. But *your* father had the audacity to tell me that he's worried about our relationship getting you hurt in all this Jeremiah crap. Like I would ever intentionally put you or anyone else in a position to get hurt?" I crossed my arms in front of my chest, "so can you do me a favor and just leave the state or something when my vision comes true so that I don't have to worry about your dad getting mad because we're friends."

Vlaine's brow furrowed then he started laughing. "What is so funny, Vlaine? He said it like it was my fault, like I'm dangerous." I stomped my heel churlishly, "and you know what, he is the one that had you be my teacher and he gets to decide what classes I take. Why would he have me paired with you like 60 hours of the week if I'm such a hazard? Argh!" I threw my hands up, infuriated.

"So you're not mad because one of the academies pretty much took your dad from you when you were a baby and he's been teaching in Scotland for most of your life and this life-altering bomb got dropped on you right before finals, but you are mad because my dad pointedly expressed concern for my safety?" He put his elbow up and leaned against the wall by my side, "and just to be clear, I asked my dad for permission to teach you. You were going to get put into a class with Professor Wylden."

I felt ridiculous standing in front of Vlaine while he was laughing. I sighed and uncrossed my arms, "I never asked you to stand up to Tracy and I don't know what made you do that dimension thing to that kid, but I'm sure no one asked you to do that either. He just made me feel like I'm a pernicious being." His eyebrows were raised in surprise and I rolled my eyes, "sorry for overreacting."

"Who told you about the 'fourth dimension thing'? That was a while ago."

If he wanted to he could read me and find out the truth so there was no reason to cover up for Will when he probably would not be coming back to Glaston anyway. "Will told me about it when he was giving me the stay-away-from-Vlaine talk."

"Will wasn't a student at Glaston when that happened," he stroked his jaw while replaying the memory in his head then shrugged it off. "I have something to show you that will make you feel better, I think."

"Wait, I need to talk to you about some things since I am finally allowed to be part of these meetings." He willingly agreed. I put my hands over my face in shame, "but first I need to know how often you read me."

I kept my hands over my face while he answered. "Since October, just when we're working on your barrier so I can see how you're doing. I put mine up for privacy so I like to extend the same courtesy to my friends."

I dropped my hands from my face slowly. "Let's start from the beginning of the questions and work up to the most recent. I'm just going to do a speed round then answer them once I'm done. Why was Draxe 'spying' on our lessons that day? Why did you think your dad sent him and why would they have wanted Draxe to take over the class? What happened with Erik? Did he just disappear? Why is Jeremiah trying to get me and not your dad? We've had the same vision about me turning invisible now, what does that mean? I'm sure there are more that I have but those are the ones that have been on my mind."

"Draxe was just curious because he knew you're a replicator but I thought my dad was looking for reasons to send you into the think tank prematurely. Erik was alive, admitted that he was spying for Jeremiah and then disappeared the day the guys came in and attacked us. I'm sure that once Jeremiah has enough men he will try to take my dad, but my dad is very powerful and it isn't going to happen easily. Did I cover everything? Oh, and I don't know what us having the same vision means, it was probably just a coincidence."

"This is a really awkward and embarrassing

question that I've already asked you but I am going to ask you again." I looked away so I could not see his reaction. "When I was having visions of Draxe I felt really strongly about him, like I would wake up feeling safe and loved and when I saw him in person I was absolutely in lust. Those feelings started to disappear then they were completely gone once the vision happened. I think Draxe is an amazing person, but I have no romantic feelings for him whatsoever now. Do you have any relatable experiences?"

He was silent for so long that I had to glance up just to see if he was still there. He remained silent even longer and I felt like I needed to further explain myself.

"I have a theory that I had seen Draxe's face for so long that it was familiar, I saw it from childhood into teens and it just turned from someone familiar and safe to someone that I was almost obsessed with because I wanted to know who he was and why I was seeing him all the time. As I started to know him there was no chemistry and then the vision happened and I looked at his face and I felt everything I had for so long but because I was relieved that I was alive and that it had finally happened. I didn't have to worry about waiting for the vision to happen anymore."

Vlaine tucked his hands into his pockets and leaned against the wall. "I think our situations are a little different."

I nodded, "I'm probably just a weird anomaly once again, mixed with the emotions of a teenage girl."

Vlaine leaned in towards me. My breath hitched as he closed the space between us. "I wanted to protect you in the vision and that hasn't changed but I didn't start falling for you until after I met you."

The air in my lungs escaped and I was frozen, just like earlier when he had his arms around me. Was he being serious? I must have heard him wrong.

"What?" I searched his eyes for integrity.

He leaned closer, his forehead was touching mine. "I'm falling for you, Abrielle."

I searched for something to say but I had nothing. My back was against the wall and there he was leaning into me. For a few seconds nothing else existed, it was just Vlaine and me. He had to know I felt the same; there was no way he hadn't read it at that point.

I fought for words, the right words to tell him how I felt. "Vlaine," I breathed, "I…"

"Vlaine?" a voice called from down the hall. The breath I had been holding exhaled all at once. Vlaine pulled away and looked down the hall.

"Jay! I was about to go down there." Vlaine motioned for me to follow him. We met the man in the middle of the hall and they gave each other a handshake with a pat on the back. "Abrielle, this is my brother Jackson. Hagan sent some security measures to help out with the Jeremiah predicament."

Jackson was in his late twenties and looked like a perfectly even mix of Draxe, Osiris, and Susan. He had Susan's ruddy hair, his father's facial features, and Draxe's frat boy stance.

"The replicator," he did a slight bow like I was royalty, "I've heard a lot about you."

"Oh," I glanced nervously at Vlaine, "good things, I hope."

I hoped he knew more about me than the fact that some ill-reputed men attacked a school because of my gifts.

"The tank gets updates when its prospects do something impressive like turn invisible or heal little squirrels."

I blushed, "I'm glad the tank can appreciate the lives of little fuzzy rodents."

Jackson slapped Vlaine on the back and told him they needed help setting up the perimeter.

"Nice to meet you," I nodded before I let them get to work.

24

Liz was just getting out of the shower and I jumped onto my bed and threw my sweatshirt on the floor. "You're taking a shower in the middle of the day?"

"I needed to warm up." She slipped on sweatpants and a sweatshirt.

It was below freezing outside but I hadn't paid much attention to the temperature since that morning.

I fell to my back and stared up at the ceiling. "Vlaine told me he's falling for me," I put my hands over my face and let out an excited squeal. "Can you believe it? I don't even know why he would like me."

Liz tittered exuberantly and sat next to me. "What did you say?"

"I didn't say anything. At first I was silent because he took my breath away. How corny is that? Now I know what they mean. And then I was about to say something but his brother Jackson had impeccable timing."

"Jay's here?" Her eyes lit up and she started combing her hair with her hand quickly. "You're going to tell him you feel the same, right? I mean he put his heart out there on the line for you so you had better do the same."

"Yeah, they sent some people here from the tank to help out with security and Jay is one of them. I'll tell Vlaine how I feel when I see him next." I sat up and laughed unbelievingly. "Me? I still cannot believe he likes me."

"Abrielle," Liz's face was kind and serious, "you're the nicest person to ever step onto Glaston grounds and you're absolutely gorgeous. Why else do you think I was worried that Draxe was going to fall for you?"

I hugged her tightly, "thank you for being so sweet." *And for being a girlfriend when I needed one,* I thought.

"This is no time for sentiments. We have our first final in three days so let's start studying. Your boyfriend will be here soon and you can give him doe eyes and tell him how you're madly in love with him, but until then we need to make sure we nail that physics exam."

"It could be your boyfriend that stays here tonight too," I mumbled.

She giggled and pulled out her study cards. Getting hurt and staying away from classes had distracted me more than I thought because I was struggling to keep up with her practice physics questions.

Draxe came into the room and I asked if he could take over studying with Liz so I could study for the other classes I had. Liz glared at me as if I had given her secret away, but I made myself busy so he would not suspect anything.

I kept staring at my phone while I was studying hoping to get a phone call or message from Vlaine. Impatience won and I picked up my phone to start texting Vlaine that I felt the same but just before I began typing my phone started to ring.

"Hey Steph," I answered then left the dorm so I would not disturb Liz.

"Hey Abrielle, so I just swung by Nicholas's house. His mom said that she hasn't seen him since last night. He wasn't in his room. What time did you say he called you?"

It was not rare for Nicholas to spend nights out without letting his mother know, but Steph was usually with him when it happened.

"He called somewhere between 5 and 6. Is he still dating Molly? Maybe they went on a romantic journey to a motel or something."

She was silent for a few moments, "no he broke up with Molly the day after that time I saw you at the diner and he hasn't really been dating anyone since." Her voice trailed off as she was talking.

"Are you worried?" I was pacing around the

foyer of the residence hall.

"Kind of," she sighed. "Speaking of dating, how are you and your very own James Dean?"

"James Dean?" My stomach dropped.

"Yeah," Steph let out a longing sigh, "that handsome, perfectly messy hair, bad boy exterior, but you know he's actually a softie on the inside."

"Can we call him something else, like another icon that didn't die at a young age."

"Does Marlon Brando sound better?"

"Yes," I laughed, "he's pretty amazing, isn't he?"

"I love you and all Abrielle, but I'm breaking the girl code if you two ever break up."

"That's fair," I laughed, "but I have to study for finals because they're next week. Let me know the second you hear from Nicholas."

We hung up then a voice close to my ear whispered, "Who's amazing?" I dropped my phone in surprise and turned to see Vlaine.

"Jeez, Vlaine, you'll give a girl a heart attack sneaking up like that." He was smirking like he was trying to keep a secret but was about to lose his restraint. "Nicholas is missing and it sounds like no one has seen him since yesterday."

"That's strange, he usually runs everything by

you and Steph. Didn't you get like thirteen text messages from him the other day?" Vlaine actually looked concerned.

"Yeah, we're usually the first ones to know everything, sometimes even before he does." I tucked the phone in my pocket then crossed my arms. "I never told you about the text messages." I gasped, "You have been reading me!"

His expression was innocent, "I have no idea what you mean. I do that for educational purposes only."

It was my turn to give him a devilish grin, "then you know I feel the same way about you." It was his turn to be speechless. "I have to go study. I'll see you later," I smiled and flipped my hair like I saw Steph do so many times and left before the realization that I admitted my feelings for Vlaine could sink in.

I lay on my stomach trying to study but thoughts about exploding targets, worrying about the school getting attacked, and Vlaine revealing his feelings for me kept my mind preoccupied. I fell asleep on top of my study material and woke up a little past midnight. Liz was sleeping peacefully and Draxe was lying on his back tossing a stress ball in the air and catching it.

"Hey Draxe," I whispered trying not to wake Liz.

"What's up Abrielle?" Draxe stopped tossing the ball and turned towards me.

"Do you think those students are alive?"

He responded without hesitation, "absolutely. There is no reason for him to take people if he was just going to kill them."

"So do you think they're okay or getting tortured?"

"I think thoughts like that are the worst ones to have when you're falling asleep. Something happened that was beyond your control and it wasn't your fault. For all we know they could have ran when the attack happened and they're all at pizza hut thinking they just got out of final exams."

"We have really strong telepaths here and they can find people if they needed to. I know you guys are hiding stuff from me. I just wonder if I should just let them capture me so maybe I can try to help those people out."

Draxe sat up and leaned forward, "Abrielle, I know you want to help them but keeping you away from Jeremiah is the best thing that we can do to help everyone. What do you think he's going to do to you if he gets you? In the world of replication you're a baby and he'll hang you up like a calf."

"Ew, that was graphic," I shook my head, repulsed. "I know there's not much I can do, but I wish I could do something."

"Just keep practicing and do your best to stay safe. We have guards here now for some extra security measures plus me or Vlaine will be around you at all times of the day. Maybe we can change that vision of yours." He walked over to the side of my bed and sat down next to me. "What's the best memory of your life?"

I smiled thinking of our fake camping weekend, the memories Steph and I had through our years of sleepovers, adventures with Nicholas, summers by the lake with Steph's family, the serenity of brushing Cinnamon, the feeling I felt every time I sat with Vlaine for my skill class and put my hands in his.

"I must have one hundred favorite memories, Draxe."

"Pick one of them," he pulled my blanket on me, "and know that whoever shares that memory with you smiles every time they reminisce on that moment because you made it as special for them as they made it for you." He tucked my phone under my pillow and smiled, "and before you say anything don't give me any credit for that pep talk. My sister would put me to bed after my mom passed away saying that, only replace 'someone' with 'mom.' So which one are you going to choose?"

"I'm going to think about something that happened earlier today." I replayed Vlaine telling me that he was falling for me.

"Good. Sweet dreams, Abrielle." He patted my knee quickly and went back to his cot.

"Draxe?" I spoke softly "is there any way you can get a recent picture of my dad?"

"Yeah, I'll get one for you," he promised.

"Goodnight, Draxe," I whispered appreciatively.

"Grab my hand," Liz shouted holding her hand out. I knew this vision all too well. We would head towards the rear exit, both of us invisible and Jeremiah would come through the door as we were about to escape. As the vision played through I tried to blast Jeremiah, I tried to fight back but it was to no avail. I could not change the vision while I was having it, only watch in horror while explosions shook the building and peers screamed as chaos ensued.

"No, no, no!" I sat up in bed. "I can't change it," I cried, tears were streaming down my face. Someone was rubbing my arm gently, but I could not see through the blur of tears. I wiped my face and saw Vlaine was by my side. Liz was sitting up in her bed watching me with a sympathetic expression. "Liz," I shook my head crying, "I tried to alter it but I couldn't."

"Abrielle, it was a vision not a lucid dream, "she pouted, "nor was it real life. There is nothing you can do until it happens except to try and learn from it."

I nodded in agreement. "You're going to grab my hand so we can both be invisible and we're going to run to the back of the residence hall to try and escape but Jeremiah is going to walk through the door we try to escape through. Maybe if we go against the wall instead of through the door first or try for a different exit."

"We'll figure that out later hun, but right now I'm going to go back to sleep. Try and do the same. We're going to need you to be well rested." Liz pouted sympathetically then turned on her side to fall back asleep.

Vlaine was by my side rubbing my hand. "So this is what I've been missing the past few days?"

"Sorry, I can't really help it." I hated the way I felt after I had the vision.

"I know," he wiped a few stray tears with his thumb, "try to get some sleep. I'll be right here."

I nodded and pushed myself to the far side of the twin bed against the wall so he could take a seat on the mattress instead of balancing against it while kneeling on the floor. Instead of sitting he lay down by my side and folded his hands beneath his head and stared up at the pink star on the ceiling.

"Goodnight Abbs," he whispered and wriggled into a comfortable position.

"Goodnight, Vlaine."

I woke up with Vlaine's arm under my head and my ankle over his. Slowly I moved my leg off his and tried to get off the bed without waking him. Draxe was sleeping on the cot and on my desk was a picture of my father. I held it delicately in my hand, like it could disappear at any moment if I was not careful.

My dad had auburn hair like me, crystal blue

eyes, and laugh lines. I got all my facial features from him, except my eyes were a swirl of my mother's green eyes and his blue ones. Vlaine was right, looking at the picture of my father was much more emotional than I expected. I tried to push the resentment for my fatherless childhood that Valdor and Aldershaw Academy had a hand in creating. I put the photograph back on the desk and tried to swallow the feelings threatening to surface, the feelings that I had spent my entire life locking away in a place deep inside my heart.

The hot shower water soothed muscles that I did not even know were sore. I let myself cry. I let the emotions I had buried come to the surface and wash down the drain. I would allow myself enough time to feel angry, hurt, and betrayed but just long enough to get it out of my system without letting self pity take over.

There were no more tears. *You exploded a freaking target with someone else's power, Abrielle,* I told myself. *You have two friends and a mother that loves you and took care of you so get your ass up and put on some mascara so you can't cry again without looking like a raccoon and get ready to change that vision when it happens in real life.*

I nodded at my own pep talk and stood up. I would get ready and not let any new information about my father make a hole in my chest where I never allowed one to be before finding out why he wasn't there when I was growing up.

I decided to go to the kitchen to grab coffee and breakfast for Liz, Vlaine, Draxe, and myself. It was strange walking out of my dorm and seeing a man posted at the top of the stairs and another at the bottom. Jackson was standing by the entrance of the residence hall.

"Good morning Jay," I smiled as I slipped my hands into my glittery aqua gloves.

"Hey Abrielle, where are you off to?"

"I'm going to grab some coffee and bagels for the scurry up in 217."

"Scurry? Oh, like a pack of squirrels! I got you." He laughed and nodded his head approvingly of my joke. "Do you want some company?"

"Sure, I'll take a hand or two."

He called out for the guy at the bottom of the stairs to take his place at the door while he helped me in the kitchen. Another guy was stationed inside the kitchen and I poured some coffee for each of the guys we had walked by including Jay. The men gave me a quick nod to say hello and thank you for retrieving coffee for them. I wondered if they knew that I was part of the reason they had to be wasting time standing around Glaston Academy just waiting for some psychopath to attack the school. I was sure they were well aware of who I was and my influence on their current assignment, but I hoped they did not blame me in any sort of way.

Liz was awake when I got back to the room. Vlaine and Draxe were sleeping until their older brother whistled a strange siren sound. Both boys jumped out of bed like they had just been mustered. Jay laughed and said something to the effect of "I've still got it," and went back downstairs to his post.

"Militant family?" I chuckled as I passed out the beverages. Vlaine and Draxe gave each other a knowing glance and settled back down but offered no explanation. I sat on the bed next to Vlaine and crossed my legs beneath me.

"What exactly is the plan after finals? Do I go back home and pretend that there is no boogie monster trying to steal me from my bed or are these guards going to follow me home?"

Draxe slurped his coffee greedily then spoke before Vlaine offered an answer. His voice flowed smoothly as he offered me the option to stay and take a winter semester of school or for someone to go home with me. I wondered if they had planned for Draxe to discuss this with me since his bedside manner was far superior to Vlaine's. He was pushing the idea of taking an additional semester at Glaston Academy through the break that I was sure it was my only option and he had given me the second only to make me feel like my opinion mattered.

I leaned my back against the wall and chewed on my breakfast slowly as I thought about the guards at the school sent to protect the students. It felt terrible knowing that I could be the reason they would not be able to spend Christmas with their families.

"My vision showed me at Glaston when

Jeremiah came, if I went home no one would have to worry. It could be next semester or even years from now considering how long it was before my vision of Draxe actually happened."

Vlaine turned his body towards me and offered a sympathetic expression. "That vision was incomplete, Abbs. This one is probably too, but it is happening every night. We can't take any chances."

"What's the worst thing that can happen if he gets me anyway?" I hadn't meant to actually speak but my frustration opened my mouth for me. Three incredulous faces were staring at me, but none made me feel as guilty as the hurt look that was also on Liz's face. I began to apologize but Vlaine spoke before I could.

"He could torture you, kill you, kill the people you love. Who knows what he is capable of before he figures out the genetic mapping for a person with replication? Once he learns the secret to what makes you different no one is safe."

My mind trailed off to the different abilities that the students at Glaston had. There were certainly more at the other academies and more people in the world with abilities that were not attending the academy. I looked up at Liz; her thousand yard stare proved she was in another place in her mind, a darker place.

"Liz," I spoke softly, "I'm really sorry about seeming so nonchalant about Jeremiah."

Her lips quivered for a moment as she began

to speak. "Jeremiah called his facility his 'tree house,' like it was just a hangout for him and his friends. Everything was labeled with Replyx Corp. That was the actual name of his lair." Her eyes were still fixed in a stare and she made no move to look towards any of us. "The testing was not the horrible part of being held captive by him, it was the mind games." She finally looked up at me, "trust me when I tell you that the worst thing that can happen to you is something that you have never experienced and it is nothing close to death."

The room fell into a short and dour silence before I asked if I could have a short internship at Hagan Think Tank during the winter break. It would allow the men standing guard to go back home and I would actually be able to see the place where Osiris wanted me to go once I completed my education. Vlaine left to discuss the option with his father and Draxe stayed to keep watch over Liz and me.

As I watched Vlaine leave the room I searched my mind for ways that I could possibly stop Jeremiah. My gifts, as Vlaine had described them, were restorative in nature. I could emulate destructive gifts, but it took much more concentration than using my innate healing and telepathy. Suddenly, I realized how I would stop Jeremiah, or any terrible person.

"I'm going to go visit Cinnamon," I stood up and left without allowing Draxe the chance to protest or accompany me.

I caught up to Vlaine in the yard before he had gotten to the main school building.

"Vlaine," I called to him, "I need to talk to you." He turned slowly and my insides melted watching his handsome face greet mine. My breath caught and for a moment I could not find oxygen. "First, I wanted to say thank you for making me feel so safe."

His lip twitched into a partial smile and he gave me a quick nod before continuing to find his father.

"I might be a novice, but I can fix this." I pulled my shoulders back defiantly.

"What?" His voice was laced with confusion.

"I'm going to heal Jeremiah," I said with determination. "Bad people are a product of mental illness and that is something I can cure."

Vlaine turned to me, equal parts adoration and concern. "Your ignorance of the evil in this world is a dangerous delusion, Abrielle. There's only one way to rid the world if it," he furrowed his brows into a menacing gaze, "to snuff it as if it were a candle."

"No, Vlaine." I broke the trance of my thousand yard stare. "Negativity leaves a residual effect, an open well for more atrocities. You need to heal the source to cure the madness."

He glared dubiously at me, "are you going to heal every horrible person in this world?"

I smiled at the possibility. "No," I stated matter-of-factly, "but I'm going to clear a nice path for whoever supersedes my endeavor."

Vlaine sighed and placed a gentle hand on my cheek. "If only there were more people like you in the world, "he kissed my forehead lightly, "it would be such a better place."

I basked in the comfort of his proximity. "I really am going to try to heal him," I whispered.

"I hope you succeed." His thumb rubbed my cheek twice before he continued back to the school.

Cinnamon seemed as restless as I felt. I was only going to brush her but the moment I was in the stables I grabbed a saddle and took her out. The morning was uncomfortably cold but she seemed to enjoy the chance to stretch her muscles.

The melody of her hooves trotting against the snow filmed trails was soothing. Her peaceful canter was the only thing keeping the thoughts of finals, my father, winter, Jeremiah, or Vlaine at bay. Somehow when I thought of Vlaine everything else just paled in comparison. He was handsome, strong, protective, and he liked me of all people. I could not understand why he liked me out of anyone else at Glaston Academy, but I was not going to question it. Humans have a way of letting relationships get too complicated when they should be simple. Love should be simple. Not that I necessarily loved Vlaine, but I did love to be around him.

My mind wandered and I allowed the euphoric feeling I felt when Vlaine told me he was falling for me to take over. The more I thought about him, the more I wanted to see him. I urged Cinnamon to head back to the stables quickly. I put her back into her stall and fetched more hay and a thick sheet for her.

"Need a hand," Vlaine's deep voice was beside my ear and I felt warmth on my back. My body hummed and time slowed as his body moved closer to mine. I nodded, but could not find the words to speak. I was frozen in elation and his hands slid on either side of me as I put the sheet on the horse in one quick movement. I turned my body to face him and my breath caught from our proximity.

Vlaine's deep blue eyes twinkled with mischief and the corners of his lips tugged up. His warm hand cupped my chin gently and he pulled me close to him. The feeling of panic began to rise as I realized what was happening. The alarm ceased as the warmth of his breath caressed my lips. His nose brushed against mine lightly as I tilted my face. Vlaine's hand slid slowly back behind my neck and he placed the other on my lower back and pulled me into him.

Our bodies were touching and I could feel my heart beating against his chest. I looked into his cobalt eyes to see the mischief vanish only to be replaced with concupiscence. His lips were parted, fuller and redder from the winter air. His hands tightened and he pulled me into him, his warm lips pressed against mine. At first I froze as every sensation flowed through my body but then I slid my hands up his chest and around his neck and parted my lips in a deep kiss.

Nothing existed except for Vlaine and me. I

could feel his pulse, every breath as we kissed. My perfect moment was shattered as we heard someone clear their throat at the other end of the stables. I pulled away quickly to see who was there, but Vlaine remained where he was and his eyes were focused on me. I licked my lips, now swollen from our osculation.

"Um," Draxe shifted uncomfortably, "come on over to the dorm when you get a minute, I just want to tell you what dad said." He turned away quickly leaving Vlaine and me alone in the stables.

My face was flushed crimson. I did not know if I should follow Draxe back to my dorm or talk to Vlaine about what had just happened. There was only one thing I knew at that moment and it was that I wanted nothing more than to kiss Vlaine again.

He was still watching me with the same expression from before we had been interrupted. I put my hands on either side of his face and pulled him towards me, pressing my lips against his greedily. His hands tugged my hips gently towards him and the existence of anything aside from the two of us was gone once again.

"We should see what your brother needed to tell us," I finally whispered after a few minutes.

His lips formed a trail from my chin to my forehead before giving me a final tender peck on my lips. "Okay, let's go see what he wants."

We left the stables and walked back to the dorm, his arm was looped around my waist and his hand rested on my hip. The gallant gesture was unfamiliar but comforting. My footsteps were slow as I tried to make the embrace last as long as possible.

Liz raised her brow when we walked into the dorm, Vlaine's arm still firmly around my waist. Her eyes met mine and there was nothing I could do to stop a smile from forming. Fortunately, Vlaine could not see that I was smiling like a buffoon and hardly able to suppress my ecstatic giggling.

"So," I sat on my bed and tried to hide my grin, "what did you need to tell us?" I looked at Draxe and sucked my cheeks in, forcing a solemn expression.

"My dad said that he sent out a favor to Hagan and you just need to fill out a few forms to get an internship there over the winter break. I put them on your desk if you want to fill them out quickly I can bring them back over to my father."

Vlaine picked up the forms and swung his leg behind me and pulled me against him. I leaned back against his chest and scanned the paperwork with him. Our bodies were ergonomic, like it was natural for us to be together. It was strange how he was so affectionate, but it felt incredible to have his strong arms wrapped around me.

I finished filling out the forms and handed them to Draxe. He took them and shrugged on a jacket.

Liz stood up and grabbed the doorknob, "I'm going with you before I get stuck in a room with these two necking one another."

I laughed and shook my head as they left the room. Vlaine's fingers brushed mine lightly and I rested my head against his chest enjoying the few moments of relaxation the proximity gave me. His muscles flexed involuntarily against me; it was soothing.

"Now what?" My whispered question was so broad and I had meant it in any way that he could answer it.

"Now," he kissed my temple lightly and leaned over to grab my text books from the floor, "we study for final exams."

25

The weekend was spent studying with Vlaine, Draxe, and Liz. I had every flashcard memorized and knew how to complete every problem we had been given in physics. When Monday rolled around Liz and I walked into our classes feeling confident and sure of ourselves but left feeling like we had just left a celebrity roast and we were the guests of honor.

The examinations were done on scantron sheets and the professors promised us our grades would be ready the very next day. My confidence was diminished and I wanted to feel Vlaine hold me. I searched for him only to find out from Jay that Vlaine was in a meeting with Draxe and Osiris discussing something about the think tank internship.

Aside from Vlaine the only thing at Glaston that was able to calm my nerves was Cinnamon. I jogged to the stable and was greeted with her whinnying behind the small gate. I saddled her up and took her for a short walk. The smell of an oncoming snowfall was in the air and I tried to hurry before the precipitation began.

Jay was waiting in the stables for me but neither of his brothers were in sight. I smiled a hello but felt angst; his angst. My empath gift was particularly sensitive to him.

"What's wrong?" I looked over to him while I walked Cinnamon to her stall.

"Nothing," he shrugged nonchalantly, "I was just awaiting your return." The last part was said as if it was supposed to be ironic humor, but I knew better.

"I'm an empath and you're an easy read," I gave him a sensitive but cautious smile, "if it has nothing to do with me I won't push you for answers, but with the whole Jeremiah threat I am a bit wary."

He tapped his fingers against his thighs then walked towards me. "Your friend was in here while you were taking your horse out."

"Liz?" With Erik and Will gone the only friends I had at the school were Liz, Vlaine, and Draxe. The word friend reminded me of Nicholas and Steph and I remembered that Nicholas was still missing. "Was it Nicholas," I hopped in place, "was Nicholas here?"

"Not sure," Jay tucked his hands into his pockets and shrugged, "he was African American and about yea high." He lifted his hand an inch above his head. "He's got a big goofy smile and pearly whites."

"Will was here?" I ran outside to look around then back to Jay. "Where did he go? I have been looking for him for weeks!"

"Right here," he laughed and suddenly Jay's features melted into Will.

I stepped backwards confused. "Will?" I jogged back outside to look at the residence hall. I could see the real Jay standing at the post he normally took. "I forgot manipulation was a gift of yours, but I didn't know you could look like someone else. Where have you been?" I kept distance between Will and myself, but I was close enough so he would not be suspicious of my apprehension.

"I didn't actually change my appearance, just changed how you saw me," he took a step towards me. "I got a job," he chortled jubilantly, "I've been working at this awesome place. I was about to graduate from here anyway but when I was given the offer I just couldn't refuse it." Will rested his hand on an overhead beam. "You know, I think you'd really like it there, Abrielle. The hours are great, it's got good pay, and my coworkers are awesome."

"Oh," I nodded and took a small step backwards. My back was against a low beam in the barn. "Where is this place?"

"It's called Replyx," he moved towards me closing the space between us.

Oh God. Will was working with Jeremiah. My stomach dropped, but I tried to appear calm. "You know, you really had me worried. You should have called or something." I tried to step around him but he grabbed my arm and held it tightly.

His grip tightened around my arm and a burning

pain pulsed around where his fingertips dug into my flesh. "Come with me and check it out. I'm telling you that you would love it there."

Lessons from my self-defense class flashed in my mind and I shot my knee up into his groin, kicked his legs out from underneath him, and ran towards the residence hall to get Jay.

"Jay!" I screamed as I opened the door. His hand pulled up the Glock that had been resting on his hip. "Jay, Will is here in the stables. He works for Jeremiah."

Just as Jay nodded towards the other men in the area a loud explosion erupted from the second floor of the residence hall. Papers, debris, and sparks shot out of my dorm room. My chest was heaving as morbid thoughts of Liz came into my mind. Screams filled the air and students began running out of their rooms. The flood of students was coming straight towards the door I was standing in front of. I could not get my legs to budge from their position and I was sure I was about to be trampled.

A hand tugged my arm and dragged me out of my stupor. "Let's go," Liz screamed, "this way!" Screams and explosions shook the building and I tried not to look back at the chaos. "You need to replicate my invisibility Abrielle," Liz's voice was loud and assertive. I hesitated and she yanked my arm, "now, Abrielle!"

I closed my eyes and blocked out the terrifying screams that were filling the building. I focused on the beauty of Liz's gift and willed myself to be invisible. I opened my eyes to find that I had succeeded. We were a few feet from the rear exit of the residence hall and clarity took over. I knew what was going to happen. Just as I skidded to a halt Jeremiah entered the room just as I had seen him do so many times in my vision. I pulled Liz against the wall with me to get away from him and out of his way.

Against the wall Liz was silent and undetectable. I tried to control my breathing to make myself as imperceptible as Liz. Jeremiah circled the room as if he was admiring his chaotic handiwork. Luther stood by him; his young brooding sharp features seemed even more menacing below thin silver hair. He spoke something to Jeremiah before they both turned to face my direction.

Liz's hand began to tremble and I gave her hand a quick reassuring squeeze. Jeremiah sauntered towards me as if he was about to step onto a dance floor at a ball, poised and determined. His dark hair was slicked back in such a manner that it almost did not match his casual jeans and button up sweater. Had his green eyes not been so full of determination I would not have thought he could be evil in any way.

His movements were fluid; he knew exactly where I was. I sucked in my breath and tried to hold it while shoving myself against the wall, trying to be undetectable. An explosion sounded upstairs giving me the chance to take a quick breath as the floor shook and wall behind us rattled.

Jeremiah's hand went towards my face as if he could see me, like the invisibility did not work for him. His thumb traced my cheekbone and he sighed, "There you are."

My legs began to tremble and the floor felt like a trampoline. He had found me despite my invisibility.

I let go of Liz's hand so that she would not be found. Just as I let go of her hand Vlaine walked in through the doors, a look of fortitude spread as he ran towards Jeremiah with outstretched hands. I could see a bald man with olive skin step behind Vlaine. *Slade is behind you!* I screamed telepathically to Vlaine, but he was only focusing on the man that was gripping my face.

The room was moving in slow motion as I saw Slade draw a gun and aim it at Vlaine's head.

"Vlaine," I screamed as I replicated his power. All the energy I could muster I shot in a tight concussive ball at Slade's chest. Slade's body whipped across the room as if it had been propelled from a slingshot, the force only stopped by a wall now adorning a hole from the impact. His body crumbled and he lay motionless on the floor.

A horrible guttural scream escaped my lips as I fell to the floor in pain. I searched my body for blood but found nothing. Jeremiah lifted me in his arms and I was still screaming. Pain clutched my entire body, it felt like all my bones had been broken.

Jeremiah shushed me like a baby and cooed,

"oh, the quandaries of being an empath."

I fought through the agony and tried to search for Vlaine. In my peripherals I could see silver hair coming closer then Luther rested his hand on my forehead. My eyes rolled back as consciousness slipped. Shaking my head I tried to regain composure and I forced my eyes to open. A warm hand touched mine and in an instant the pain was gone. My eyes fluttered open to see a white room equipped with various medical machines. I was still in Jeremiah's arms and as I looked around panicked, he lay me down delicately on a gurney.

"Where am I?" Tremors shook my body as I propped myself up onto my elbows.

"Shhh child," Jeremiah shushed me, "you're safe now." He turned to Luther and the other man, "we shall let her rest today."

The strange person who was holding my hand was wearing a hooded sweatshirt and I could not see a face. I tried to read the hooded person as they walked away but I barely had the energy to sit up, let alone get into someone's head. Whoever it was had made the pain I had felt from the attack stop instantaneously.

I watched them walk out of the room then I felt a breeze by my left side. I turned and looked up to see Erik standing by me. His long hair was tied back and ash was smudged onto his cheeks. He stroked my arm gently and a calm sensation spread throughout my body. I shook my head and tried to fight the serene feeling his touch left.

Erik leaned over my body, his face inches from mine. He brushed my hair back gently and grinned. "Welcome to the tree house, Abrielle."

ABOUT THE AUTHOR

While daydreaming and delving into imaginary worlds is her favorite thing to do, C.C. Lynch also loves to hike, read, and play video games. Though Glaston is the debut novel for this author, many other projects are in the works and will, hopefully, soon make their appearance on the shelves. C.C. Lynch holds a biology degree from Salem State University where she met her husband. Their pets, Gunner and Rocko, keep C.C. Lynch company while she gets to fulfill her passion of writing.